D0555291

The Great Pretender

a Hector Lassiter novel

CRAIG McDONALD

BETIMES BOOKS

First published in the English language worldwide in 2014
by Betimes Books

www.betimesbooks.com

Copyright © 2014, Craig McDonald

Craig McDonald has asserted his right under the Universal Copyright Convention to be identified as the author of this work

All rights reserved. No part of this publication may be reproduced, copied, stored in a retrieval system, sold, or transmitted, in any form or by any means, electronic, mechanical, print, photocopying, recording, or otherwise, without the prior permission of the publisher and the copyright owner.

ISBN 978-0-9929674-2-0

The Great Pretender is a work of fiction. Names, characters, places, and incidents are either the product of the author's imagination or are used fictitiously. Any resemblance to actual persons, living or dead, events, or locales is entirely coincidental.

Cover design by JT Lindroos

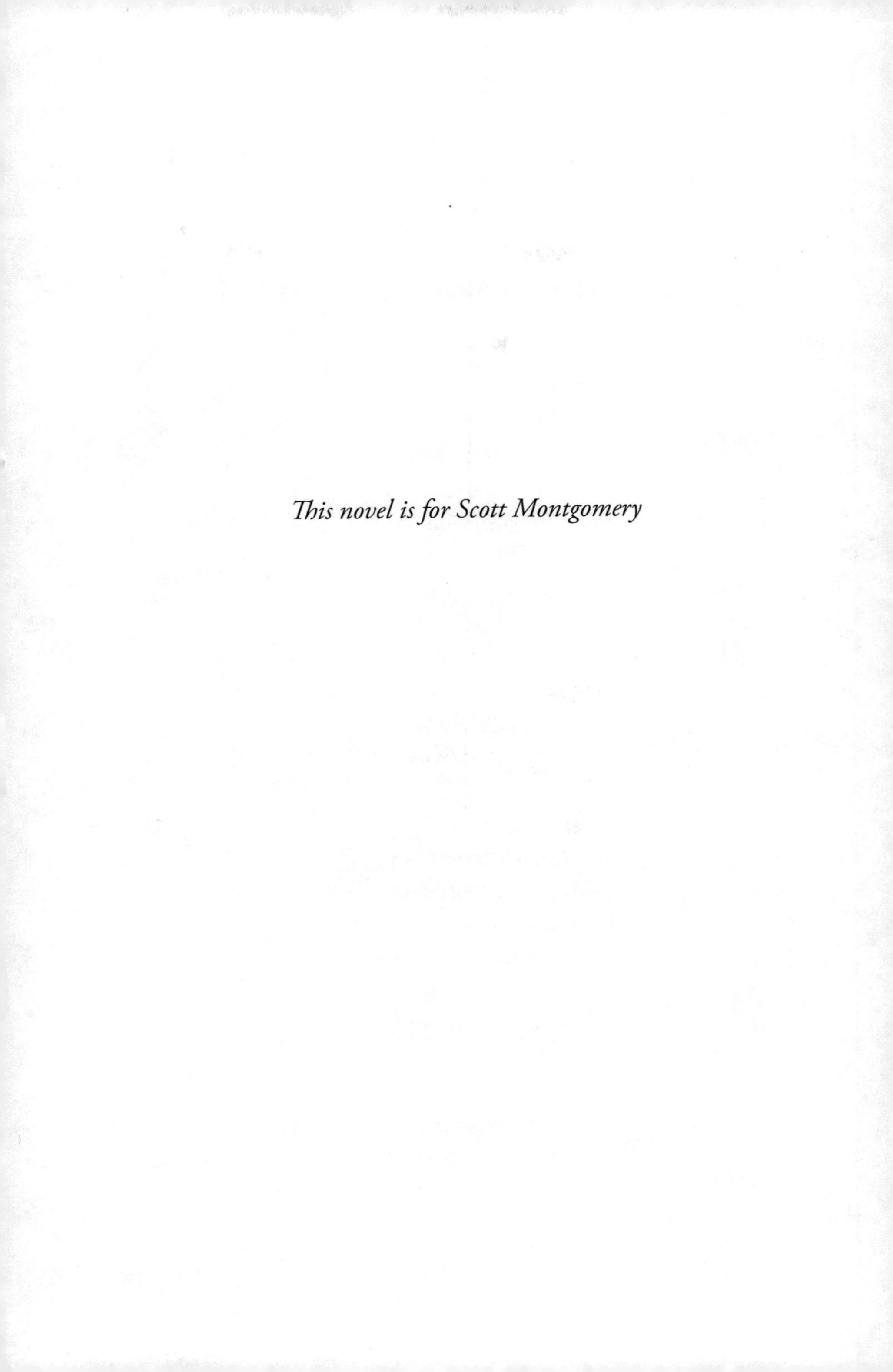

This novel is for Scott Montgomery

ALSO BY CRAIG McDONALD

The Hector Lassiter Series

One True Sentence
Forever's Just Pretend
Toros & Torsos
Roll the Credits
The Running Kind
Head Games
Print the Legend
Three Chords & The Truth
Write from Wrong (The Hector Lassiter Short Stories)

Standalones

El Gavilan

The Chris Lyon Series

Parts Unknown
Carnival Noir
Cabal
Angels of Darkness
The Daughters of Others
Watch Her Disappear

Nonfiction

Art in the Blood
Rogue Males

PRAISE

“With each of his Hector Lassiter novels, Craig McDonald has stretched his canvas wider and unfurled tales of increasingly greater resonance.” —Megan Abbott

“Reading a Hector Lassiter novel is like having a great uncle pull you aside, pour you a tumbler of rye, and tell you a story about how the 20th century ‘really’ went down.” —Duane Swierczynski

“What critics might call eclectic, and Eastern folks quirky, we Southerners call cussedness – and it’s the cornerstone of the American genius. As in: “There’s a right way, a wrong way, and my way.” You want to see how that looks on the page, pick up any of Craig McDonald’s novels. He’s built him a nice little shack out there way off all the reg’lar roads, and he’s brewing some fine, heady stuff. Leave your money under the rock and come back in an hour.” —James Sallis

“Craig McDonald is wily, talented and - rarest of the rare - a true original. He writes melancholy poetry that actually has melancholy poets wandering around, but don’t turn your backs on them, either.” —Laura Lippman

“James Ellroy + Kerouac + Coen brothers + Tarantino = Craig McDonald.” —Amazon.fr

INTRODUCTION

If any label best describes the Hector Lassiter series, it's probably "Historical Thrillers." These books combine myth and history. The Lassiter novels spin around secret histories and unexplored or underexplored aspects of real events. They're set in real places, and use not just history to drive their plots, but also incorporate real people.

As a career journalist, I'm often frustrated by the impossibility to nail down people or events definitively. Read five biographies of the same man, say, of Ernest Hemingway, and you'll close each book feeling like you've read about five different people. So, I've concluded, defining fact as it relates to history is as elusive a goal as stroking smoke or tapping a bullet in flight.

History, it's been said, is a lie agreed to. But maybe in fiction we can find if not fact, something bordering on truth. With that possibility in mind, I explore what I can make of accepted history through the eyes of one man. The "hero" of this series, your guide through these books, is Hector Mason Lassiter, a shades-of-grey guy who is a charmer, a rogue, a bit of a rake, and, himself, a crime novelist.

Some others in the novels say he bears a passing resemblance to the actor William Holden. Hector smokes and drinks and eats red meat. He favors sports jackets, open collar shirts, and Chevrolets. He lives his life on a large canvas. He's wily, but often impulsive; he's honorable, but mercurial.

He often doesn't understand his own drives. That is to say, he's a man. He's a man's man and a lady's man. He's a romantic, but mostly very unlucky in love. Yet his life's largely shaped by the women passing through it.

Hec was born in Galveston, Texas on January 1, 1900. In other words, he came in with the 20th Century, and it's my objective his arc of novels span that century — essentially, through each successive novel, giving us a kind of under-history or secret-history of the 20th Century.

Tall and wise beyond his years, as a boy Hector lied about his age, enlisted in the military, and accompanied Black Jack Pershing in his hunt down into Mexico to chase the Mexican Revolutionary Pancho Villa who attacked and murdered many American civilians in the town of Columbus, New Mexico. Villa's was the first and only successful assault on the United States homeland prior to the events of September 11, 2001.

Much of that part of Hector's life figures into *Head Games*, the first published Hector Lassiter novel and a finalist for the Edgar and Anthony awards, along with a few similar honors. That novel is set mostly in 1957. Its sequel, *Toros & Torsos*, opens in 1935. Subsequent books about Hector similarly hopscotched back-and-forth through the decades upon original publication.

The Betimes Books release of the Hector Lassiter series will try for something different, presenting the books in roughly chronological order—at least in terms of where each story starts as the novel opens. The series now opens with *One True*

Sentence, the fourth novel in original publication sequence, but the first novel chronologically.

Set in 1924 Paris, that novel is now followed by its intended sequel, *Forever's Just Pretend*, enjoying its first-ever publication and completing a larger story revealing how Hector became the guy we come to know across the rest of the series: "The man who lives what he writes and writes what he lives"; friend to Hemingway, Orson Welles and other 20th-Century luminaries.

The rest of the repackaged series unfolds in similar fashion, a mix of the old and new titles.

The Lassiter novels were written back-to-back, and the series mostly shaped and in place before the second novel was officially published. It's very unusual in that sense—a series of discrete novels that are tightly linked and which taken together stand as a single, larger story.

Welcome to the world of Hector Lassiter.

Craig McDonald

"Almost any story
is almost certainly
some kind of lie."

—Orson Welles

OVERTURE

Breathless, the chubby-faced boy spied on his grandmother through the closet's cracked door.

The boy watched the old woman chanting, preparing to sacrifice a pigeon to The Dark Prince who lived on the far side of the dusty looking glass. Chirping, beating its wings, the terrified bird struggled in the old woman's grip.

George's grandmother Mary had increasingly given herself over to conflicting and even sinister obsessions. The little grand dame seemed to regard herself as part Christian Scientist and part wizard. She styled her latter, darker interests after the diabolical teachings of Aleister Crowley and Madame Blavatsky.

His grandmother also had this small, insanely detailed miniature golf course on the third floor of her rambling home, occupying what was once an upstairs ballroom but most lately partially converted into her idiosyncratic and slap-dash vision of a black magic shrine.

Still muttering in some unintelligible, guttural language, she knelt before a rustic wooden altar and stained glass-window. She deftly wrung the pigeon's neck and placed the bird's twitching body on the altar adorned with a golden pentagram.

The old woman crossed the pigeon's corpse with a bronze dagger, her incantations veering into faltering Latin. Young

George Orson Welles began to whisper, over and over, "You'll burn in hell for this, you old witch. You'll surely burn in hell, you monster!"

BOOK ONE

PANIC BROADCAST

Thursday, October 27, 1938

"I have a great love and respect for religion, great love and respect for atheism. What I hate is agnosticism, people who do not choose."

—Orson Welles

1

THE STRANGER

"Perception is reality, that's how the saying goes, isn't it, Hec?"

Hector Lassiter, novelist, screenwriter, and for the moment, literary executor, looked down at all the chilly pedestrians scurrying through the autumn wind tearing along Fifth Avenue. The fierce wind made eyes water and noses run down there. Up here the wind cut to bone. He called above its roar, "That's indeed what some say, Mathis." Hector lit a cigarette with his windproof Zippo, engraved with the legend, "One True Sentence." He slipped the lighter into the pocket of his overcoat.

Standing on the eighty-sixth floor of the world's tallest and most famous building, Hector pulled on his right glove and took another hit from the coffin nail as he stared up at the dirigible mooring mast—a pointless novelty—looming higher above them.

Hector wasn't crazy about heights and the view up made his legs tremble. Taking a deep, icy breadth, he looked back down the side of the Empire State and said, "Suppose as clichés go, that one is true enough. Least so far as it runs. Take those people down there. They only look like ants, you know."

They were supposed to be having this meeting over coffee in a cozy place downstairs. But Hector had talked his companion into coming up here in the wicked wind where only fools, would-be suicides or stubborn tourists would venture on a blustery, late autumn day. Hector had his reasons.

Peter Mathis, rising New York publisher, smiled and said, "Sure. Anyway, this is a remarkable turn to say the least. Imagine, the popular and mysterious mystery writer, Connor Templeton, and the cult crime author, Bud Grant, being one-in-the-same. But, no, that's not enough! Both of those male writers were actually the pen name for a raven-haired stunner named Brinke Devlin! My publicity people are going to go berserk in the best sense with this, Hec. It transcends the merely remarkable. And it's surely money in the bank. Having seen some snapshots of Brinke, this wife of yours who wrote like a tough, lusty he-man and yet looked like a far prettier, bustier Louise Brooks? All I can say is, this will be huge."

"Money isn't the point, not for me," Hector said. "And certainly not for her. Publication, long-term, hell, permanent publication, is the aim. This is about her legacy. This is about Brinke's long game. Literary immortality is the objective."

"Well, of course," Mathis said. "That's one of the things you pay me for, isn't it?"

Hector nodded. "Just making sure we're clear on my primary goal in signing with you to at last publish all of her books under Brinke's *real* name." It was a Hail Mary gambit on Hector's part. His first wife's literary oeuvre under both her pen names had lately gone out of print. Hector simply couldn't stomach that. Brinke could never slip into literary obscurity, not so long as Hector lived.

The two men shook gloved hands. Mathis said, "To my last comment, I'm in danger of being late for a meeting about some of Thomas Wolfe's posthumous works. We're in negotiations about trying to do something more significant with *O Lost*. I still can't believe he's dead. And gone so young. Did you ever meet Tom?"

The North Carolina novelist and Ernest Hemingway's *bête noire* had died last month. Tom's was a sudden and bad death, like Brinke's, only of natural causes.

Hector let go of the man's hand. "Crossed paths two or three times, I suppose. Seemed a nice enough fella in the moment. A decent, if undisciplined, fiction writer. He drove Hem to distraction, I know. Anyway, thirty-seven is far too young to be dead, regardless of what you did or how well you maybe did it."

"Indeed. Well, at least Tom didn't have to suffer too long. There's real comfort in that, yes?"

"Sure there is."

They said their goodbyes. Hector watched the publisher go, then checked his watch. His next appointment was characteristically late. He turned up the collar of his overcoat and thrust his hands deeper into its pockets, looking out across the city but also watching the other lone man standing a bit off to Hector's left, the author's presumed stalker—his reason for dragging the publisher and the actor yet to come up here in the roaring, cold wind.

But there'd be time for that later, if indeed the man was really following the writer. For now, for better or worse, Hector's head was elsewhere. Dead at thirty-seven? Jesus Christ, didn't that resonate? Come January, Hector would be thirty-nine. Brinke would have been, what? Forty-three, forty-four? Something like that. Hector damned himself for not being certain. Either way, his first and truest love had never seen 1926.

That voice—it rose above the roar of the wind. "Hector, old man! Don't you look well?" It was *l'enfant terrible* himself, George Orson Welles, twenty-three, red-cheeked and already the toast of the Great White Way and the radio airwaves. Orson, still tragically baby-faced, was sporting the sparse shadow of a beard he was growing for a stage role.

Hector had first met the dramatic prodigy in Ireland, when Orson was indeed a boy actor. Back then, Orson regarded Hector as a kind of worldlier older brother. Eventually, after a brief return to the States, the two had shared an idyll across Spain, followed the bullfighting circuit together. That fraternal dynamic defined their friendship in its early going.

Now, despite their age difference—one of fifteen years, give or take—they comported themselves more or less as peers. Hector supposed that owed chiefly to his young friend's precocious but universally acknowledged—if untamed—genius.

As he had the last time they'd met, Orson looked to be firing on pure adrenaline, caffeine and nervous energy. Maybe something else, too: Hector was betting on Benzedrine or perhaps amphetamines to kick-start the boy-giant's metabolism. Even as a kid, Orson was fighting his waistline. Eyes already tearing-up, Orson cast his watery gaze down at the sidewalk far below. "The call of the void, yes? Did you hear about Dorothy Hale, old man?" Orson's voice was already growing breathy, the cold wind aggravating his asthma.

Hector shook his head. "What's a Dorothy Hale?"

"What *was*, you mean. Or *who* was she, rather." Orson smiled sadly. "Socialite and struggling actress. Pretty, but lacking talent. She threw a big farewell party for herself in her penthouse in the Hampshire House on Central Park South. Then she hurled herself off her terrace. It was only a few days ago. It was in all the papers. Suicide, though some say murder.

Would they really dig for a bullet after a fall like that some have wondered. Anyway, I'm surprised you haven't heard."

"Been on the road mostly these past few days," Hector said. "Haven't been keeping up with the news. Just grown more than tired of all the war drums, you know?"

"Understood, and anyway we haven't much time, old friend," Orson said. "We need to take our meal and then for you to tell me what was so pressing for us to have to meet—delighted though I am for any excuse to spend time with you. Then I need to get to my place with all haste. You can sit in tonight, if you'd like to, and listen to the probably vexing wax disc coming my way later. I'd frankly love it if you did. I'd be very grateful for your reaction. They're rehearsing and recording our next Mercury production tonight. It's a corker, at least in theory. My spin on H.G.—that *other* Wells, though he spelled his last name the wrong way—and *The War of the Worlds*. We're giving it the new broom treatment. Projecting it all through the prism of our modern mass media. Basically, in the early going anyway, it will play as a developing radio news story. We have a fake orchestra, fake news breaks. Hell, even a fake F.D.R., more or less."

"Can hardly wait," Hector said. "But about us meeting now, I'm confused. You telegraphed me for this meeting, don't you remember?"

"I did no such thing, old man. You sent for me." Orson frowned. "*Urgent* was a word used at least three times in various forms in your telegram, you'll recall."

"I don't recall that and I could say the same of your wire to me," Hector said. A new chill that had nothing to do with the autumn cold made him shiver.

"This is very strange," Orson said. "Clearly, we do need to talk more." Orson smiled uncertainly and pulled the brim of his hat lower against the gales. Of the same, he said, "This wind… Still, not as bad as last month's, I suppose. The remnants of that hurricane killed over five-dozen in the city and injured hundreds here. Whatever the reason for us being here together now, is there some good reason we're at the top of this absurd building, in this ridiculous cold, old friend?"

"Maybe, and it could be tied to this other little mystery about our respective wire communications," Hector said. "My previous meeting was here, but I was also testing a theory. We can surely go inside now. Know of any restaurants close-by and with a fireplace?"

Orson smiled and took Hector's arm. "We'll find such a place. It's colder than a witch's you-know-what up here. Maybe Billingsley's Club Room, or Dickie Wells, in Harlem, we might find some delectably dusky female companionship."

Orson smiled and impulsively tousled the hair of an eavesdropping, equally red-cheeked boy. The child frowned, then looked like he might cry. His pretty young mother glared at Orson. For his part, Welles held up gray-gloved hands to show them both empty. He said in his most sonorous tone, "Now, watch out for the slightest hint of hanky-panky, good sir."

With raised eyebrows, Orson reached behind the boy's ear and produced a quarter that he folded into the tyke's trembling hands.

All seemed to be forgiven.

Smiling and shaking his head, Hector said, "Always with the magic."

Orson winked at the boy's comely mother and said, "Always. Of course." An at once cherubic and satanic smile spread across the actor's face. He said, "I am, after all, a charlatan."

2

THE OTHER SIDE OF THE WIND

There was no fireplace, but the joint was snug and warm enough. Orson had taken Hector to Chinatown. After a whirlwind pass through a couple of shops looking for some joss sticks, they headed to this lately discovered haunt of Orson's. It was a new, downstairs joint on Mott Street called Wo Hop's. They lingered long over soup and their entrees, mostly sipping belly-burning tea to wash it all down.

"Not what you expected, I'm fairly certain, but I do so love this place," Orson said. "It's got promise, don't you agree?"

"It's more than fine," Hector said. "I've lately been coming around to Chinese fare. And, frankly, this city's Chinatown's always fascinated me, much more so than Frisco's." He frowned, then added, "Japan on the other hand?" Hector grimaced.

"Indeed," Orson said, talking while wolfing down roast pork with oyster sauce. Hector and Orson were presently at extreme ends from one another on the political spectrum, but current conditions were such that, left or right, all Americans were skittish, anticipating being dragged into the European mess once again.

Orson said, "I confide this only to you. All of that's kind of what we're hinting at with our next radio production, you see. The whole world, and America particularly, is desperately on edge, and yet, strangely complacent in the most vital sense. Unprepared. Tonight's show—you must understand, it will be broadcast live Sunday night in finished form—it's really about *all of that*. My—that is to say, the Mercury's—Martians are just a kind of audience-friendly boogey-man. They are a stand-in for the Hun or the Yellow Menace, to use the popular, pulp magazine parlance for those two evil empires."

"Christ, don't forget the Italians." Hector forewent another sip of hot tea for some ice water. He broke open a fortune cookie and read to himself, "Run! Do that now!" Startled, Hector set fire to the slip of paper and tossed it burning into the ashtray along with the stub of his own still-smoldering Pall Mall.

Frowning, spoon poised with a bowl-full of steaming egg-drop soup, Orson said, "Your fortune was that bad, was it?"

Hector shrugged. "Queer, anyway. Been a disappointing and unsettling day on several fronts, not including the circumstances of us being together here, now. Even the fairly innocent stuff has rubbed me wrong of late. You know, I caught a discount matinee this morning just to kill some time. *The Saint in New York*. I frankly didn't love it."

Orson blew on his spoon to cool his soup. "I saw that movie too, upon release. But only because the critics said the star was like some down-market version of me. How could I not see what they meant by that, yes?"

"Even worse, before the cinema, I roamed some art galleries," Hector said. "You know I collect in a minor way. Well, I stopped in at this place called the Julien Levy Gallery. Seems they're preparing for a showing of works by Frida Kahlo next month. Not good."

Orson frowned. "What do you mean by that? What's wrong with Kahlo's works?"

Hector shrugged. "My life has been rather lousy with Surrealist artists of late. Stuff I can't describe and you wouldn't believe. Anyway, just seemed another very bad omen. It's been a rough year or two."

"I've heard you and Papa are on the outs," Orson said. "What happened with Hem?"

Hector shrugged. "Ernest walks in his own world presently. I wish him well. Anything else is rearview mirror stuff." He scooped up another fortune cookie. There was no fortune inside this one. The author raised his eyebrows.

Orson said, "Now what do you make of that? What on earth does that mean for you?"

Still frowning, Hector said, "Aside from the fact I've been robbed? Maybe that my future's all used up?"

Orson wrinkled his nose and said, "Wouldn't that be the hell of a statement?" Hector could tell his younger friend was dwelling on this strange development of being deprived a fortune in a fortune cookie, and also on Hector's observation about it. Hector was doing that, too. He figured he could use that bit in some way in a novel or short story down the road. But the question in these awkward situations in terms of artists and shared, resonant experiences—every *damned* time, be it Hemingway, be it Orson Welles with an extra "e" or, hell, be it recently gone-south-of-the-sod Thomas Wolfe—was who would get there first?

Their waiter, ancient, barely able to handle English, said, "All is good? More? You want check, mebbe?"

"We want check, definitely," Orson said, nodding at Hector.

The novelist-screenwriter rubbed his jaw and said softly, "Sure, the check is mine." He showed his empty cookie to the waiter and said, "I was shorted, brother. No fortune in this cookie."

"That *very* strange," the old man said. A hopeful smile. "But mebbe you better off?"

"Or maybe I'm not," Hector said, holding up his wallet. Their waiter scurried off and came back with a handful of fortune cookies. Hector thanked him and skidded off some bills. The old man went to make change and Hector eyed the pile of cookies. He picked one at random and opened it up to read aloud, "Want to make someone disappear? Make them keep a promise."

Hector looked up to see Orson studying him. "That one's surely better than the last?"

"But still less than I'd hoped for," Hector said after sharing it aloud. "Seems much more up your alley. I mean you being the amateur magician and all."

"Amateur?" Orson blew his nose. He said, "I still have the sniffles from being on top of the infernal Empire State. You said you had a specific reason for being up there in that goddamn cold and wind. What on earth was it?"

"Testing a theory," Hector said. "Figured only a man who was following me would trail me up there in this weather. I was right. Fella did."

Looking troubled, then starting to look around the restaurant, Orson said, "You're being followed?"

"Yeah, by that hombre over there in the black coat and hat," Hector said. "The one who ordered only a pot of tea. The chain-smokin' fella with the scar down his cheek. That's the man for certain."

"So you confront him," Orson said, "we find out what he's up too, yes? See if perhaps he has something to do with our obviously fake telegrams to one another?"

"Nah," Hector said. "Like I told you, seems I've got all kinds of enemies this season. They run the range from crazy painters to disgruntled Feds." He checked his watch again. "We head to the studio now?"

"No, to my home, as I said before," Orson said. "There, maybe you can help me edit the script for a final pass after we hear the rehearsal recording. You know how I love a last-minute polish." That noted Welles smile—at once bemused, playful and challenging. "What's the old line, and wasn't Wilde who in fact said it? No work of art is ever completed, only abandoned?" Hector shook off another little chill. Orson rose and began to button his overcoat. "What about your sinister shadow, though?"

"Figure we'll lose him in traffic," Hector said. "In this city, and with a few cab changes, shouldn't be so hard at all to do that."

Another frown. Orson said, "But won't it drive you positively crazy? I mean not ever knowing *why* he was watching you?"

Hector just shrugged and said, "When do we ever know anything?"

Brown eyes twinkling, Orson said, "Touché."

Together, they wandered back up the creaking stairs and out onto the twisted streets of Chinatown. Cursing in Chinese, a little woman two floors up rushed to pull laundry from the railing of a third-floor fire escape as the rain and wind whipped at her sheets and pillowcases.

Orson took a deep breath and spread his arms. "Chinatown in the rain. Exhilarating, isn't it?"

"Sure it is, but now let's find the first of what's likely to be several cabs," Hector said, very aware of the scar-faced man indeed dogging their trail.

3

MURDER ON APPROVAL

At last satisfied they'd shaken his shadow, Hector said to Orson, "Time to tell our cabbie our final destination."

Orson said, "You're sure that we've lost him?"

"Close to certain as I can be," Hector said. "Let's roll those dice."

Upon arriving at Orson's place, they were greeted by his pretty young wife, Virginia, Irish—ivory-skinned and, by all accounts trickling back to Hector through channels, calamitously cuckolded by her precocious, only slightly older husband.

It was their first meeting, and Mrs. Welles exuded an immediate and immense sadness that pierced Hector and made him actually hate his young friend, at least a little, in the sorry moment.

Virginia Nicolson married then-nineteen-year-old Orson in 1934, two days shy of Christmas. They now had a seven-month old daughter, bewilderingly named Christopher.

Virginia, perhaps with the hastening assistance of Orson's increasingly feckless philandering, had more than shed her baby weight. She was very desirable in Hector's eyes, yet she exuded boundless despair.

Fair-haired Virginia said to Orson, "We've barely seen you in three days, darling. I can make sandwiches and the two of us..." Her lilting voice trailed off. Hector immediately began to formulate his exit line, feeling every inch the unwanted third wheel. But things didn't go that way.

"Make the sandwiches by all means and with haste," Orson said curtly, pressing blunt fingers to his pretty wife's lips. "I'm surely famished." Hector couldn't grasp how that could be after all that just-devoured Chinese grub. Smiling, Orson took Hector by the arm and dragged him to his den, where the younger man poured twin tumblers of whiskey. He handed Hector a cigar and a glass, then set about placing the wax disc with the "War of The Worlds" rehearsal performance on his CBS-furnished, state-of-the-art turntable.

Soon enough, Virginia arrived with a plate of ham sandwiches and a glass of milk for herself. The three of them settled in to listen to the first-run of the Mercury Theatre of the Air's next "classics adaptation."

The recorded rehearsal went at least in form much as Orson had described it to Hector. Roughly the first half of the radio play was structured as a breaking news event—purported coverage of an unfolding invasion by the planet Mars. But the melodrama was couched in familiar conventions of current radio journalism practice, with repeated interruptions of this damned band playing from the ballroom of a fictional Gotham hotel.

In the end, the program was potentially bracing, but a bit too meandering, Hector thought. It wasn't yet honed sufficiently to drive home the verisimilitude of an authentic and unthinkable unfolding news event. It sounded just a bit too polished, too studied.

When the recording was complete, Orson asked, "Your thoughts, Hector. And, yes, by all the Gods, do be brutally frank. Art affords no room for diplomats, as we both know from hard-won experience."

Hector well knew Orson would certainly recognize a kind lie, so he said, "The first half, as it unfolds as an invasion, is terrific in concept. But it needs to be a bit more ragged. It needs more of an air of desperation and confusion. And it must be pared down. The thing is far too polished and stylized. When the mayhem is unleashed, it should be choppier, far crazier than it is now. And when it becomes just you in what I guess is the second act, wandering in what I suppose we'll call the wasteland, well, that's a tad of an anticlimax." Hector shrugged. "But that second half is necessary of course. There's simply no coming down from what you've all built in up front. It brilliantly paints itself into a corner in that way."

Orson, dejected said, "You hate it, in other words." He looked to his wife. "You too?"

Hector shook his head. "I don't hate it at all. It's still compelling as hell. Just more conventional when it turns to straight up melodrama after the news treatment drops out."

Orson looked as though he'd been stabbed. But there was still time to fix it before Sunday night's live broadcast, and they both knew that.

And, in the end, Orson was enough the honest artist to accept Hector's assessment. False praise would kill their friendship, Hector had known that from the start.

"Please stay on tonight, and we'll tackle the editing together," Orson said. He smiled at Hector and Virginia. "After, I'm sure we three will find some mischief for ourselves."

Hector was uncertain what Orson meant by that last, but he was pretty sure he didn't want to find out. As he grew older, Orson seemed more the libertine to the increasingly circumspect Hector. Or maybe the brash, randy actor was just looking for someone to begin assuming responsibility for his unwanted wife.

"No way," Hector said. "I've got more than a few years on you, kiddo. Need my beauty sleep." He nodded at Virginia. She held out an ivory hand and Hector kissed it. He pointed at Orson's pretty wife and said, "Besides, you've got every reason standing right there not to burn the midnight oil playing radio wizard. Hell, this Sunday is just an hour of one night of another year, right? This program a mere holiday toss-off for the kids?"

Orson glowered. Then he snapped his fingers. "I forgot. I'm supposed to meet Houseman at midnight, at the Mercury. Still another project we're trying to whip into shape against the clock. This one for the stage." Hector wasn't sure he believed his younger friend. Probably, he decided, Orson was more likely off to the arms of some other *inamorata* of the moment. They were all ballerinas these days, or so Hector had heard.

Somehow, Orson managed to get on his coat and hat and actually preceded Hector out the door.

Awkwardly standing there at the threshold after Orson had deftly bolted, Hector held his hat in both hands and shrugged. "That young man never seems to rest. Long as I've known him, he's been like some vaudeville performer—rushing from one trembling pole to the next, trying to keep spinning all these crazy plates he's set in motion."

Virginia smiled sadly. "As good a description for it as any, I suppose." She pulled Hector's coat's lapels closed and appraised him, standing very close. He could smell her perfume, some heady, musky scent. She said, "Orson lately has a favorite saying that I don't like at all." Falling into a feminine impersonation of the grandiose Welles' voice, his wife said, "Human nature is eternal. Therefore, one who follows his nature keeps his nature in the end." She shrugged and said, "You're very different from all his other friends, you know, Mr. Lassiter. At least far different from the ones I've been allowed to meet."

Her lilting voice continued to beguile Hector. He was also intrigued. And he was made more than a bit uncomfortable by her sudden familiarity in adjusting his coat. He said, "How so? Oh, and you please call me Hector going forward."

"There's a calmness about you, Hector," she said. "I'm not sure how else to say it, but that you seem very… you seem deliberate. You seem steadfast, despite the charisma you have. Focused is maybe the word I'm looking for. A word I don't associate with my genius husband. You just don't seem afraid to be still for a time."

"Former friend of mine was fond of a phrase," Hector said carefully. "Hemingway cautioned always against the danger of confusing movement for action." A smile. "Or maybe I'm just lazy by nature."

"Your ex-friend's words seems fine ones to live by," she said. "Anyway, I don't believe you and lazy are acquainted, not for a second." Virginia squeezed his shoulder and said, "I hope we meet again, Hector. You're a wise and good influence on Orson, I think. He's much calmer around you. So please know you are always welcome here."

Hector smiled and said, "Then I hope we cross paths again soon."

"I do, too."

He kissed her hand a last time, then found his way back down onto the street.

Outside the Welles' building, Hector shook out a fresh cigarette, got it going, simultaneously looking around for a cab. *Nada.*

He thought about it, then decided to walk at least a little ways back in the general direction of his hotel. Hell, maybe he'd even go the full distance if no hacks for hire presented themselves in the brisk and breezy interval. He could use the exercise.

But about three blocks along in the chilly night air, Hector realized his shadow had found him again.

It wasn't necessarily the trickiest of feats, not if the man had recognized Orson. If his stalker had identified the young actor, then Hector's mysterious pursuer or any associates had only to stake out the theaters, studios or domiciles most associated with Welles in a gambit to re-acquire Hector's trail. Christ, it didn't even have to require that much effort—not if whoever was following him was tied to the false telegrams sent to both Hector and Orson.

Well, contrary to what he'd said to Orson earlier, Hector decided he now very much did want to know what the stranger's game was about.

His shadow was about five-ten and looked quite thin under his black overcoat, so Hector figured he had crucial height and weight advantages over the man. That was all possibly fine if it came down to something hand-to-hand, but the stranger might also have a gun or two tucked away in the folds of that long, loose-fitting coat. About any of that, Hector simply couldn't be certain.

Then he caught a break: a panhandler put the arm on the stalker. This new player asked the man with the scarred face if he had a light, if he couldn't bum a smoke.

Hector's pursuer insisted he didn't have a light or a spare cigarette. The scar-faced man's accent? Was it *German*?

The beggar who wanted a smoke kept badgering.

It was just enough distraction. Hector got in close behind his shadow and pushed two fingers up tight and hard against the man's left kidney. He said softly, "You don't want to die here tonight, do you friend? Please don't make me shoot you through." Holding out his Zippo and a few Pall Malls with this other hand, Hector said to the little man who'd made his ambush possible, "There you go, old pal. Breathe deep and move on along jiffy-like, right?"

The beggar got his first cigarette going, winked his thanks and pushed on.

When it was just the two of them, Hector reached around, patted about the scar-faced man's torso, and pulled out a forty-five and the stranger's wallet. The former seemed to make more of an impression upon the stranger. He said, "And *now* you have a gun?" His stalker spat on the pavement. "That is how it is, isn't it? You tricked me." The stranger was definitely German.

"Let's take a little walk, buddy," Hector said. "You out in front, at least six-feet ahead. Make your way around that corner and down that alley to the adjacent street. Do it nice and easy, or I swear I'll cost you a kidney. Or maybe I'll just put you down in an easy jiffy."

The alley was all shadows and shafts of light in which sewer gases swirled from rusting grates and manhole lids.

As they walked from cone of light to cone of light, Hector said, "How about a name, true or even false? At very least, it would just be useful to have something to call you, don't you know."

"Kaspar Barth." The unremarkable name was offered up so readily and unaffectedly Hector sensed it might actually be the man's real handle. Either way, Hector said, "Okay, Kaspar. I suppose, for starters, you know who I am?"

"Of course. Don't waste our time with the obvious."

"Of course," Hectored repeated. "You—or you and some friends—drew me here to New York to meet with Orson, didn't you? So why are you tracking me? Why try to force this rendezvous with Mr. Welles?"

Silence. They reached the alley. Still, the man wasn't talking.

"Stonewalling isn't a winning strategy," Hector said. He flipped open the man's wallet and found some cards that supported the stranger's stated identity. So, Kaspar was apparently not a liar—not in that respect at least.

There was another card inside, mostly white and decorated with this strange image: the card was emblazoned with a black sun in which were centered two crooked crosses. A single word was printed on the card. Scowling at the piece of thin cardboard, Hector said, "What, or who in the hell, is *Thule*?"

More silence. Hector said, "What is it exactly you want that makes you follow me like this?"

Kaspar said sharply, "Just this. Do you still have it? Does Herr Welles perhaps have it instead?"

Hector shrugged. "Do either of us still have *what*? What the hell are you after?"

His captive put his hands into the pockets of his greatcoat. He looked dejected. "If you have to ask me that then it's clear you don't possess it."

"My patience has never been much worth remarkin' on," Hector said. "That's by way of a warning in addition to a lament, partner. Call it a warning — the polite part of our discussion is very near to drawing shut, I fear. I'd really like not to hurt you, you know."

"*Feh*, just shoot me now if that is so," Kaspar said. "I'll not talk, so why waste anymore of your time, or mine?"

"I'd do that because I think you're underestimating how far I might go to compel you to cooperate," Hector said.

Kaspar said, "And you're underestimating me if you truly think I'm alone."

A gun at Hector's back. Another German accent ordered him to keep still, then a gloved hand reached around him. "Surrender *your* weapon," a new voice said to Hector.

Cursing, Hector did that.

But then there was a *third* voice and this one was female. "You drop *your* gun, now, *bekannter*," the woman said to the second German. "Do it *gently*!"

Hissing, the second man did that, stooping to place his gun on the ground.

Hector started to half-turn to get a better look at this providential female stranger. She handed Hector back his gun. As she did that, the scar-faced German suddenly dove for one of the discarded guns. Hector fired and the back of the scar-faced man's head disintegrated in a pink spray, splashing a tattered poster touting *The Cradle Will Rock* at the Windsor Theatre.

The second German raised his hands in surrender, but the woman shot him cleanly between the eyes. She turned the gun on Hector.

He raised his hands, said thickly, "So he wasn't your friend, after all? Not either of them?" His mouth was suddenly very dry, his underarms damp. "Am I next in line?"

"Don't be absurd," the stranger said, her voice all silk and smoke. She was apparently American, but Hector, who'd spent many years in Paris after the Great War and through the early 1920s, thought he detected a little French accent in there, as well. She said, "Isn't it clear I'm here to save you? I rearmed you, after all."

"It is clearer now, but only for you having said it," Hector said, forcing a smile. "Can I please put my hands down? Might I fetch a fresh smoke?"

"Of course," the woman said. "You speak some German?"

"Some," Hector said, pocketing his gun and getting another Pall Mall going. "A little, here and there. Strong on Spanish and French, got some Italian… and I have a smattering of German. At least know the word 'friend' in Kraut."

The woman was backlit, so Hector couldn't make out much yet other than the fact she was slender yet shapely. And very tall. All-in-all, she presented an enticing silhouette.

The woman slid her gun into the pocket of her Black Watch tartan overcoat and put her own cigarette between her lips. She leaned into his lighter, grasping his hand to guide it there, then said, "Tell me, Hector Lassiter who knows at least a little German, are you familiar with the name Rudolf von Sebottendorf?"

"Definitely not," Hector said carefully, slipping his Zippo back into his pocket.

"What about Adam Alfred Rudlof Glauer?"

"Not that fella, either."

"They are the same man," the pretty stranger said. "Dear Lord, we really do need to talk it seems."

"So let's do that before cops or pedestrians start finding us, or worse, finding these corpses." Hector pointed at the dead men. "Ever been to the Cobalt Club?"

"Never," the woman said. "Certainly sounds better than the Pink Rat."

"Never heard of that joint," Hector said. They were shrouded in shadow and it was still hard for Hector to get a clear look at the woman. Hector said, “This Pink Rat sounds like the perfect dive.”

“Oh, it’s more than that,” the woman said. “It’s on the West Side, near the wharfs. These,” she pointed at the corpses they’d just made, “seemed to favor that dump.”

Hector offered an arm and the woman slipped hers through. “So we’ll find a cab before anyone else finds *them*,” he said of the dead Germans. “The Cobalt Club it is.”

4

THE WHITE LEGION

The rain pounded harder as they drove through the glistening streets of Manhattan; the thunder and lighting stepped up their pace, too.

On the cab ride over, Hector tried to study his savior in the gloom of the cab, but he was still unable to get a good look at her.

A bit later, inside the lobby of the tony New York night club, Hector could at last get a much better view as he helped her off with her stylish coat.

The woman wore a black dress that emphasized a generous bust. The dark dress was cinched at her trim waist with a wide, black patent leather belt adorned with an Art Deco-style buckle emblazoned with ziggurats. Crisply pleated, her skirt reached half way between knee and ankle of her long and shapely legs.

When she removed her black fedora to pass it to the nearly as sleek but more skin-baring hat check girl, Hector saw his accidental companion wore her long, glistening blue-black hair in a loose-curled up-do. There was some natural wave in that hair, he thought.

She had a sensual, full mouth, painted dark crimson. The woman also boasted high cheekbones and coppery skin, just shy of suggesting "high-yellow." That made Hector wonder if she was perhaps of mixed race.

But it was her eyes that truly startled and engaged him. They were candid, wide and the palest shade of gray. Hector found them at once unsettling and bewitching.

"We're about twenty minutes in," Hector said, offering her arm as they made their way to a table, "and I still don't know your name."

A smile, with dimples. "That would be Cassie Allegre."

"I really like that, not that it maybe matters to you. What'll you drink, Cass?"

"How about an Old Fashioned?"

"Sounds perfect," he said.

He caught a waitress's eye. Their server was sleeved in a metallic silver gown that bared proud shoulders and plenty of back.

Cassie watched Hector watching their server go and smirked. "Such a wolf. It appears you do live down to your reputation as a lady's man, Mr. Lassiter."

"So tell me about yourself," Hector said, smiling and striving to look apologetic. "You're the perfect mystery to me and clearly have all the advantages in terms of knowing something about me and my too widely reported foibles. Tell me, please, about all this tied to you. Chiefly, what terrible thing have I evidently done to Germany I know nothing about?"

"What is it you and Mr. Welles have done might be the cannier question," Cassie said. "Or, more exactly, what is it that you have that the Germans want?"

Hector scooped up some pretzels from a bowl sitting between them. "Okay. Sure. I'll bite. What might that be, exactly?"

"And there we have it, yes?" A rueful smile, bracketed by her enticing dimples. "The fact you have to ask me what this is all about underscores you don't even know what you may have." A hand wave. "If you even still possess it." Still another qualification followed with a pointed finger, "*If* you ever actually had it."

"Spoken more than a bit like our dead German friends," Hector said. "So I'll confess I'm at sea. On that note…" Hector reached into his pocket and showed her the wallet he'd taken from one of the dead men. "What I know I *do* have is one Kaspar Barth's billfold. That, and this strange card bearing a single word, *Thule*. What is *that* exactly? Do you have any clue?"

Cassie tapped the end of her cigarette on their shared ashtray. "Here's where you laugh. Thule is a secret society. A malevolent one. You've truly not heard of the Thule?" She pronounced it differently from Hector, as *too-lee*.

Hector shook his head. "Truly. Not. About tool-lee, I mean. Do please illuminate me." He raised his eyebrows. "And malevolent? Really?" He couldn't remember the last time he'd heard that adjective actually used in conversation.

She wetted her full bottom lip, laced her fingers on the table. "You are familiar with the Nazis, Mr. Lassiter?"

"Please call me Hector. And yes, painfully aware of those sorry bastards. The whole world knows about them, of course." He blew smoke out both nostrils, settling back in his chair. "What I really want to know is about you and Thule." Softer he said, careful not to be overheard, "You shot that German, summarily. Hell, your hand didn't even shake, darlin'."

"Yes." Cassie shrugged her padded shoulders. "As to shooting him, I was protecting you. They'd have killed you soon enough, please believe me about that."

Hector did happen to believe her about that much. He said, "You're Creole aren't you?"

"Why do you say that?"

"Your looks, your accent… and your last name."

"From New Orleans, yes. Studied in Paris a few years. But as to the rest, what's in a name?"

"Plenty, too often," Hector said. "So, on that note, tell me about Thule."

"It begins, more or less, with that man with the two names I asked you about. The German you said you've never heard of. I guess he kind of started all that. Thule is a secret occult society. One filled with killers now. Nazis of all stripes. Some of them are formidable men. They view themselves as actual realizations of the *übermensch* ideal. They see themselves as virtually invulnerable, rather like that comic book character—you know, Superman."

Whispering again, Hector said, "We killed those men tonight with little to no fuss. I didn't see any bullets bouncing off 'em. So much for German supermen."

"Those were merely foot soldiers. Grunts or minions. But still, they were Nazis, and so hardly human in that sense." She searched his face. "It actually bothers you I killed that man? You don't seem the squeamish type."

"He was in the process of surrendering."

"Or do you think it was just the appearance of surrender?"

Hector didn't answer. She pressed on, "Do I scare you then? Do you regard me as a killer now?"

Hector loosened his tie, then decided to remove it entirely. He rolled his necktie up and shoved it into the pocket of his suit coat. He rarely wore ties, hated them in fact. Loosening the top button of his dress shirt, Hector said, "Anyway, what is this secret society all about? What binds these crazy birds?"

Cassie settled back in her chair, quiet as their waitress brought their drinks. Hector kept all attention on his companion as their server sashayed away, the practiced swing of her hips wasted on Hector this round.

Alone again, they tapped glasses and Hector said, "*Santé.*"

Cassie smiled back and said, "*Ochan.*"

"So, back to it. These Thule?"

She sipped her drink, played with the cherry, then ate it. A sigh. "I keep hesitating only based on what I know about you from your reputation. I expect there'll be little patience on your part for what's to come."

Hector smiled. "Not necessarily. I'm intrigued as hell. And, clearly, I'm in some danger from these Germans, regardless what I might think about the supernatural or occult, which, as you correctly guess, is pretty much nil."

"Just not the spiritual type, Mr. Lassiter?"

"Oh, I'm plenty spiritual, or so I like to think. Just not particularly religious."

"Fair enough. I think I know what you mean by that. So, the Thule Society as we know it now, as we and these Germans care about it, traces it roots back to around the time of the Great War."

"It is truly occult?"

"To its black bones," Cassie said. She leaned across the table into the candlelight. "You have to open your mind to this much at least, Hector. The Germans, the Nazi Party—at very least some key figures close to Hitler, and maybe even Hitler himself, if some stories are to be believed—they set real stock in the Thule Society and certain valuable religious artifacts it covets. Artifacts they believe bestow their keepers almost God-like powers. They actually are seeking the Holy Grail, the Ark of the Covenant and the item that concerns you and Mr. Welles."

She was too right: everything Cassie was telling him now struck Hector as well beyond daft. Still, two men were dead because of all of this crazy nonsense. Two dead that he *knew* about. There was no reason to doubt others might have also been killed for this farce. He said, "And this Holy Roller item that apparently should matter to Orson and I, what is that exactly?"

The candlelight burnished her pale gray eyes. She sipped more of her drink, then said, "Have you ever heard of the Holy Lance of Longinus? Of his spear?"

"Nah, but that is surely an odd handle," Hector said, sipping his own drink. "This old boy and his spear sounds more than a little like the makings of a Tijuana Bible. Who is this Longinus character?"

"Who was he," Cassie corrected.

"Okay, who was Longinus?"

"He was a Roman soldier purported to be present at Christ's crucifixion. Some legends have it they were contemplating breaking Christ's legs to hasten His death. Longinus thrust his spear into Jesus' side to see if He was still alive. Blood and water gushed from His wound. So, the Savior's blood came in contact with the spear's tip. Ever since, that weapon has been believed to possess boundless supernatural powers. Most call the Holy Lance the Spear of Destiny. Any army or leader that controls the spear is said to be unstoppable." She hesitated, then added, "And those who lose possession of the Holy Lance are said to die almost immediately after its loss. They always die violently."

"So Thule is just some kind of crazy religious cult, just as you've described it," Hector said. "Just a load of mumbo-jumbo and wrong-headed faith?"

A shake of the head. Cassie said, "A faith? No, that's grossly understating it. Thule is an occult secret society. Its members believe their cult descends from Gods you or I would dismiss as Norse myths. But they really believe in these ancient deities and legends. They do that like all those around here in this gaudy place likely believe in Jesus Christ, I suppose. Thule is quietly but potently central to the Nazi movement, whether Hitler himself realizes it or not. The concept of Thule and racial purity underpins the whole concept of the Master Race that fuels Himmler's vision of the S.S."

Hector raised his glass again, hesitated, then said, "And you? What are you exactly, in terms of all this? Avenging angel? Christian soldier, marching boldly onward?" A smile. "Cassie, are you some kind of Vatican operative, or the like?" He reached out and squeezed her hand. "Hell, maybe British Secret Service?"

"That last is probably closest. But I'm not working for the British. We'll come to what I am, in time." She withdrew her hand from his.

Hector tried to plumb the depths of her arresting gray eyes. He rubbed his jaw. It had already been a long day; he could feel his five o-clock-shadow-and-then-some as his fingertips rustled across his stubbly cheek. "You saved my life, so I guess you have a right to tell your story anyway you care to. I promise I'll stop derailing you. Tell me more about Longinus and his spear and what on earth it possibly has to do with me."

Watching for his reaction, Cassie said, "Your part in all this, it begins in Ireland, several years ago, during your travels there, when you met the younger Mr. Welles."

"Hell, he's still young," Hector said. The smoke from his cigarette resting in the ashtray rose in a swirling column between them, twirling into the blue, overhead light.

"Yes, three years younger than me, in fact," Cassie said, "though I somehow think of Mr. Welles as much older than I am."

"Near or far, Orson has that effect on most, yes," Hector said. "I met him in Ireland in 1931, I reckon. He was just getting his start on the stage. A plucky teen who talked himself into his first role there in Dublin. I was frankly astonished to find this old soul living in this bombastic young man's oversized body. Maybe tellingly, even then, Orson excelled at playing old men on stage, even though he was only sixteen at the time."

"And in Spain you traveled together, too," she said. "That was about 1932, wasn't it?"

"Somewhere in that range," Hector said. "We did some traveling together there, yeah. He was alone in Morocco first, then we met again in Spain, mostly chasing the bulls and the festivals. The *ferias*. We finally came back to the States long about 1933. He was like a mooching kid brother back then. Now? Harder to define the relationship, though I still seem to pick up all of the tabs, despite Orson's growing fame on the radio and stage. Still, he's grown up, at least a little, I think."

"Just so. What else do you remember about that time, Hector? What do you remember about Ireland, particularly?"

Because he was the man he was, an author notorious for living what he wrote and writing about what he lived, Hector reckoned he remembered plenty.

5

THE HYPNOTIZED AUDIENCE

Dublin, 1931

Young Orson's name preceded him: Hector had read a notice in one of the daily newspapers that said the teen Welles had "descended on Dublin and taken it by storm."

Shopworn clichés aside, that attitude seemed to characterize the reaction of most in the critical theater community in Ireland regarding the imposing, already six feet and-then-some, sixteen-year-old American.

Still, none of that was really any enticement or inducement for Hector to take in Welles' act. Hector was never one for the theater, preferring instead the cinema—for which he occasionally wrote—when indulging his very limited leisure time.

Hector was only going to tonight's show because a friend's relative with whom he was staying, a pleasant enough colleen named Teagan Hanrahan, loved to see stage shows but rarely had the money or company to do so.

Hector's longtime friend, an Irish ex-pat cop named Jimmy Hanrahan, had pleaded that while Hector passed through Dublin he please try to get Jimmy's female cousin out and about a bit. Seemed that Cleveland, Ohio-based Jimmy's clan back home on the Emerald Isle was convinced Teagan was toiling under threat of spinsterhood.

The night's play would be the third Hector had endured with Teagan for Jimmy's sake. On this night, she had selected a show at the still newish Gate, a play called *The Dead Ride Fast*.

Orson Welles was to play an American in this production. The play's plot pivoted on black magic, so in the end the production was just pulpy enough to hold Hector's attention, something he couldn't say of the more classical first two productions Teagan had dragged him to.

After the performance, Hector presumed to take a clearly smitten Teagan back stage to meet Orson. He figured as a fellow American working in the field of the arts, a possibly homesick boy-wonder might welcome the unexpected visit from a Texas-born novelist of some small renown of his own.

As it happened, Orson's ego was such Hector could have been from Mongolia or Galway for all that the teen actor cared. Welles was still early in his career, and eating up any and all admiration from *any* source.

Bent before a dusty mirror, Orson finished removing a false nose with some alcohol, then stood and shook Hector's hand. He bowed and kissed Teagan's hand.

Up close, young Orson was a charismatic figure with intense eyes, an unruly mop of hair and this voice that didn't at all fit his age or face. The kid was also the near giant everyone went on about, standing perhaps six-two and looking Hector straight in the eye or a bit better as he pumped his hand and, to Hector's pleasant surprise, praised his novels. Orson correctly rattled off the titles of three or four of Hector's books the young actor declared to be personal favorites.

"I'll confess I've wanted to try my hand at writing stuff similar to what you publish," Orson told Hector. "You should give me writing tips and I'll trade you acting lessons."

It would have been a one-sided exchange, as Hector harbored no theatrical ambitions whatever. But then he saw how Teagan was basking in the young actor's presence. "Maybe we should talk those terms out over a pint," Hector suggested, just trying to stretch out their meeting for Teagan's sake.

Combing his hair and studying Hector in a mirror, Orson said, "Your treat?"

"Certainly," Hector said. "I—*we*—invited you."

"Delighted to come then," Orson said. "Just give me a moment to finish becoming myself."

They claimed a snug in the pub a block's walk from the Gate. To Teagan's disappointment, Orson confessed he was contemplating leaving Dublin soon. He'd come to Ireland with romantic misconceptions about the country and about Dublin's theater scene—talking himself into his first role by exaggerating his prowess and experience, as well as lying about his age.

Local fame had virtually followed Orson's first curtain call. The kid actor already felt he'd crested some hill as rave notices had also been published back in the States in key newspapers. Orson increasingly felt it was time to move on before he began to slide down the other side of the pinnacle in "increasingly claustrophobic" Dublin.

"Where will you go, then?" Teagan asked.

"New York, of course," Orson said. "Or maybe Chicago first. My notices here have reached both those places, I'm told. I should now have a solid foothold in either city."

Orson turned his attention to Hector. Over the rim of his pint of Guinness, the actor said, "I came here to make my name. What brings you to Ireland, Hector?"

The novelist tried for something glib. "I live in the Florida Keys. Just ducking hurricane season."

Orson swatted that aside. "Absurd. Why are you truly in Ireland, old man?"

Old man. Even though was born in Kenosha, Wisconsin, there was something about Orson that almost convinced you he was vaguely British by birth. Hector said, "Just flirting with a change. Needed distance from the island."

It was six years since Brinke's death, and Key West still felt strangely empty to Hector. His friend Hemingway's now permanent presence on the last Key only drove it in harder, evoking memories of 1924 Paris, when Brinke, Hem and Hector had potently roamed the City of Light as a trio of sleek and ambitious, experience-hungry up-and-comers.

"We should go back to the States together," Orson said. "Gentlemen of the road, so to speak. I don't think they even have hurricanes in New York City." He blinked, contemplating, then said, "Certainly they don't in Chicago."

"When were you thinking of going back?" Hector nodded for another Guinness for himself.

"End of February," Orson said. "My stage commitments will be complete then."

Hector couldn't explain why he was congenial to traveling with this young near stranger, but he felt something immediately clicked between them.

Orson's brown eyes glistened. "Can this schedule be made to work for you?"

Hector accepted his fresh pint with its faint impression of a four-leaf clover floating in the foam. "Gives me more that a month to see more of Ireland," he said. "Maybe I'll even bump around Scotland a time. Fish a bit in those lochs."

A flash of lightning. Thunder rumbled and shook the glass. Orson grumbled, "My God, the weather here I surely won't miss."

Teagan nodded in commiseration, looking as though the young man's remark upon the weather came as a revelation, apparently not realizing she would be left to endure that weather long after the two Americans had moved on.

Orson smiled at her and said, "Dublin's fair ladies on the other hand? They will be much harder to part with."

"So, it went like that," Hector said to Cassie. "We came home in the early spring after some time in England, and a brief time in Paris, which is still my favorite city in the world."

Cassie bit her bee-stung lower lip. "Almost sounds like a romantic idyll, the way you paint it. I mean, if you clearly weren't such a legendary skirt-chaser."

"To be sure, I don't have tendencies in that other direction," Hector said. "Orson either. Anyway, things didn't go as Orson had envisioned for him back then. All those theater doors here or in Chicago were anywhere near as open to him as Orson anticipated. So, after a few months, Orson got the itch to travel abroad again. I was pretty flush at the time and I've always liked to wander, to mosey. He went ahead to Morocco while I finished a novel. I met up with him a bit later, in Spain, like I told you. Hemingway had just published his bullfighting bible, *Death in the Afternoon*. Orson had the bullfighting bug from that book. Young Welles had it bad."

"So you two rogues went to Spain," she prompted, seeming to sense some other tangent might otherwise loom.

"So we went to Spain," Hector said.

"And there you met Mr. Rosenblum, and you took possession of the medallion," Cassie said. "Tell me about *that*. It's really what matters in the end, you know."

The young actor and elder author met up in Seville; they settled in Triana.

Orson, eager to immerse himself in the culture, "to live among the common people of Spain" as he phrased it, put up in a little place above a brothel or "fuzz castle," as he termed it.

Hector had first chosen a slightly smarter hotel on the edge of the pottery district. There he took up with a dusky beauty with blue-black hair, named, of all things, Carmen. In Spain, between bars, bullfights and time lost lolling in the arms of his tempestuous, back-scratching Gypsy lover, Hector honored his pledge of tutoring Orson in the dubious art of fiction writing for the pulp magazines back in the States.

Orson's resulting sales were fewer and farther between than Hector's, but they generated sufficient scratch to oil Orson's working-class lifestyle. Incidentals beyond that Hector still covered for young Welles, an intimation of years of check covering on Hector's part seemingly yet to come.

They were in the city's Gypsy quarter, sitting in a *barra* not far from Orson's place above the brothel, savoring a sweating pitcher of sangria and plotting a path through the coming season's bullfighting circuit to points further out in Spain when a haggard and panting old man collapsed onto the bench next to Orson.

The sweating old man identified himself only as "Rosenblum." He had gray-streaked black hair and olive skin; a prominent nose and skittish yet penetrating anthracite eyes.

He said in Spanish, "What are your names you two young fools? Quickly! We have hardly any time, you know!"

Confused but somehow game, Hector readily supplied his real name; Orson did likewise. Commotion at the entrance of the bar: the old man urged something wrapped in a paisley handkerchief into Hector's hands. It felt like a metal disc, roughly the size of a baseball. It was heavy.

"You must keep this safe," the old man said. "I'll make it more than worth your while. Meet me at noon tomorrow in front of the Giralda. Return this to me then and there. Do that and I'll pay you both. I'll make it well worth your trouble."

The old man didn't wait for an answer. He rose unsteadily and said, "I'll go out the back. When the men after me leave that way too, you should dash out the front. You run too, but the other way. Questions might be asked of others here. Then they will look for you like they do for me. Believe me—you don't want to be identified or caught by the men chasing me."

As predicted, a band of strangers—five of them—swiftly passed by Hector and Orson. All of the men were blond and blue-eyed. One of them, very broad-shouldered and with closely cropped yellow hair, stood at least six-six.

When they had passed, Orson wet his lips and said, "At the risk of sounding cowardly, I feel compelled to follow the old man's urgings that we leave, Hector. I think we should do that and with real haste, just as he said."

Hector nodded. "No argument here." They slipped out into the harsh afternoon glare, losing themselves in the crowd.

Back in Orson's room above the brothel, they at last got a look at the clunky metal disc the old man entrusted to them.

6

DON'T CATCH ME

Hector contemplated Cassie. He waved a hand, trailing cigarette smoke. "Anyway, we kept our promised noon appointment next day in front of the minaret. As you'll probably have guessed, the old man didn't show. So we tried again the next day and even the day after that. We looked for any word of the codger in the local papers. Then we simply stopped being stubborn. Orson and I pushed on from the city, chasing those bulls, just as we'd planned. Long about the summer of 1933, we at last came home. Orson and the medallion—this hunk of metal he thought theatrical looking—went to Chicago. I finally settled in again in Key West before moving to another island a while back. I live out Seattle way these days, more or less."

Cassie took a slow deep breath. She stroked a wave of dark hair back from her beaded forehead. The place *was* feeling a little close, Hector thought. The posh club was certainly more crowded than it had been when they arrived.

They were also starting to draw stares from neighboring tables, Hector noticed. There was something about the quality of the amber stage lights as they further bronzed Cassie's flesh, something about her own dewy sheen from the heat that burnished her skin, drawing stares and narrowed eyes.

Back in the lobby, under the brighter, whiter lights, it seemed to Hector she'd easily enough passed for Caucasian. But here in candlelight and the reflected, many-hued footlights, tawny Cassie looked just possibly something *else*, even in Hector's far gentler estimation. She was too exotic; too bronze for the lily-white bluebloods.

He figured he was of-a-sudden flirting with some misperception of miscegenation and therefore near certain trouble with the club's strapping bouncers. His sultry companion seemed to read his mind as she scanned their neighbors' accusing eyes. She said softly, "I don't want to cost you a haunt, cowboy. We should move on from here. I hate this joint, anyway. We'll pick up the tale at my kind of place, okay?"

"Your kind of place? Where would that be?" Hector refrained from testing an unworthy theory by guessing at possible nightspots elsewhere in the city, Harlem for one.

She rose and took his hand. "It's a new place, in Greenwich Village." She flashed him that dimpled smile to which he feared he was already growing dangerously accustomed.

And her move to take his hand in hers, now that they were departing? That also set his mind to work on it all. But maybe she just wanted to rub their neighbors' faces in their racist perceptions a little, Hector thought. If so, he gamely cooperated, wrapping an arm around her trim waist and pulling her closer.

Another part of Hector wondered despite her dismissal of him as a "lady's man" if she wasn't perhaps actually taking an interest in him in that way.

She said, "Come on, Mister Hector Lassiter. Let me broaden your horizons. Maybe I'll at least give you something or someplace new and fresh to write about."

She gave their second cabbie of the night, a gruff and beetle-browed man named Moe, an address at number one Sheridan Square.

Looking back through the rear window of the cab as they merged into traffic, Hector said, "Fairly certain we're being followed. See that Chrysler Imperial, three cars back?"

"I did," Cassie said, "and I'm all but certain you're right. But here's the good news. Broad-minded as the place we're going to is, even would-be Aryans will stand out in there like a tarantula on a fig leaf, so I think we'll be just fine. At least until we eventually have to leave this next club."

This next club proved to be "Café Society," a hot-spot just a few months old that featured decidedly non-white musicians performing for a mix of white and black clientele as well as a hearty contingent of lefty theater types.

As they rolled up out front, Cassie squeezed Hector's arm and said, "I already love this place, though it's hardly been around any time at all. They tout it as 'The Wrong Place for the Right People.'"

Hector laughed. "As slogans go, that one's pretty god-damned wonderful. I may have to appropriate that for use in book or a story somewhere."

"Sorry, think it's trademarked now."

Hector shrugged, pushing his fedora back on his head with two fingers and softly said, "Well, now that's a heart-breaker." He paid their driver, then held Cassie's kid-gloved hand to help her from the cab.

The doorman, tall and dark, looked them over, smiled and then winked and licked his lips at Hector as the novelist frowned back. Hector sighed and followed his striking companion down the stairs. He caught himself concentrating on the curve and sway of her hips and as she made her way down the stairs on stiletto heels.

The patrons were indeed a racial mix. The walls were a riot of murals by Berman, Groth, Hoff and Refregier—emerging artists whose work Hector was pleasantly surprised to recognize.

Billie Holiday was performing on stage under smoky blue light, belting out a yearning version of *When a Woman Loves a Man*. The last time Hector had seen Billie perform was at the Cotton Club. Even for its location, that famous Harlem nightspot where the ritzy white classes liked to "slum" remained racially segregated in a way that this newish place strikingly did not.

An elderly old dark-skinned man led them to a table not far from the stage, then beat Hector to the punch scooting in Cassie's chair. They ordered two more Old Fashioneds, cocktails that turned out to be stronger and far better made than those at the Cobalt Club.

Nursing his potent drink, Hector said, "I've heard old Heinrich Himmler, S.S. honcho, actually believes Atlantis was real. And that it was maybe in Tibet of all places?"

Cassie smiled, savoring another cherry. "So you know more than you pretend to about Thule."

"Not really, just a little more about the Nazis and those at their crazy upper echelons," he said. "I'm a novelist, never forget that. Always seeking grist for the fiction mill, just as you said. But candidly, all of this is too out there, even for the likes of me, Cass. I don't write fantasy or science fiction stuff, you know."

She said, "Fair enough. Then what became of what you must therefore see as the meaningless medallion that fell into your and Orson's hands? Where did it go after reaching Chicago?"

Hector shrugged. "Truly have no clue. Orson was an up-and-coming actor. The young makeup genius and tyro costume designer. He thought the medallion theatrical looking as all hell, just as I said. So if memory serves about something that seemed so inconsequential years ago, I reckon I let him keep it in that vein. As to whether Orson still has it or not?" A weary shrug. "Hell, by now it could be in the traveling trunk of some two-bit, round-heels actress making the Borscht Belt circuit for all I know. Orson's nothing if not impetuous." Hector ended with another shrug. "This gewgaw is really that all-important?"

"It's far more than just some ornament," Cassie said. "It's a key *and* a map. A key and a map to a crypt where a legendary relic is stored. A treasure that the Thule—the Nazis—are desperate to lay hands on."

"And that's this so-called Spear of Longinus?" Hector scowled.

"In theory, Hitler already controls the Spear of Destiny," she said. "Sadly, it fell into his hands when he seized Austria. It was housed in Vienna back then. Supposedly, Hitler has since had it moved to Germany, to St. Katherine's Church in Nuremberg, specifically."

A funny smile. "Here's the thing, Hector. It's almost certain the spear Hitler has is a fake. The story goes it was swapped for a replica in 1931 by a Jewish mystical secret society, done in hopes of keeping it from falling into Thule—or Nazi—hands. The real spear is believed to be now hidden in a crypt somewhere in Rome. The man who stole it from Vienna was an elderly

Jewish solider of fortune allegedly known as Rosenblum. That's your *aha* moment there, of course. This Rosenblum succeeded in secreting the spear somewhere in Rome, then he was pursued across Europe by one of the early converts to Thule and his minions. Mr. Rosenblum eventually died in Spain almost immediately after giving the medallion over to you and your friend. The finally caught up with the poor, brilliant man just seconds after you met him. That very last part, you two having the disc, remained unknown until just recently. You see, it all kind of stopped there in Spain, the trail, the legends of the medallion. At least until a few weeks ago."

Hector said, "So what happened a few weeks ago to change all that?"

"The Nazis got wind of what happened with Mr. Rosenblum and realized their spear might be bogus," Cassie said. "Apparently, this Thule whom you and your friend saw in passing in Spain years ago—the very, very tall one, their leader it's believed, a man named Rune Fuchs—ran afoul of the law shortly after killing Rosenblum. He served several years in prison, which more or less bought you and Orson a few years of peace and quiet from the Nazis and Thules. When this man got out of confinement, and he started to talk to his fellow cult members again, the Thule—now some of them S.S., in actuality—resumed their search for the medallion and the real spear. They resumed the search with gusto and with the belief you or Orson Welles have what they want."

"So the actual Spear of Destiny is still in play, or so these idiots think." Hector rubbed his jaw again. A wry smile. "Gotta say, Mussolini is such a prize idiot, it almost makes me believe something supernatural *is* propping him up after a fashion. That sorry bastard could drop a rock and miss the ground. Old Benito's every inch that incompetent."

Cassie said, "Anyway, that's what the medallion is for, a map to the real spear's location, and a key to opening the vault in which it is hidden."

"Yeah," Hector said, grinding out his cigarette, then draining his drink. He nodded for another libation. "This is leagues past crazy for sure." Those two dead men nagged at Hector's mind however. He said, "They came at me directly tonight, as you saw. Jesus Christ, that means Orson, Virginia and their child are probably sitting ducks."

"Yes, they'll eventually move on your friend, and his family, too, if need be," she said. "You two are the last men definitely known to have seen the medallion, to have held it."

A smile and her hand closed over his. "Rest easy for now. I'm not the only one on this from our side you know. Your friend is under a kind of guard, even as we speak. It also doesn't hurt that FDR and members of his cabinet so fawn over Mr. Welles."

"Orson's got the right kind of politics for Roosevelt's lefty crowd." Hector considered her hand touching his, faint bronze on still-tanned white. "You said *us*. Who is *us*? Who exactly do you work for, Cassie? You still owe me that much."

"It's a kind of civilian arm of military intelligence," she said, carefully choosing her words. "I was recruited and then trained in firearms and the like, because I have special skills, you might say that…"

An announcer stepped into the smoky spotlight, holding up his hands and calling for silence. "Your indulgence, please," he said. "Ladies and gentlemen, we need some quiet."

When everyone was silent but for a few scattered coughs, he continued, "As has already become custom here at the Café Society, all food service will cease for Miss Holiday's closing number. In order for you to focus on the true message of her song, there will be no food or drink service, and no encore afterward."

The lights went down, plunging the basement room into blackness. Then a single, stark beam fell on Billie Holiday's face, a huge violet flower pinned up in her glistening black hair.

She began to sing "Strange Fruit," a dirge-like ballad about racially motivated lynching, a song said to have been inspired by a photograph of two young black men dangling dead from a tree branch, ropes digging into their ruined necks.

Southern trees bear a strange fruit,
Blood on the leaves and blood at the root.

Respectful silence hung over the room throughout her performance. She ended to thunderous applause. When it was done, Hector settled their tab and said, "I'd suggest a brisk walk in the crisp autumn air around the Village to clear our heads and finish your filling in about the matter and nature of your employment. But as we likely still have stalkers out there lying in wait—"

Cassie suddenly gripped Hector's handed and nodded toward the entrance. "We need to move, Hector, *now*." Four men, all blond and blue-eyed, were brazenly brandishing guns and pushing diners out of their way, stalking toward Cassie and Hector. So much for "lying in wait."

A woman screamed, yelled something about guns and then the Ku Klux Klan. Others took up the cry, some diving for cover, other's rising and scattering while screaming.

The place erupted as more diners, black and white, scrambled toward the stairs leading up to the front door and the street.

Hector spotted an illuminated sign that promised a second, rear exit behind the stage. He reached for Cassie's hand but the crush of panicked diners was carrying her the other way in the resulting stampede.

Cursing, Hector made for the rear door, two of the men breaking off to pursue him, the other two still trying to reach Cassie.

7

JOURNEY INTO FEAR

Hector retained the automatic he'd taken earlier in the evening from one of the men Cassie had killed. Ruling out the value—let along the prospects—of potentially taking any prisoners, Hector ran up the steps and then pressed his back to the wall. Feet were pounding up the stairs as he rounded the corner; words were urgently exchanged in German. Hector raised his gun to the level of his shoulder.

As the two blond men emerged into the windy cold from the cozy club, Hector fired twice. The blond men staggered and fell.

He chanced a look down the staircase to see if the other two men had maybe broken off their pursuit of Cassie in favor of chasing Hector. He saw more diners had at last realized the place had a second exit; they were just making their way to the foot of the stairs.

Hector pocketed his gun and dashed around the side of the building before anyone could see him.

He reached the front of the club in time to see a cab peel off from the curb at speed: Cassie was in the back seat with a gun to the driver's head.

A Chrysler Imperial with two blond men in the front seat tore off after her cab.

Cursing, Hector stalked away from the melee of the dinner club and the hopeless scramble for cabs and cars on the part of its terrified patrons.

After walking deeper into the Village, Hector at last found his own cab and asked to be taken to Orson's theater on West 41st Street. He checked his wristwatch in the taxi's dome light and saw it was now Friday—12:30 a.m., in fact. That was typically a prime-working hour for night owl Orson. That was if the randy Mr. Welles wasn't instead spending the early morning hours tangled in some dancer's arms and legs.

Checking over his shoulder, Hector said to the cab driver, "Understand, I don't want to go directly where I told you, pal. We're going to take some alleys and back roads getting there. Indulge me, yeah?"

The cabbie just winked in the mirror. "The more we drive, the more you gotta pay me. We can go to Atlantic City and back, just the way youse want. Just say the crazy word, pal."

This time, Hector was firmly committed to shaking any tails.

Hector experienced trouble at the theater door. A balding and imperious man of indeterminate accent refused him entry to the crumbling building. Hector at last managed to catch sight of Welles and called out, "Orson, can you tell this fella I'm truly your friend?"

Smiling uncertainly, Orson made his way to the theater door. The balding man sniffed in Hector's direction and said to the young actor, "I suppose this is some other yellow journalist or pulp scribbler whom you mean to try and bring into our cash-starved fold?"

The man sniffed again and said in a Mid-Atlantic English accent that set Hector's teeth on edge, "Clearly, this creature is a writer. That fairly comes off him in fetid gusts."

Hector smiled ruefully and thrust out a hand. The man, now John Houseman but born Jacques Haussmann, gripped Hector's bigger mitt reluctantly and shook it limply. Self-important, prissy and condescending—these were Hector's sorry first impressions of Orson's primary and increasingly uneasy creative partner on this still-young Friday morning.

Houseman was rather distantly known to Hector as a name and vexing personality to his young theatrical partner, and the author supposed that what little he thought he knew via Orson colored much of his initial perception of John. Hector had endured Welles' endlessly bitching on about the growing creative friction he was experiencing with Houseman.

John had also had a hand in producing some sort of opera that Hector's one-time mentor, Gertrude Stein, had written a few years ago. Predictably, Gertrude had had strong opinions about all of that, not all of them charitable.

On the other hand, Hector and John were much closer in age, and so probably experienced many of the same challenges and frustrations in coping with the often petulant boy genius whose friendship they shared. Maybe, Hector thought, the two of them could find fair footing in commiseration about all of that at some point.

Still, Hector felt a need to needle back, at least a little bit. Letting his Texas tones leak in deeper, he said, "I've spent a lot of time in Europe over the years, rangin' here and there, but your accent is a positive mystery to me, old pal."

Obviously pleased by Hector's digs, Orson split a smile between the two older men and said, "It's bastardized Romanian.

That accent, I mean. What's the sad saying, John? Being Romanian isn't a nationality but instead a profession? That is it, isn't it?"

Orson's jibe elicited a frosty smile from Houseman. Hector said, "Anyway, no worries about another artistic mouth to feed. I have no intention or interests in joining the Mercury family, so please don't fret. I'm a maverick. Never been much of an effective collaborator, and I always pay my own way."

Houseman said, "So what is it exactly that you write, Mr. Lassiter?"

"Doesn't matter a lick," Hector said. "Tonight, or this early morning I should say, I'm just an old friend of Orson's." He showed Houseman his broad back. "Speaking of which, we need to talk, Orson. We need to do that right now."

Hector led his young friend deeper into his own theater, to a quiet corner. He said softly, "Remember that man who was following me? Well, he's shot to death."

Orson looked up sharply. "You killed him?"

"Not that one specifically, no. There are some others who've died since we last talked. They died just as badly. You're tied up in this, too, I'm afraid. It spirals from stuff years back, from when we were in Spain together. We need to get back to your place. You and I need to get your family and put you and them some place safe."

Orson held up his hands. "Slow down there, old man. What on earth is going on? I have deadlines, several commitments. Performances."

Hector took his young friend by the arm. He roughly pulled him toward a back exit, simultaneously drawing his gun.

"I'm serious, Orson. You're just going to have to trust me on all this. I'll explain on the way."

8

CONFIDENTIAL REPORT

On the cab ride to Orson's place, Hector caught Welles up on his strange and bloody Thursday night. Hector lit a cigarette as he unfurled his tale; Orson worked at a pipe. The novelist closed his Zippo, pocketed it and cracked his window; he'd always hated the smell of pipes. He said, "Our politics—our differences there—I have some sense of."

Orson struck a match and at last got his pipe going. He flung the match out the window, cranked the window closed and shivered. "Yes, yours are narrow-minded and wrong. Even selfish. *Republican,* I suspect. Where are you going with this, Hector?"

"Religion," Hector said. "Faith. About those matters, I don't have a strong sense where you're concerned."

"Oh, I try to be a good Christian," Orson said, settling back in his seat, wreathed in pipe smoke. "But I don't pray too often. Don't want to bore God, I suppose."

Hector smiled. "That's a swell line." It also struck Hector as one that was very practiced, a celebrity's bon mot for the wags along the Great White Way. He turned in his seat so he could watch their wake. "What about the occult," Hector said.

"Do you set any stock in this Thule stuff about ancient weapons and their supernatural powers? In all this satanic stuff?"

"If you believe in God, you must be prepared to believe in the Devil, Hector." Orson blew more smoke. "As it happens, my grandmother was a witch." He said it matter-of-factly.

Hector shook his head and said, "My condolences."

"No, I'm being quite serious." Orson's voice grew sonorous. "I loathed the woman, the smelly, evil dwarf. She had a black magic shrine on the top floor of her home. I watched her perform a sabbat there, little me spying on her from a closet. She actually put a curse on my parents' marriage, the sick bitch. I'd discount that but for the fact she so loathed my mother, who then died quite shockingly when I was nine."

That million-dollar radio voice cracked. "At my father's funeral, the old bitch actually managed to have crept in satanic nonsense from Madame Blavatsky and Aleister Crowley, had it wedged in there in stinking dollops between the Bible verses. Did you know Blavatsky placed a swastika on the cover of her book years and years before the Nazi's appropriated the symbol? It's quite true."

Hector didn't know that. Layers of pipe smoke now filled the cab. He cracked his window wider. He noticed their driver doing the same. Hector checked the street behind them. All seemed to be clear behind them for the moment.

Orson said, "Hector, you actually met Crowley—the so-called 'Wickedest Man Alive' in person, didn't you? I seem to remember hearing from someone that you did."

Hector caught himself massaging his fist. "Once. Fleetingly, in Paris. February, 1924."

The actor nodded. "And your thoughts about the Great Beast of the Pit, or Lucifer's Leviathan, based on that meeting?"

Hector shrugged. "Not much other than old Al had a glass jaw."

Orson roared with laughter, slapping his thigh. Once he was spent, he frowned at his suddenly extinguished pipe and worked at getting it going again. They were approaching his apartment building. Hector said, "Is there some way in there other than through the front door, kid?"

Virginia struggled to close her suitcase. Hector smiled and said, "Please allow me."

"When I said I hoped we crossed paths again soon, I meant it Hector, but certainly not under these circumstances," She watched him work at her suitcase. "You're sure we're actually in some kind of real danger? This seems positively mad. We should just call the police."

He nodded. "Four men are dead that I know of. It's all crazy sounding, I grant you that. But in a situation like this, the aggressor sets the terms of engagement. These men, these alleged Nazis, they mean business. So we have to react accordingly. Police won't be of use."

A sigh. She said, "So where will we go?"

"We'll spend some time on the road, making sure we're free of tails," Hector said. "Then we'll get you all in a hotel somewhere, under another name. Hopefully, in a day or two, we'll get this sorted out. Get it behind us all, nice and neatly."

The flint was dying in Hector's Zippo so he scooped up a hotel matchbox emblazoned with "Monolith" and got a cigarette going. He watched Virginia tuck in her daughter.

The little girl said to her mother, "Should I be afraid?"

Her father said, "Of course not. Remember, I'm the Shadow, yes?" Orson assumed his radio voice as the invisible avenger. "As you sow evil, so shall you reap evil! Crime does not pay. The Shadow knows!" Then that evil cackle. Yeah, Hector thought, that should surely help the kid have sweet dreams.

Orson moved to the window and looked down at the street, all beetle-brow and frowns. "I simply can't be a prisoner here, you know, Hector. I have Sunday's broadcast to see to, as well as this infernal *Death of Danton* to whip into shape for the Mercury Theater—for the *actual* theater, that is to say. I have obligations that must be kept."

"It's two in the morning," Hector said. "You damn well can get some sleep now. Later in the morning, I'll see you safely get to all the places you need to be. By then, maybe we can even manage some kind of proper protection for you, so you can keep playing radio and stage impresario."

Orson said hopefully, "The bar downstairs still appeared open. Perhaps we can just relish a nightcap and the two of us can have some of the good old deep talk and—"

"You sleep *now*," Hector repeated. "You've got a family to watch over. For my part, I'm just on the other side of that panel. Knock or holler if you need help." Hector nodded in the direction of the connecting door. "Oh, and focus on remembering what became of that damned medallion years ago. Seems everything—most importantly our good health—hinges on that damned relic." He hesitated. "You're *sure* it might not be in some storage or costume closet back at the theater?"

"Sure as I can be of anything that never really mattered much to me," Orson said. "It almost certainly never made it to the Mercury. You know how I was, then. I'm pretty sure I gave it to an actress or some dusky Gypsy girl. To some fancy of the moment all those years back. It's just a question of which one." Hector fought the urge to wince; he saw Virginia's eyes flare.

"Still..." Hector said, "If it is still in the theater and these bastards should decide to look this morning?"

Orson waved his pipe, dismissing all that. "They won't have the opportunity to look. As close to premiere as we are now, and with my work tempos, I'm telling you, the theater is full, day and night, much to the chagrin of my actors and crew, let alone some superstitious German fools. There'll be no digging around there now by so-called Thule, that I can promise you, old man."

Hector waited in the corridor to hear that Orson followed his instructions in securing his own door. At last satisfied that was done, Hector went to his room.

He was about to place his key in the door when he heard a noise from his room. It sounded like water running in there. Standing to the side of the door, Hector drew his gun and rapped knuckles on the panel. He said, "Let's not do this the stupid and probably bloody way. Come out now so I don't have to come in shooting."

The door squeaked and it opened a crack. A female voice said, "It's not like that."

Hector lowered his gun. He said, "Cassie?"

The door opened wider. Hector shoved his gun into his waistband.

Cassie was dripping wet, wearing only a towel. Her jaw was bruised, her throat scratched. He caressed her cheek, simultaneously closing the door behind him with a foot. He locked the door with his other hand.

He said, "It was bad?"

She nodded at the soiled heap of her clothes. "Bloody, anyway. I've got nothing to wear presently."

Her looked her over again—bare legs, bare shoulders and arms. Her hair was slicked back and her face fresh scrubbed of makeup. Hector preferred women in this natural state—devoid of makeup and all the current season's too-chic shellac. He felt this stirring. He said, "That's not your blood on all those clothes, I take it. I surely don't see much damage below the neck." That didn't sound right, but he sensed she knew what he meant.

"No, it's not mine," she said with a half-smile. This soft drip-drip on the tile. "Sorry, didn't quite have time to fully dry off. I should go do that now."

He placed a hand on her bare shoulder. "Hell, there's no rush." Hector lifted her hair. "Just as well you don't finish toweling off. I think you're headed straight back into that shower. Afraid there's still quite some bit of blood matted in your hair."

Cassie wrinkled her nose. "Oh, yuck. I'm so sorry."

"Not your fault," he said. "And it's hardly the first blood I've seen. Although this looks like it must have been from a slaughter. And how on earth did you find me here?"

A shrug of those shoulders. "I have government connections, remember? Every hotel in the city has got your description. Finding you wasn't hard at all with that advantage. Your friend and his family are next door?"

"Just through that door," Hector said, inclining his head leftward. He looked again at the ruin of her bloody clothes. "Those two I saw chasing you? You killed the both of them?"

"Two turned into four. And two on my side also met bad ends."

"I'm very sorry for all that." He tried to lighten the mood a bit. "Good news is, there are plenty of smart shops with fancy threads downstairs. Bad news is, they don't open for several more hours. Guess that bad news for you is very good news for me. I very much approve of you staying just like this." A smile. "I hope you like that towel."

A knowing smile back. "So how much do *you* like it, Mr. Lassiter?"

Pushing his coat and jacket over his shoulders, she said, "You can just loan me that shirt of yours to sleep in. There's plenty of floor for me and I'm told I don't snore, so I shouldn't be any bother." He pressed a finger to her lips.

"Beg to differ." Hector finished helping her remove his coats. He threw them carelessly over the back of a chair. "More bad news," he said. "My own luggage and spare shirts are in another hotel across town. Joint's probably lousy with Thule about now. Good news is, the bed here is king size, because I tend to sprawl. Still, there's probably some room for you in there." He fiddled with the buttons of his shirt. "I feel positively overdressed. Could use a shower myself."

She rubbed his jaw, smiling at the sound his whiskers made. "You could sure use a shave, too."

He said, "I know where I stand in terms of being on the market, but I'll confess I'm just now getting around to remembering to do this." He checked her left hand, pleased to see no rings. He kissed her wrist at the pulse, then said, "Despite that naked ring finger, anyone else I should know about?"

"Not presently," she said softly. "But that doesn't mean this is a good idea. That it's the *right* idea."

Hector cupped her chin. "First we need to finish getting the rest of this blood off you. We can debate after."

Cassie pressed a hand to his chest as he tried to gather her closer to him.

"Hector, we both know this world doesn't like people like us together. I mostly pass, sure. But sometimes—" She faltered, said, "Doesn't it bother you, even a little, that I'm not—"

He cut her off with a kiss. Soft and tender at first, it became harder and deeper as she responded.

Still, she resisted. Cassie said, "We *can't*. It's crazy for you, Hector, I mean as a public personality who the scandal rags and columnists can destroy. I'd say eighty percent of the time I pass with no problem. But there are times I just don't and then it can become pretty bad. The right—or maybe wrong—kind of artificial light, like back in the first club?" She shrugged. "The right or wrong people who make that connection? That could be a calamity for a man like you. Every now and then, I actually get turned away at some restaurant, or ordered to the back of the bus. You need to know the fire you're playing with. You have things to lose, Hector."

He kissed her again, emboldened to go further as she once more responded. He pulled away from her just long enough to say, "Darlin', I have never, ever cared about the opinions of others." A smile. "Well, maybe a rotten book critic or two, but beyond that?" He smiled and shook his head. "Water off my back."

This time she took the lead, their tongues tangling.

Panting, she fumbled with his belt. Lips still touching his she said, "You're absolutely sure about this? This isn't something you want to do just because of what I am is it?"

"You mean a woman?"

"Don't be coy. You know what I mean. Some men are just drawn to the exotic notion of being with—"

"I'm certain, and it's because you're you, Cassie, not about what you may or may not be. This isn't about skin color."

She smiled and stroked his chest. "Then you'll help me with my hair?"

"For starters," he said, "certainly."

9

THE BRIDE OF DEATH

His heart racing, slick with sweat, Hector said thin-breathed, "You're a marvel. And us together? Beyond words."

Cassie gave him a troubled smile. "You're sure that's not because of what I am in other people's eyes? Does the thought of sleeping with the likes of me bring something to it for you?"

That set him back on his heels. He brushed her hair back off her damp forehead. "It's because of what we just shared, and not anything more than you just being you, just as I promised." He ran his nails down her back, squeezed her bare hip. "Despite it all just now, you still owe me some critical answers, you know."

"I do, but I'm also starving. How about you order us some room service while I freshen up? After all, I've still got nothing to wear and so can't answer that door."

Dressed in Hector's only shirt, Cassie smiled and tapped flutes by the rain-kissed hotel room window.

She said, "Not sure I'd ever have thought of scrambled eggs and champagne together, but I confess, it's pretty wonderful."

"Like to say it was my inspiration, but options were scant at this hour," Hector said. "Call it a happy accident." He freshened her glass. Little bubbles ran up its sides, catching the light. "So what are you exactly? After what we've shared it's time to stop keeping *all* secrets. Are you FBI? Some other new government alphabet soup as yet unknown to me?"

"No acronyms," Cassie said. "It is apparently quite new, this organization I'm attached to. Nearly as I can tell, the thinking was if the Nazis have Thule, then Uncle Sam needed his own occult brigade, I guess." A little shrug. "So you've got us."

"One last time, who is *us*?"

Cassie looked down at her plate. She stirred her eggs with her fork. "One year ago, I ran a struggling little shop on Bourbon Street. You know, in New Orleans."

"I know the city, certainly. Drank my way down that raucous street more than a time or two, I reckon."

"But I bet you never took the time to stop in a shop like mine along the way. I sold all kinds of things from that little space. Things I'm sure you've never heard of and would set no stock by, even if you had known it existed." She hesitated and said, "I did some other things there, too. Read cards, read palms." She took another bite of scrambled eggs and raised her glass. "Just gets crazier and crazier with me, doesn't it? Please never forget I warned you about us together like this. What I can do—what I have to believe in to do all that—it's a world apart from what you've known or obviously take stock in."

Hector said, "So you're hinting you were drafted to be, what, a kind of supernatural consultant for our government? You're some kind of warrior witch, is that the gist?" Hector drummed fingertips on the table. "Guess you're right in a sense. Every time I think we've touched bottom on crazy, there's this whole new level that comes to light."

"Like I said."

"So, you really are Uncle Sam's Voodoo secret agent?"

"That's a misunderstood, misused term, Voodoo," she said. "More like *Gris-gris*, but more narrow even than that. That damned Béla Lugosi movie, *White Zombie*, has twisted everything people believe about Voodoo, what they think they know of it. It's not evil. In fact, it's all tangled up with Catholicism. At least as we practice it in Louisiana. It's about helping others in the end. It's about doing Good through nature, through spirits and our ancestors."

Hector said, "Can you do anything about Orson and his straying from his wife?"

"As a matter of fact, maybe. But I seriously doubt Virginia would cooperate."

Smiling, Hector said, "What would it take?"

"Just a few drops of her blood in his coffee. Some whispered words. He'd never do her wrong after that. Be faithful to the grave, though I'm not sure that would be any favor to her." She smiled and said, "And, even though you don't believe in this stuff, you just decided I will *never* brew you coffee, didn't you?"

Hector laughed. "Only because I'm particular about how I make it outside the restaurant-bought stuff. Developed odd tastes along the dusty trail back when I was mounted cavalry. You see, as a kid, much like Orson, I lied about my age, only I did it to get in to military service. Consequently, to me coffee is best made in a pan over an open fire, outlaw-style. Damned near everyone else calls it appalling." Well, Brinke, in time, had developed a taste for his style of java.

"Odd as my life has been, I'm betting you can give me a run for the money on many fronts," Cassie said. "In whatever time there is for us, I look forward to getting to know more about you, Mister Hector Lassiter."

Hector stroked the back of her hand. "Likewise, Cass. In the meantime, anything I should be especially on guard for? I mean if Uncle Sam or the Germans should throw an evil version of you back at me?"

Cassie withdrew her hand from under his and picked back up her fork. She smiled and shook her head. "If a woman tries to kiss you twice on one cheek, and once on the other, brace yourself and run—it's a spell." She stirred around her eggs and said, "For what it's worth, you should know I do have some of what I guess you'd regard as serious education. I've got a university degree in folklore. I minored in comparative religions, which probably is even more useless than my major in the real world."

"Yes, your studies in France, I take it," he said. "I'm just envious you've got the sheepskin. In the end, that's what really counts, or so I've heard. Hear tell nobody really uses their degree in that sense. But hell, I never finished high school. You should probably know that up front."

"You're plenty intelligent. Worldly and you have a facility for languages. What happened with you and higher education? Is it because of running off to war?"

"Pretty much," Hector said. "I thought it would be romantic to ride a horse for your current employer. To carry a gun and ride behind the flag. No need for me to say to you that isn't at all so, right?"

"Right."

"After, life just kept getting in the way of any more schooling. But this is getting maudlin," Hector said. He held out a hand, palm up. "What are the damages?"

"You mocking me, Hector? You know you don't want to do this."

"I'm not at all mocking you. I'm truly curious to hear what you say."

"A test?"

"That's not the right word for it. Let's stay with honest curiosity."

He spread his fingers slightly, drawing her attention back to his outstretched hand.

She took it in hers, traced a line or two there with a fingernail. She turned his hand on side to check its cutting edge and sighed. "Whatever else you take away from this, don't worry about giving up smoking," she said.

"It's that bad?" Hector was truly taken aback by her simple statement; surprised by his own immediate sense of angst. He figured she must mean he was a near-term goner. Cancer? Emphysema? Either way, it felt like he'd just been dealt a death sentence.

"Quite the opposite," Cassie said. "You've got a long, long road ahead. It won't always be smooth—far from—but whose is?"

"That's a load off, I reckon." He reached out with his other hand and turned over her hand to better see her palm. He said, "What about you?"

"Haven't a clue," she said.

Hector stared at her hand. "You can't read your own palm?"

"No. That's another crazy story but one I won't share now." A funny smile. "You're bravely out this far on the crazy limb, I flatly refuse to saw it off behind you, darling."

He said, "The bottom line though is that you truly believe?"

She met his gaze. "I do. Things I've seen, and the things I'm sure I've made happen? I can't *not* believe." She squeezed his hand. "I don't ask you to embrace any of it in the end,

Hector. Lord, the man you are, the artist you are, I'd have you not believe, I think."

"What about you?"

"What about me? Are you asking how I ended up going down this path? Why I'm not just a believer, but a Voodoo witch to use a term you probably thought of in the early going?"

"Your questions," he said, "your words. Not mine. But I'd welcome those very answers."

"Guess you'd call it a family enterprise," she said. "Five generations on my mother's side, reaching all the way back to Haiti. How crazy does that sound?"

Hector pushed his plate away. "Crazy doesn't cover it for me, not that word, not as a writer. Maybe, instead, sublime?" He held up his hand. "You don't have to respond to that. It's your life after all. I mean, it's your calling, right? But maybe consider telling me this much, please. Did you choose this for yourself, or was it foisted on you, maybe because you were simply next in that long and crazy line?"

He wondered how to best describe her smile. Rueful? Yes, we'll go with just that word, Hector decided.

Cassie squeezed the bridge of her nose. "Oh, they told me it was my choice, but just as you implied, when you're fifth in line for anything stretching so far back in time, can you really say no?"

Hector said thickly, "Christ, sweetheart, I'm sorry."

"Could be a lot worse," Cassie said. "There *are* worse things. Whore, dance hall girl. Maybe secretary." She entwined her fingers with his. "This career, if you can even call it that, at least let me get to know a broadminded and noted writer in the lustiest biblical sense. That's not nothing, right? We've surely had a time in the shower and in that bed. And if, in the bargain, I can keep the Spear of Destiny from Hitler's hand, well, that's honest and important work isn't it?"

"Regarding that last, you best hope Orson recalls what round heels ingénue he maybe gifted that sucker to. So far, we're hitting dry wells in terms of prospects for recovery of that medallion."

Cassie said, "There are really that many women in the kids' past? I find that pretty hard to believe. I know he's your friend, but I just don't see it. He doesn't send me, not even a little."

"Well, plenty of others he *did* send," Hector said a bit sourly. "*Does* send. Mostly they're women in his same line of work. He's a genius, remember? He also has a lot of roles to fill in a lot of projects at any given time. Call it a kind of aphrodisiac for a certain kind of woman working in a certain type of trade."

"Is that what they call the casting couch at work?"

"That's probably the politest term for it," Hector said.

"So what does the rest of Friday portend for Hector Mason Lassiter?"

"Aren't you supposed to tell me?"

"I didn't look that closely," she said evenly. "Where you're concerned—where we together are concerned—I think we should try to take life as it comes, Hector. No shadows and no intimations. No expectations of any kind. No tremors of intent."

He leaned across the narrow table and kissed her. This time it was soft and slow and lingered. He said, "That said—and agreed to—I see in your future some early morning clothes shopping looms. I figure to put you in Virginia's hands for all of that as you've literally nothing to wear downstairs to do your own shopping. While you two see to suiting you up, I mean to get my own luggage back here, jumping it through some crazy hoops on its return to me, trying to make it sure it's not followed. And it sounds like I'll play body guard to Orson until memory dredges up some starting point for this medallion search."

She raised her eyebrows. "And that's it? That's our plan?"

"Not quite," Hector said. He took her hand and drew her back toward the bed.

10

OUT OF DARKNESS

"This Cassie sounds not only exotic, but like a woman of action, too," Orson said. "How did you talk her into staying at the hotel?"

"Lack of un-bloodied clothes for one thing," Hector said. "Though Victoria should be seeing to that soon enough."

Orson smiled and said, "You deeply surprise me. I've crossed color lines for lust—if not for love—but I didn't think you ever would. Your home state sided with the Confederacy didn't it?"

Hector drummed his knuckles on the seat. "What on earth does that have to do with me or with anything?"

"Heritage? Prejudice is ground into us, we're not born with it, you know."

Hector had nothing to say to that. He just looked out the cab window, watching storefronts slide by. It was still relatively early, so traffic was moving at a reasonable clip.

Orson said, "She'll go back to Key West with you?"

"Home's still really there, I guess, but I'm not there, presently," Hector said. "I rent that place out now for cash. I live in Puget Sound, on an island called Whidbey."

"You'll take her there, then?"

Hector chewed his lip. "Maybe especially not there. There's stuff about that place I didn't know at the time I was looking for my next good place. Maybe I made a bad choice."

"Old man, I do so appreciate you playing body guard to me," Orson said. "I truly do. But I am racing the clock on multiple fronts as I've said, time and again. I have *Danton's Death* to mount for the stage, as I've also told you, and this Sunday's radio show, which as you heard for yourself, has all the earmarks of a train wreck barring some serious attention and artistic elbow grease."

"It wasn't that bad," Hector said. "And I won't be underfoot, if that's what you're implying. I frankly don't trust your memory about the medallion, so I want permission to ransack backstage, to comb through your wardrobe trunks and lockers."

"Ransack away, but do it as neatly as you can," Orson said. "John is very fussy. I'll even let you start with my private dressing room. It's packed with the surviving detritus of the career running all the way back to that first show in Dublin. But it's a fruitless pursuit, I can already assure you of that."

"All the same…"

Orson just sighed and shook his head. "If it was me, I'd be back at the hotel with my nearly naked Voodoo priestess. You really must introduce us, you know that, don't you, old man?"

Rummaging back stage, Hector could hear Orson railing against a reluctant thespian who was screaming something back about a girlfriend's birthday.

Orson bellowed, "There'll surely be other birthdays and just as certainly other girlfriends! We only have one opening night, goddamn you." A moment passed in silence, then

Orson's voice boomed, "If you walk out that door now, you're no true artist!"

More than a tad disgusted, Hector tried to open a dusty footlocker but the lid wouldn't budge. As he struggled with the trunk, he half-listened to the ongoing ruckus on stage.

Evidently, Orson was rethinking his rough treatment of the actor. He said, "We'll break for a meal. Everyone clear out and be back in an hour. That goes for you, too, John."

Hector heard Houseman say, "No, perhaps over a meal you and I can—"

"No, quite impossible, I need some time alone to think," Orson insisted.

Hector looked around, spotted a discarded iron fireplace poker and forced the lock with that. The mechanism gave way and Hector folded back the trunk's lid. His eyes were immediately set to watering by the acrid stench of mothballs. That same scent tickled the back of his throat and started Hector on a coughing jag that made him see spots.

When he at last regained some composure, Hector dug through Shakespearean robes and myriad wigs. Stirred dust set him to sneezing between continuing, lighter coughs.

Still digging, he put hands on a box—wooden and secured with a brass fastener. Hector pulled it out and moved it to a dressing table where he'd have more light. The box was overflowing with rings and bracelets, most of them exaggerated in size and ornamentation for stage use. There were clip-on earrings and a golden nose; a tangled assortment of necklaces.

Hector hit bottom, finding just a remaining chamois bag containing something that felt like, his fingers traced the edges—yes, by God, it felt like a disc of some kind, and about the right size.

Dry-mouthed, Hector upended and shook the bag. A heavy metal disc, about five-inches across, dropped into his hand. It might be bronze or some other alloy. Whatever it was, it had begun to acquire a greenish patina since Hector had last seen the mysterious medallion.

It bore inscriptions in some language Hector still couldn't read. On one side, there was what might be a map, but with no obvious north, south or other compass points indicated. On the obverse side, there was an image of Christ on the cross, a spear thrust into his side.

Something scuttled softly behind Hector. Startled, he drew his gun. It was a rat, gray and hulking. Hector put his roscoe away, then he paused again.

More screaming from up front: A voice, German, demanded, "Where is Hector Lassiter?"

Jesus Christ!

Hector replaced the medallion in its soft bag. He looked around Orson's theatrical sanctum sanctorum and decided no good options for hiding the disc were to be found.

Impulsively, Hector shoved the bundled medallion down his pants, right at the front. He figured if they dared look to find it there, maybe they deserved the damn thing.

That voice again, at once strident and guttural, "Search everywhere!"

Hector dug around through more accessible wardrobe cases. He came upon a gold medallion dangling from a copper chain. This one was about an inch-larger than the real item—a quarter-inch thicker, maybe. It had a spear-toting Viking on one side and what might be construed as damn near *anything* amidst some Runic symbols on the other.

It was close enough in the moment to perhaps fool them, Hector figured. He slid that disc into his coat pocket. Other dressing room doors were being kicked open and slammed shut. Hector drew his gun again. He figured to make a go of it. One man opened the door to Orson's room. The invader had the inevitable blond hair and blue eyes. "Strapping" would do as a short form description of the man, Hector told himself. As the big man edged through the door, Hector wedged his gun up under the man's cleft chin. "Steady there, Fritz," Hector said. "Let's have your gun for starters."

There was confusion and anger in the German's striking blue eyes—eyes that might make a Himmler-like racial purist swoon. Hector said, "Give me your goddamn gun."

The younger man finally did that. Hector said, "Now you lead on, Macduff. Your friends and I are going to have a little chat. You're my hostage."

Hector figured if it was only two or three of the Thule he might yet prevail.

As they walked into the theater proper, Hector saw he was faced off against eight other men. Two had guns pointed at Orson.

Another of the Thule pointed his gun at Hector's head. That man was a giant—six-six, easy—and had a face that tugged at memory. The giant smiled and said, "Hector Lassiter. I'm Rune Fuchs. It's been some time, but you've changed little. If I'd only known then what I know now. So many lost years…"

"Hell, pal, who can't say the same," Hector said. "Here's how I see us moving forward. We both have one hostage, so it's clear that we're not going to—"

"A moment." Fuchs smiled and shifted his aim. "Let me save us both time and toil." The tall man pulled the trigger on his Luger and shot Hector's hostage between the eyes."

Hector stood with his gun at his side, staring at the dead man sprawled before him. Hector shifted his feet to evade the spreading blood puddle.

Six guns were now trained variously on Orson and on Hector.

The tall man broke off and walked toward Hector. He punched Hector hard in the stomach, dropping him to his knees. As Hector doubled over, the man began to pat him down. Hector said, "You better not hurt us more than this. I'm pretty well known, but Orson is *very* well known. Christ, he's a friend to the damned President. You know—to FD-goddamn-R."

An evil smile. "I don't need to hurt you anymore it seems. I have this!" Fuchs held up the chunk of ersatz Viking jewelry Hector had hidden in his pocket. It twirled, catching the stage lights and reflecting them back, making Orson and Hector squint.

Still trying to get enough air, Hector gasped, "Okay, you win, Rune. At least have the decency… to carry out… your own dead… Do that before my friend's friends… wander back in here and… somebody else gets… hurt." His breath was still ragged, had him talking in huffy bursts, like damned old jowly Ford Madox Ford back in Paris so many years ago.

Two of the Thule tore down a curtain and rolled their fallen comrade inside. They dragged the dead man along as they left.

When the door slammed behind them, Orson cursed. "Goddamn me to hell," he raged. "Curse my short memory!"

Hector held up a hand and said, "Help me up, will you? Jesus Christ but that hurt. Son of a bitch can surely throw a punch and he does it starting from on high."

Orson hauled Hector to his feet. Still getting his breath, Hector looked around, then snatched up a scrap of paper and a crayon. He scrawled on the sign, "Theater closed by order of the Mercury Theatre Management until further notice. Cast and crew, please await direct contact from Mr. Welles before return."

He thrust the piece of paper at Orson and said, "Post this out front, right now. Do it if you value your co-workers. After, you and I are running out the back door, pronto."

Staring at the piece of paper, Orson said, "Why on earth would I do that? Why would *we* do that? The Nazis have what they want."

"Gotta keep your cast and clientele safe," Hector said. "Right?"

"But those damn Thule already have the medallion," Orson said. "And, hell, my cast is already rebelling as you no doubt heard."

"The Germans have just taken some of your worthless Viking costume jewelry," Hector said. "When they see that's what they fled with, they're going to be well beyond rage. Hell, by now they may already know they were taken in and be doubling back here. They won't be so nice the second time around, believe me. So you see, kid, we really need to exit, stage right. We need to do that two minutes ago."

Orson shook his head and said, "Yes. I see. Thank Christ at least that Houseman saw none of this. Anyway, we've been having trouble with an elevator that's key to the production's execution, so to speak, of *Danton*. I'll use that as a pretext for a brief closing, but only for a day, Hector. It's truly all I can afford."

11

THE IMMORTAL STORY

Much of Friday afternoon and evening were lost in more hotel moves and Hector arguing with Orson against a return to the Mercury Theatre.

"I'll say it a last time," Hector warned. "Next time, they won't be so gullible. Next time, they'll likely go straight to the bloody mat against us."

Hector had kept the fact he'd found the real medallion a secret so far. Alone for a couple of hours, he'd bought some modeling clay and made impressions of both sides of the real disc. The true medallion he had stashed in a safe at his publisher's office.

After, in another borrowed office belonging to his present editor, Hector dialed up a fairly recently made acquaintance.

Special Agent Edmond Tilly said, "Hector! It's always a pleasure. Or at least nearly always it is. You calling me with more dope about Spain? About Franco?"

"No. This time it's for a favor." Hector said, "I need some true gen on a particular person. I need all you can tell me about a woman named Cassandra Lightner Allegre."

Hector rounded out his day with a visit to Cornell University. There, he shared his two blocks of still curing clay with Prof. Adam Lindscott.

The professor's first words on viewing the halves of clay: "Dear God! Do you have any idea what this is, Mr. Lassiter?"

Hector said, "At least vaguely, otherwise I wouldn't be here now, would I? Although I will confess I'm a little surprised you know it on sight."

"It's quite well known among the cognoscenti," the professor said. "It's believed to have become hopelessly lost in Europe somewhere. Where on earth is the original?"

"No clue regarding anything about that," Hector said. "I just have these. What can you tell me based on what you're holding?"

"But this clay is still curing, Mr. Lassiter. It seems to me you surely must have the original, or at least access to those who do. These impressions are quite fresh, still a little soft."

"Nah—don't trying playing Sherlock in that way, it won't get you anywhere. And consider this a copy of a copy."

"But *you* do know what this purports to be?"

Hector wet his lips. "Absolutely. I know the alleged stakes, too, as I now gather you do, as well. So help me to interpret it."

The scholar sat back in his leather chair. He tented his fingers. Already, Hector was starting to dislike, even to distrust, the academic. There was something too studied about the man and his mannerisms, too theatrical. "I must insist on being part of any recovery you're contemplating, Mr Lassiter. This is, well… It's *everything*, as you claim to know."

"And I can only guess what it might mean for your career," Hector said.

"There is that as well, of course."

Hector smiled and said, "Right. Clearly, I could use some expertise on this. You seem to be that man. Lord knows, I don't want to be 1938's version of Lord Carnarvon."

"Very well." Excited, the professor leaned forward and pointed at the first impression—what Hector took to be the face of the medallion. It was the side that depicted the crucifixion and the spear being thrust into Christ's side.

"This is a kind of shorthand for telegraphing what the disc represents," the professor said, "but it's also vital for reading the map on the other side." The professor pointed at the second impression, what Hector figured indeed comprised a map. "Please tell me precisely how these two images align, Mr. Lassiter."

Hector wasn't sure about that nuance at all. He said, "It matters?"

"Immensely. The image of Christ, the orientation his head on the original object, it indicates true north. It essentially gives the critical orientation for the map on the other side. But there's more that is not here. Why wasn't an accurate cast made of the sides of the medallion? Of its edges?"

"That matters as well? There's something on the sides, too?" Hector was furious with himself for not being more attentive to detail.

"There are supposed to be subtle notches along the sides of the original," the professor said. "They give the precise measurements between these various points here on the map. Without knowing true north, and without those measurements and the point of origin—which is also engraved on the rim, you have nothing useful here. In the end, these impressions are just tantalizing in the most terrible and frustrating way."

Hector stood. Reaching for the clay impressions he said, "Then clearly I'm wasting my time and yours."

That sound—a gun cocking out of view, under the academic's desk. The professor leveled a revolver at Hector's head. "We're far from finished talking, Mr. Lassiter. Where did you come by this? How do we access the original? Please, tell me now, before…"

Hector, even more furious at himself, said, "Couldn't figure out how to best phrase that last, egghead? Where *were* you headed with that sentence? Maybe, 'Please, tell me now, before my Nazi friends come barging through that door?'"

Hector gestured broadly with raised hands at the door. As the professor's eyes tracked his gesture, Hector rolled to the floor, then kicked the scholar's desk with both feet. The ornate desk slid backward, tipping over the professor's chair. A stray shot pierced the ceiling.

Reaching over the desk, Hector got a grip on the man's gun hand and peeled the revolver from his grip. He pointed the gun back at its owner and said, "So you're goddamn sellout, a turncoat for the worst kind of racists."

"Nothing about the Nazis coming to me should surprise you," the professor said, managing to do so haughtily, despite being flat on his back and pinned under his own ostentatious, oversized furniture. "You came to me for my singular expertise, you hack. So did they. They anticipated you'd be coming. I managed to buy a few moments so we could perhaps reach a separate piece, so to speak. Let me come with you, and together—"

"You pulled a gun on me," Hector said. "So all trust is gone." Voices down the hall; many feet, moving fast.

Hector gathered up the clay impressions from the floor and shoved them in his coat pockets. Hector opened the man's office windows and looked down. They were on the second floor, but an embankment halved the distance to the ground.

Hector decided he could make the jump into a bush below without probable injury. Before taking that leap, Hector said, "For the record, you can tell those bastards about to break down your door I really don't have the original and have *no* idea where it can be found."

Sneering, the academic said, "They won't believe that anymore than I do."

Hector figured that was sadly so.

As the professor struggled to get up from under his desk, Hector dropped out the window. He heard wood splinter in the professor's office. Hector ran along the side of the building to avoid presenting an easier target for a bullet.

Classes were changing. Hector drifted and mixed in with the students in their crush between sessions. He slid into a library and lost himself in the dusty, pulpy-smelling stacks.

From an upstairs library window, Hector watched more than a dozen men comb the campus grounds. To his relief, the book burners consciously or unconsciously avoided the library.

After an hour watching from the safety of his bookish perch, satisfied the frustrated Germans had at last abandoned campus, Hector phoned for a cab to pick him up at the library's delivery door.

12

NEVER TRUST AN HONEST THIEF

"The romance is already over, Mr. Lassiter," Cassie said. "You called the Feds on me, you treacherous bastard."

Hector sighed, then locked the door behind himself. When he turned, Cassie had a gun pointed at his heart. "How dare you call in Hoover's gorillas on me?"

He slipped off his overcoat and jacket. He saw his luggage had at last caught up with him after its profusion and confusion of hand-changes across New York City. "I'm truly sorry," he said. "I was becoming paranoid and maybe overcautious. I've also not been a good judge of character these past couple of years. I suppose the good news is Mr. Hoover's agency knows nothing about your current employers. Yet, clearly, word trickled back to your organization pretty quickly that I was making inquiries. Far as I'm concerned, staying off Hoover's radar is further endorsement for your side's skills."

"You're not helping yourself," she said. "Not even a tad."

Hector rooted through his suitcase. "I know," he said. "There's no worthy defense. It was a rotten thing to do. But if you were me, and had a resource like that to access, well, given what's allegedly at stake, wouldn't you have checked me out, too?"

A short shrug. "Maybe."

"Not by way of defense, but as a simple point of fact, I also remind you that you already evidently read my FBI file, a document whose size and content I really don't want to contemplate."

"It is surely hefty," she said, "and you're still only what, thirty-seven? Thirty-eight?"

"Something like that."

"What are you doing now?"

"Looking for my razor and the like. Showering, shaving. Then I'm regrouping. Assuming you don't shoot me first. Orson and family still in their room?"

"Yes, still. But rebelling, loudly. Seems to be berating his theater troupe by phone. My God, the tirades that arrogant man is capable of."

Hector found his shaving kit. He said, "Tell me, Cassie, have you ever heard of a fella name of Adam Lindscott?"

Cassie put down her gun and opened a closet. She hung up his suit jacket and coat. "As it happens. Why on earth do you ask?"

"Credential-wise, he struck me as a potential resource for us," Hector said, watching for a reaction.

Cassie rolled her eyes. "Why do you know about him?"

"Result of research and just casting around for expertise."

"You have me for that," Cassie said coldly. "Or you *had* me. Anyway, Lindscott is an opportunist of the worst stripe, or so I'm told. He thinks only about himself and ways to enhance his own shot at tenure. Worst of all, he's a Thule stooge. Everything he's done in the past four years is secretly underwritten by the National Socialist Party. He's secretly an occultist. He's something worse than Thule, if I hear right. You see, Thule is kind of like, DeMolay. You start there and move up to the Masons. Above the Thule are the Vril. They sacrifice children for more occult power. They take their crazy ideas from this novel written last century by Edward Bulwer-Lytton, called *The Coming Race*. Trust me, we do well to steer clear of the professor."

"So noted," Hector said, freshly cursing himself. He stripped off his shirt. "Again, I'm sorry, believe me about that."

She held up a hand. "Talk is cheap. Keep it a lonely act of idiocy, and maybe we can yet get beyond it." Cassie followed him into the bathroom. "Orson told me about your close call. By now, they probably realize you fooled them with that costume jewelry. They'll be doubly angry you know."

"Sure," Hector said. "But I simply wasn't spoiled for options in the moment."

"Your actor friend still has no idea where the real medallion is, you know."

"I know," Hector said. He began to draw the water, then parked his butt on the side of the tub as he untied his shoes. "Let's say for a moment I could make that big leap of faith and accept this ancient Roman spear is everything you believers claim. If so, we've got plenty of dubious characters on our side that from my perspective who are also a worry in terms of wielding the power you describe. Take prissy little J. Edgar Hoover for example. You rightly think little of him. He's almost Hitler without the funny moustache. Hell, I've yet to cast a vote for F.D.R. in this lifetime because what little politics I have run completely counter to that bastard's character and philosophy. I despise Roosevelt's arts and character destroying federal schemes. So I'm not crazy about even our current president having the power you describe. Candidly, more I think on it, the more appealing it seems this damned relic remain rusting in limbo, or maybe better still, destroyed."

Cassie watched him undress. "Ever read any Yeats, Hector?"

"As a matter of fact, some, yeah. If I have a favorite poet, I suppose either he or Byron is the one."

"The best lack all conviction," Cassie recited, "the worst are full of passionate intensity. The Thule, the Nazis and the Vril are fully committed to discovery. Even considering Hoover, FDR—warts and all—better that *we* get there first, wouldn't you say?"

"The only way to do that is with the medallion though, right?" Hector had this sudden compulsion to hurl the real chunk of metal into Hudson Bay.

Cassie crossed her arms. "The medallion is crucial to discovery, yes. But, of course, accidental discoveries are made. Anyway, the medallion was last known to be in yours and your friend's hands. You and Orson don't strike me as men to disappear into the mist, just like the spear or the medallion. You both lead large public lives. So as long as the medallion is missing, and you two aren't, there'll be no peace for either of you. You both could end up dead protecting these items you don't really have an investment in. Do you really think the Germans will hesitate to use Virginia and Christopher in the most violent and cynical ways to motivate you and Orson?"

Hector didn't doubt that for a moment.

Cassie said, "Do you want me to describe to you what Mr. Rosenblum suffered at their hands before giving you two up to that giant of a Thule?"

Hector had finished undressing. Naked, he fiddled with the taps, drawing a hot bath. He usually preferred to shower, but this one time, he wanted to soak. "No thanks, Cass. I've got enough imagination to supply the bloody details."

"I've read a novel or two of yours, you know. I suppose your imagination can do that very dark thing." She shook her head. "The man who lives what he writes and writes what he lives. That's what the press people call you, right?"

"Afraid that's so," he said. He tested the water, then stood and settled in.

For the first time, Cassie candidly surveyed the back of his body in good light. Shuddering, she said, "What in God's name caused all those scars on your upper back?"

"A whip of sorts. It was Paris, the winter of 1924. Someday I'll write about that bit of living, too, I expect. I always seem to get around to putting it down on paper. Some things just take longer to endure living again, that's all."

"You're a white man. In Paris of all places, why would anyone take a whip to you?"

"Just cruel and crazy cultists, a little like your Thule or Vril. They were fanatics."

Cassie sighed and began to unbutton her blouse.

Watching her undress, Hector said, "I guess, however, I can take solace in the fact you've already told me I've got a long life ahead of me."

Cassie unzipped and peeled down her skirt and the last of her lacey under-things with it; the faint impression of garter straps on bare thighs. Nude, she stared him down, hands on hips. "Sure you do. And that's a true thing. But I said nothing about guarantees of a happy life."

"That's certainly so," he said. Hector held out a hand. She took it and he steadied her as she stepped into the tub, crouching and wrapping her legs around his waist. "You're doing wonders for my morale and confidence," he said.

"In some ways it feels like I'm doing just that," she said. "And just returning the favor, I suppose."

He debated then confessing his discovery of the medallion to her. Her cautions about a lifetime of Thule harassment also resonated—that was all too undeniable in terms of cold-light logic.

Still, it struck Hector there must surely be some third alternative.

Cassie said, "They will be much more ruthless next time. This goes to the very top. Himmler, Hermann Göring, Alfred Rosenberg, Rudolf Hess, Martin Bormann. That last one is an avowed devil worshipper."

"I do know that," Hector said. "I go forward with little else but those happy thoughts uppermost in fevered mind, believe me."

At two a.m., Hector awakened with an inspiration.

He untangled himself from Cassie's arms, dressed, and slid from their hotel room.

Hector hit the lobby and found a pay phone. The young woman on the other end of the line, an artist in her own right, said, "Mister, do you have any idea what time it is?"

"I do. And time is getting shorter. They tell me you have remarkable skills with metal. I have the money to make it worth your while to use those skills, but time is truly wasting, even at this wicked hour, darlin'."

13

A SAFE PLACE

Saturday, eleven a.m. and an uneasy lunch.

Orson, Hector and Cassie sat at one table; Virginia and Christopher were at a small table, far enough away to keep the child out of earshot of hearing talk of stalkers or the potential bloody consequences of their discovery by German occultists.

Orson said, “I will avoid the theater tonight—we’ll keep it closed a while longer for the sake of cast and crew’s safety—but I have to complete Sunday’s broadcast, at bare minimum. I *have* to do that.”

Hector said, “We’ll see what we can do about making that one happen safely. Really, I want us both out from under this, and I mean yesterday. I want us both to go on with our lives, buddy. I’ve never been one to look over my shoulder for any time at all. Not happily.”

After brunch, as Orson retreated to his hotel room with his family to continue taming the scripts for *Danton’s Death*, *The War of the Worlds* and three other prospective projects for stage and radio, Hector and Cassie wandered the rain-kissed streets, coat collars turned up and hats pulled low, a shared umbrella held low and angled against the rain.

A half-an-hour into their walk, the rain picked up and the wind gusts threatened to turn their umbrella inside out. They sought refuge in an old Catholic church.

Hector lit a single candle, then he and Cassie took their seats in a rear pew. She said, "May I ask you who that was for?" The single lit candle flickered in the slightly chilly church.

He thought about it, then told her about Brinke. Maybe the story went on too long, but hell, Cassie had asked.

When he finished she took his hand and said, "I read an interview you gave. You confessed to writing in churches and cathedrals. If I didn't already know you, if I hadn't looked at your palm, I'd be drawn to you for that admission all on its own."

Writing in churches was a practice that accidentally started shortly after Hector had met and become romantically involved with Brinke. But Cassie surely didn't need to know *that* detail. A man had to keep some secrets from subsequent lovers, some even from his readers.

This church's priest, old and portly, made his cautious way down the middle aisle in a wine-stained cassock, steadying hand moving from pew back to pew back. He eyed them, his gaze lingering longer on Cassie. He raised his eyebrows and said to Hector, "Is there something you'd like to confess, sir?" His racist implication was clear enough.

In that moment, Hector despised the priest. He thought about calling the padre out on all those burst capillaries in his nose and the gin blossoms at his cheeks.

Instead, Hector wrapped his arm around Cassie's shoulders and said, "Just to confess my love for my beautiful intended, here."

That elicited a frosty smile from the cleric. The old man made his way back toward the altar, Cassie chastely kissed Hector and said, "I warned you about us together. There's no place, I guess, where we can be together without being confronted, or at least looked at like that."

"There *are* places," Hector said. "Paris—anywhere in France—plenty of other places in Europe. We'd be just fine over there."

"All war zones, or soon to be so, for one thing. But also places that are anywhere but in this country, you're saying." She stood and offered a hand. "Let's get out of this so-called church, my warrior bard. Let's go find a book shop."

They were leaving Scribner's Bookstore, Cassie armed with a couple more of Hector's novels she hadn't yet read. She said, "We should head back to the hotel soon. I want a few hours with you alone, between the covers, figuratively and literally, before things go completely crosswise and maybe even bloody on us."

Hector stopped her walking and pulled her close. "That simple intuition speaking or something you truly see in the cards or in my hand?"

Cassie pressed her hand to his heart, studying him. "You want an honest answer to that?"

He bit his lip and said. "Now I suppose you're warning me that I don't?"

Cassie said, "You don't need a crystal ball to predict terrible trouble ahead, Hec. You don't need a weatherman to tell you which way this wicked wind means to blow." She stood on tiptoes and kissed him. "But you surely know that by this point in your storied life."

There was something there in her eyes and sad smile he couldn't quite read. She said, "You've been to and fro in the world, yes? Been some places and seen some things?"

She pressed both palms to his cheeks and held his head up so he had to meet her gaze. "I'll put that bigoted priest's question to you again. Anything you'd care to confess, Hector? Will you do that while whatever secret you may or may not be keeping still can't hurt me or someone else you care about?"

He thought about it. Hector thought about it hard.

Following some instinct he couldn't yet explain, Hector said, "No. Not a thing, darlin' Cassie. I've got nothing on earth to confess, presently."

14

TOMORROW IS FOREVER

(Sunday, Halloween Eve)

The Mercury's Trick-or-Treat special fell on the Sabbath; it struck Hector as eerily appropriate, given events.

Orson was holding court in a hotel banquet room over a massive breakfast buffet in a grand old ballroom, just twelve hours from becoming the most famous—to some, the most infamous—man in America.

He was performing sleight of hand for Christopher and neighboring diners, tricks with coins, cigarettes, unused coffee mugs and wadded up balls of napkins. His daughter giggled and clapped hands at each trick as Orson beamed. "If you can fool a child, then you're truly a magician," he said to the room.

Hector rose and tossed his napkin across his plate. "Excuse me for a couple of minutes, please."

Cassie scooted back her chair. "Where are you going, Tex? I should tag along."

"Huh-uh," Hector said. "This is nothing sinister. I'm supposed to sign a contract for Brinke, tomorrow. Now I'm thinking I best get it done today, before Mr. Welles here has to show up at the CBS studios for his radio show. I just can't miss this window, so I've got a call or two to make. Please put the arm on our waiter for me while I'm gone, won't you? He's just not diligent in terms of keeping the coffee coming and hot."

"Here, here," Orson, who practically breathed coffee, boomed in accord. "More java!"

Hector did head toward the lobby and its bank of pay phone booths.

On the way he met his Soho artist; dowdy, dirty blond hair, but something intense and knowing there in her blue eyes. She handed Hector his fake medallion, its rim now etched with random hatch marks and an impulsively chosen starting point Hector had selected for a go-nowhere search—St. John in the Lateran and the Cloister. It was a choice Hector hoped just might run a Thule search party crazy until the end of time.

Hector's found-on-the-fly artist Bricky Callow said, "It's acceptable?"

"It's better than *perfect*, darlin'," Hector said.

It was anybody's guess whether Bricky's knock-off was a correctly oriented to true north, but then Hector wasn't yet fully committed to turning the ersatz medal over to the Thule.

Doing that might buy him a year's peace, or maybe just a few minutes if there was something that was also supposed to be there on the original that he'd missed. Either way, Hector figured, at some point the Germans would again come knocking at his and Orson's doors once this latest deception became known.

He paid Bricky for her work—perhaps overly-handsomely, based on her pleased expression. She said, "If you need more of those, I retained the molds and I could make a thousand or more. We could even mass-produce them. They're kind of kitschy, don'tcha think?"

It *was* possible he might need more at some point. Hector squeezed her arm and smiled. "I'll get back to you on that. Thanks a million for the lightning turnaround on this, darlin'. You're not only talented, but very sweet to do so." She offered a cheek to kiss.

Next, Hector called up his current editor to regain access to the real medallion. He also talked Peter Mathis into bringing the contracts for publishing Brinke's books under her own name to the same location, intent on killing several birds with one stone.

He was just hanging up the phone when Cassie slid an arm around his waist. "Still don't trust me? Does it bother you the feeling might be mutual?"

He kissed her forehead after she literally ducked his first effort to find her mouth, protecting her lipstick or their standing in the hotel—take your pick. She said, "Got your dates set up?"

"My business appointments," he corrected, "And yes, I do. I've now got one annoyed editor who's angry to be dragged into the city and his office on the Lord's day of rest and also one pretty miffed publisher for similar reasons. But as I represent money in both their banks, I figure they'll soldier through it just fine. Orson still playing Houdini upstairs?"

"Of course. He's an exhibitionist. He lives for the acclaim—but you know that, and probably better than most, being his friend this long."

She hesitated, then said, "I know he's juvenile, and I'll concede he's probably a prodigy, just as they all say. He's also your friend. But I don't really like him, and sense he sees his charm is wasted on me, to his chagrin."

Hector leaned against the phone booth, arms crossed. "The young man's not to every taste, I concede that readily," he said. "He drove the men who gave him his first big break back in that Dublin theater to epic distraction. Hell, he vexes me plenty and often. As to love? Orson has a favorite line on the subject. 'It is difficult for love to last long, therefore one who loves passionately is cured quickest.'"

"Grim." Cassie tightened the knot in Hector's necktie. "Passionate love or not, it's the cavalier way he treats his own family that most offends me. So long as they're fawning—playing audience—he's engaged with them. Otherwise?" She shrugged sadly.

"Sorry to say, I can't disagree with any of that," he said softly. He checked his watch. "Three hours until I play author-slash-literary executor. We better get back upstairs before Orson the Great gets in over his head and tries to saw some dowager in half or the like."

Cassie took his offered arm and said, "I hope you're not expecting me to play babysitter to the wizard and his family while you do all that book stuff. At the end of the day, I'm not a bodyguard, even if I do have a gun and can put someone down with it at pointblank range. I'm really just a spooky academic. You'd do well to remember that, Mr. Lassiter."

Hector looked around to make sure no one else was watching, then leaned down to kiss the soft, dark down on the back of her neck. "My witchy egghead," he said. "I know. You're coming with me to my publisher's, as it happens. So is Orson."

"And his family?"

"You have friends who *are* more in that bodyguard line of work, don't you? Aren't they watching, even now?"

"Quite likely," Cassie said. "You've frankly got me in a difficult place now. If I don't trust you, they less and less will come to trust me as I stay at your side. And I'm not sure the key men who are running the American side of this mess believe in the occult anymore than you do."

"It's probably okay," Hector said. "I know a guy who does do personal protection kind of stuff. It's a side thing for him, but he's formidable. I've engaged him, too. He should be taking charge of Virginia and Christopher about now. But I need to get up there and vouch for the hombre."

Cassie nodded and said, "About that little girl's name. Why on earth did they call her Christopher?"

Hector thought about it, searched his memory and admitted, "I haven't a clue." He urged her onto the wide and winding staircase up to the ballroom. "On the subject of family, Orson confided to me his grandmother practiced black magic. At least he claims it was so. I've come to regard Orson as something of a fabulist. Have you offered to read his palm?"

"Lord, no," she said. "He's the conceited kind, anyway. Maybe he's really descended from a witch as he told you. You know, I'd have loved to see that play that made his name—his so-called *Voodoo Macbeth*, but I didn't have the money to come all the way to New York for that then. Maybe Mr. Welles even believes in what I do like you don't. Even granting all that, he's far too self-centered to doubt in his own will to power."

"The will to power," Hector repeated. "That's from Nietzsche, isn't it?"

"Believe that's so." Cassie smiled sadly. "That's a writer who I do believe Hitler has read."

Hector checked his watch again. He once more thought about confiding to Cassie and Orson his discovery of the real medallion and his commissioning of a convincing fake. His FBI source had vouched for Cassie in every way that mattered.

And yet?

Mounting the long staircase, he assessed her again: Smart, beautiful, sensual, yet embracing of this occult nonsense he couldn't countenance. But perhaps that last was to *his* discredit, he told himself.

As they approached the ballroom, he took her hand and moved toward an adjacent sitting room. She resisted, said, "Your friends are this way."

"I know," he said. "He'll keep. I need… I want…" He faltered.

She misunderstood his intent. "No way, lover. It's a crazy time for it."

Hector half-smiled. "No, it's not what you're thinking. No time for doing *that* properly now, you're right. This isn't about sex. I need you to show me what you can really do, sweetheart. Not just vague talk of long lifelines or the like. Not anything that might be drawn from some goddamn FBI dossier. Can you—well, dazzle me? Hell, terrify me if need be."

Cassie gave him a worried look. "I don't like this, darling. I have a feeling giving you what you say you want now could cost you more than either of us is prepared to face up to." She wrapped her fingers around his neck, gripping hard and looking him in the eye. "I've seen it happen before, so I know. There's nothing more harrowing to behold than an atheist confronted with undeniable proof of God. And being given proof of what you must surely regard as the Devil?" She shook her head, searching his pale blue eyes.

"I know enough to know there's supposed to be black and white magic," Hector said. He thrust out his hand. "You said you don't serve the Devil."

Cassie said, "No, that's the hand to see your future. No proof to be had there, not immediately. Give me your other hand if you're really sure about risking this—your other hand shows me your past. Presumably stuff that couldn't be in any file. The stuff you maybe hide even from your own memory, best you can."

She took his offered hand and examined it for a time, brows knitted. She finally said, "My God, Hector. The things you've survived, endured…"

He still wasn't buying in but said, "What's that other line from Nietzsche? That which does not kill me makes me stronger?"

Still looking stricken by what she saw in his hand, Cassie brushed a dark comma of hair back from his forehead. She kissed him hard, wrecking her own mouth, then pressed her forehead against his chin. "You're truly sure you want me to do this to you?"

"Entirely."

She looked him in the eye. "You tried to kill your father. You shot him when you were still a child, though it appears not without good reason."

Hector felt like he'd been gut-punched. His straying mother's death at his father's hands was public record. So was his father's eventual execution by the state. But Hector's role in the bloodshed that terrible morning was not on the books or told in any of the papers at the time. It surely couldn't reside in some government file.

Grafton Lassiter had tumbled to the fact that Hector's mother was in love with another man.

Hector's father—a world-class son of a bitch—shot his mother in the face, killing her instantly. Little Hector, still just a boy, heard the fatal shot and grabbed a shotgun. He fired off one barrel at his old man, nearly severing the son of a bitch's left arm and pocking his father's face with stray shot.

But his father recovered; his arm was nearly healed when the state put Grafton down.

Hector's maternal grandfather convinced the law his daughter had gotten off a shot at her crazy husband before she was killed herself. In the face of Grafton's claims to the contrary, the court accepted Beau Stryder's account of events.

In the end, only old Beau and Brinke Devlin, now thirteen years dead, knew the truth. And now here was Cassie, the bronzed white witch, who had somehow evidently seen the sorry truth in his hand by some means Hector couldn't comprehend, much less countenance. Surely the truth of the shooting must have found it's way into some file Cassie had gained access to. It had to be that way, right?

She hugged him hard. "My God, the look on your face. I'm *so* sorry my love. I'm *so* sorry. I knew this was a calamitous mistake."

"I asked for it," Hector said, not liking the fear and uncertainty he heard in his voice. "I asked you for undeniable proof of your power and now I seem to have it."

Cassie was still holding him hard in her arms. Cheek pressed to his chest, she asked, "Why now? Why this moment for this question?"

"To help me decide something," he said.

"To help you decide what?"

"Let's wait until we have Orson with us. I'll explain on the way to my publisher's office. You go fix your mouth. I've got to see to Virginia and Christopher's bodyguard, first."

15

MASQUERADE

Hector signed his and Brinke's new contracts and retrieved the real medallion from his publishing house's vault while Orson and Cassie loitered in the lobby.

Peter Mathis said, "This had to be done on Sunday, Hector? It had to be?"

"Afraid it must," Hector said. "I might have to hit the road back west tonight in something of a rush. Back west or to some other points to parts unknown. A cloud of dust and hearty Hi-Ho Silver."

After the contracts were signed, Hector secured a horse-drawn coach and rode around Central Park while confessing to his friends his recovery of the true medallion.

Cassie, eyes flaring, said, "You have it now? Can I see it?"

"You could, but I don't have it on me," Hector lied. "That would hardly be good strategy with all these Germans running amok, now would it?"

In truth, the fake medallion was in the left-hand pocket of his gray wool suit jacket, but the real article was in a small pouch he'd secured to his right leg, just below the knee. "It was in my publisher's safe. I put it, boxed, in the hands of a courier. Another friend should be placing it in a locker in Union Station soon. I'll arrange delivery of the key for that particular locker to myself before night's end."

"I come to think it should probably remain lost—the spear, I mean," Orson said in his most portentous baritone voice. "At least it should remain missing until the world calms itself one way or another. If the Spear of Destiny is indeed in fascist Italy, getting in there to find it, and getting out again with the spear?" Orson shook his head, his brown eyes glistening. "Both tasks strike me as insurmountable."

Hector looked to Cassie. "Your thoughts?"

"The risks of obtaining the spear in Rome are real and obvious enough," Cassie said. "At least for us or anyone like us. But last time I checked, Italy and Germany were allies. The medallion should at least be in our government's hands to prevent those others from laying hands on the real spear. The risks are real, just as I said, but so are the rewards for our side. And if the spear remains in play, doesn't it strike you the world may never be calm enough to recover it otherwise, or worse, that it may simply be too late for our side to make use of it?"

She took Hector's hand. "Think hard on all that."

"Oh, rest assured that's about all I've been doing," Hector said. "I've done little else since laying eyes on that damned thing."

They stopped for a late lunch before Orson set off to the studio for the Mercury's Halloween broadcast of The War of the Worlds. Hector settled for Orson's favorite joint, 21, on West 52nd Street. He did so despite the demand that he wear a tie in order to be permitted entry.

Cassie had excused herself to the phone. Orson poured himself more wine and said, "She's possibly calling in the Marines, you know. Or J. Edgar himself."

"Possibly," Hector said. "It was a calculated risk. Here, take this. Keep it in your pant's pocket until I tell you otherwise."

Hector passed Orson the false medallion, wrapped in a silk handkerchief.

"My God," Orson said, quickly placing the packet in his pocket. "Is this what I think it is?"

"Yes and no," Hector said. "The images on the front and the back are exact copies of the original, but they are about six-degrees out of proper phase to one another. You see, Christ's head on the real item points to true North. The hatch marks you'll find on the rim are supposed to measure precise distances between map points. On the real item, they presumably do just that. In this case, however, they're randomly assigned. This medallion might make an interesting paperweight, but it's no treasure map."

Orson said, "Eventually, whether it's Uncle Sam or the Germans—even these so-called Thule—this will be seen through as the hoax that it is, you know. The trick will probably be discovered and sooner rather than later."

"Probably so," Hector said. "It's mostly just a gambit to buy you time until I can figure out a way to deal you and I out of this farce, forever. In the meantime, think of that metal disc in your pocket as a one-use-only escape hatch. As we've agreed, tonight particularly, you're an easily acquired target coming and going from the studio. If you run afoul of Germans this evening, if I'm not there to help you, that's when you use that disc as needed to get them off your back."

Orson nodded. "What do you intend to do if caught? Do you have a copy of your own?"

"Seems too risky we might both have to pony up the disc tonight," Hector said. "That would just underscore a hoax. As to plans tonight, I mean to stay glued to your side until the broadcast is over and you're safe and sound with family somewhere. On the other hand, Cassie and or her employers may have other things in store for me." Hector checked his wristwatch and rose. "Going to go see if I can scare her up, in fact. So sit tight. There's only one way in or out, so no worries on that front."

Orson smiled. "If you truly think that, then you clearly don't know this place's history during prohibition. It's connected to the sewers for quick liquor disposal and riddled with secret passages and hidden wine rooms. This establishment is a sieve, in that sense."

"Terrific news," Hector said. "Try not to get lost in the sewers, then."

Hector found Cassie hanging up a pay phone. He held her hand as she stepped from the mahogany booth. "Go ahead and ask," she said.

He smiled. "How much did you volunteer?"

Cassie let go of his hand. "Your secret is safe for now. I'm trying to buy us more time so I can talk you into doing the sensible—into doing the *right* thing."

"How are you doing that—buying that time for us, I mean?"

"I said I thought you might have a hot lead on the location of the medallion. I could use some of your storytelling powers to fill in some details on that, I expect."

"I can help with that, as needed," he said. "Fiction writers make terribly effective liars, I'm afraid. Thank you for keeping the confidence, honey."

"It's probably a terrible mistake," she said. "You hiding this medallion from our government certainly seems a terrible threat to me."

"Maybe," Hector said, "but candidly, and certainly selfishly, I haven't yet figured out a way to turn it over to you all if I ever even incline that way. Not to do it in any way that will save me future grief from the Germans, that is to say. Let's face facts, darlin'. If I give you the medallion, the U.S. government is hardly going to take out an ad in the dailies saying something like, 'We have it now, so Thule, leave poor Hector and Orson alone.' Right?"

"That *is* a problem for you," she said. "Now that you say it, I can see it. Still, your arrogant, philandering friend is just one big advertisement for himself tonight, a huge target for kidnapping while you two are still viewed as possessors of the medallion."

"Seems to me your side can do something about that potentially," Hector said.

"As an American, my side should be your side, too, Hector. Anyway, I have tried to have the surveillance on Mr. Welles stepped up, through tonight at least."

"Good. And I'm working some angles of my own on the Orson front." Hector paused and then said, "By the way, if you haven't already gathered, I plan on spending the evening with him at the studio. You want to go with us, or…?"

"With you, of course," she said. "That's where the action will be. I told you, I'm really no bodyguard and so not keen on the notion of sitting around with the Welles girls. I don't want to spend my night cooling my heels with Virginia and Christopher and that ex-boxer turned bodyguard you've hired for them. Virginia and I? 'Different worlds' doesn't begin to do it justice."

Hector said, "There's time for one more drink maybe, then we hit the studio for prep work. Let's go find Orson before he starts calling attention to himself by reciting Shakespeare or some damned thing to pass his time alone."

16

MESSAGE FROM THE HILLS

Before they headed to the CBS studios, Orson threw Hector a nasty curve ball, uncharacteristically insisting upon going to the hotel "to say goodnight to my girls. I know you think we're going to the studio and then the hotel after the show tonight, but that's simply not the way it can be," Orson insisted. "I *have* to get to the theater afterward to knuckle down and fix *Danton' Death*. The whole future of the Mercury Theatre may well ride on how that play is reviewed by the goddamn critics."

"So it's about posterity," Hector said. "Is that really worth your life?"

"Posterity?" Orson made a face. "Posterity is another form of worldly success. Jot that down, if you will, please, on a slab of marble. It's about remaining commercially viable so I can continue to create. It's about my career." He studied Hector's face and said, "It's about providing for my family."

Reluctantly, Hector agreed to the insisted-upon side trip.

At least, Hector consoled himself, his young selfish friend was evidencing some heartening family sentimentality.

As Cassie and Hector sipped coffee and watched from a corner, Orson pushed his crew threw fragmented rehearsals, changing beats and shortening bits here, elongating silences there.

At some point, as the Martians emerged from their ship and their faces were being described, Orson called out, "Dear God, this piece of shit is worse than shit! It's corny, too!"

In another corner of the studio, very much to himself, actor Frank Readick was listening over and over to a recording of Herbert Morrison's Hindenburg broadcast, prepping for his role as Johnny-on-the-spot newsman Carl Phillips.

Poor "Carl" was destined to die in some field in Nowheresville New Jersey, some place called Grovers Mill, where the invasion from Mars was improbably slated to begin.

It became clear as the run-throughs continued that Orson had set aside two roles for himself, that as narrator, and as astronomer Richard Pierson, the scientist left to wander a burned-out New Jersey and New York wasteland in the aftermath of the invasion.

Orson leaned into the microphone, polishing his own opening lines for the night's melodrama. "We now know that in the early years of the Twentieth Century, this world was being watched by intelligences greater than man's own…"

Hector glanced at a clock on the studio wall. Six p.m., eastern. Just two hours until broadcast time.

Cassie whispered in his ear, "Seeing all this may ruin radio for me, you know. It's like that line about newspapers and sausage-making. You know? You may enjoy eating it, but you do not ever want to see it made?"

Hector thought about films, and how he regarded them since he'd become a scriptwriter and said, "Believe me, I get it."

A little man with glasses and a beaky nose tugged at Hector's sleeve. He said, "It is Mr. Lassiter, isn't it?"

"Yes…"

"You have a phone call. If you'll follow me outside…"

Hector trailed the little man to a small office off the control room. He realized Cassie was dogging his heels, one hand in her purse. He presumed she was clutching a gun.

A pretty blonde with cat's eye-frame spectacles and a rather daring neckline passed him the phone.

Virginia Welles said, "Hector? Thank God it's you. I'm so sorry, but your friend, Mr. Moreno? He became quite ill. Some reaction to room service shellfish, it seems. They swear he'll be okay, but they're about to take him away and we'll be left quite alone and so…"

"No worries," Hector said. "Cassie and I are headed your way now. Traffic allowing, we should be there in thirty minutes. Sit tight and don't answer the door for anyone but us. I'll find someone else to watch you and then get back here to fetch Orson before the show's end. This is nothing but a complication, honey. Nothing to fret over."

Hector hung up the phone and told the bespectacled blonde, "Please tell Orson something came up. Tell him not to worry, but Cassie and I will listen to the show from the hotel with his family. Tell him I'll be back to get him here and to take him to the theater as earlier planned."

They seemed condemned to hit every red light between the CBS building and their most recent hotel. Their cabbie said, "What time have ya got, brother?"

"Seven-twenty," Hector said.

"Good," the driver said. "Don't want to miss Charlie McCarthy tonight. That Mortimer Snerd is priceless, you ask me."

Hector thought this everyman's assertion might well send Orson off a cliff. Any given Sunday night, Orson's audience was a fraction of that garnered by Edgar Bergen and his coterie of wooden sidekicks.

And then there was that other absurd aspect that set Hector's head spinning: the idea of a ventriloquist performing on radio? Yet the more he thought on that, the more Hector figured it was probably some kind of accidental favor to Bergen, whose lips visibly moved when he spoke for his dummies.

By seven-thirty, they were still six blocks from the hotel. Cassie said, "We could get there faster on foot I think."

Hector agreed and paid their cabbie, left him sitting there alone in stopped traffic.

Passing by the doorway of a residence room as they made their way down the street to the Welles' family's current hotel, Hector heard the overture music Orson had selected to open each broadcast of the Mercury Theatre on the Air, Piano Concerto No. 1 in B-flat minor by Tchaikovsky.

17

THE PHANTOM VOICE

Leaves chased discarded newspaper pages across Times Square as Cassie and Hector neared the hotel. A large group of men—most of them blond—were gathering outside. Hector stopped counting at a dozen.

"This has become a disaster," Cassie said.

A hand suddenly on Hector's shoulder. He spun, drawing down.

"Whoa there, Hector!" A man in a black trench coat and hat said, "Friends, remember?"

Hector frowned, then recognized Special Agent Edmond Tilly. The fed had seven men backing him up. Putting away his gun, Hector said, "Friends? Not so sure about that. Collaborators, anyway. You're with her?" He nodded at Cassie.

"Not with her side like you mean, more like collaborators to use your word," Tilly said. "More like we're with who she is with, but same sides, yeah. All with Uncle Sam, in the end."

"You do see you're also outnumbered," Hector said.

"I have ten more in the lobby," Tilly said.

Hector shot Cassie a look. She shrugged. He sighed and said, "Is this arrival of the cavalry your doing, Cass? Given the Thule contingent here, clearly you were justified sending up a flare if that's indeed what you did. He turned back to Tilly. "The Welles family okay?"

"My men say so, at least for the moment," Tilly said. "But that crowd there is clearly headed up to make it very much otherwise, don't you think?"

"Seems a safe bet," Hector said. "So what then? You all shoot it out in the lobby? That would almost certainly end in a slaughter of civilians."

Tilly pointed at three men standing off from the group of Germans. "No, you'll go up with that trio of mine. Go in through the back door of this building. My guys will explain why you go that way on your trip there. Either way, you all get up there quietly and grab the Welles women while me and my boys help those Germans cool their heels down here."

Hector quickly agreed, hoping he could lose the three FBI men on the way back down.

Slipping his gun into his right hand coat pocket, Hector said to the trio of FBI agents assigned him, "Follow us, boys. Let me knock on the door when we get up there, okay? Do it wrong—" a lie "—and you must might get shot."

The agents, holding up badges, led Hector and Cassie through the kitchen—raising eyebrows and drawing glares from hotel cooks and servers.

"All those German in the lobby…" Hector said. "Hell, the stairs' entrance is right next to the lobby's elevator bank. How do we get up there without being seen?"

"No worries," one of the agents, a smallish slope-shouldered man with mouse brown hair said. "There's a special service elevator that comes right off the kitchen." The agent waggled eyebrows. "That's why this joint's a favorite for local politicians who are looking to tryst. It was designed to speed room service delivery, so to speak. They say old Joe Kennedy himself paid to have it put in place, so when he was in town he and—."

Hector said, "Save the rest, pal. I already despise that crooked cocksucker."

One of the other agents held the elevator door. He said, "It's a small elevator. Maybe the dame shouldn't—"

"*You* stay then," Cassie said to the man, heading into the cage first. Hector followed. As the door closed on them in the cramped little elevator, Hector said, "You want the sixth floor. Having said that, where exactly does this door open on the other end?"

Furrowed brows. "Uh, not sure," the small, lead agent said. "Somewhere equally out of sight, no doubt. Some maid's quarters, maybe. It is a service elevator, after all."

The doors opened and a heavily accented German voice said, "Ah, the lift is here at last!"

The three FBI agents were still at the front of the cage. Two were shot in the face before their guns cleared their shoulder holsters. The door was now fully open. Three armed Germans were on the other side. One had a hand on Virginia Welles' arm.

Virginia—wild-eyed, terrified—was holding tightly to Christopher.

Even as the two FBI agents fell, Hector made a cold calculation. He put his Florsheim to the back of the still-standing Fed and kicked him into the arms of two of the three, heavily-armed Germans.

Hector shot the third—the one manhandling Virginia—between the eyes. To her credit, Virginia deftly managed to get her little girl's face turned toward her bosom, sparing Christopher the sight of the carnage resulting from Hector's shot.

Shifting aim, Hector pulled the trigger twice more, hitting the second Thule in the throat and then the chest. Cassie put the last of the German's down with a single shot.

The last of the FBI men, sprawling among the dead Thules, snarled, "Lassiter you son of a bitch! I'm going to—"

Hector cut him off with a wagging finger, "Language, Agent. A child and ladies are present. I'm certain Mr. Hoover wouldn't approve." As he said that, Hector pulled out his display handkerchief, shook it loose, then gestured at his own forehead and left cheek. Ashen and dazed, Virginia accepted the handkerchief and wiped the blood from her face in the places he had indicated.

Hector a extended a hand and reluctantly helped the last FBI agent to his feet. "Easy, brother," he said. "At least we're all still drawing air. Your compadres never stood a chance, you know. You all should have done your homework on where the elevator deposited us."

A familiar voice from a distant radio: "...the gas to be hydrogen and moving toward the earth with enormous velocity. Professor Pierson of the observatory at Princeton confirms...describes the phenomenon as (quote) like a jet of blue flame shot from a gun (unquote)."

The disgruntled FBI agent said, "Shut up, Lassiter. "You're not in charge here anymore. You're just—"

Another gunshot. The agent staggered, clutching at his back, then fell. The second man whom Hector had shot turned his trembling gun hand toward Hector. Cassie put the man down.

Hector heard the opening strains of "Stardust" from a distant radio, then a scream.

Through clenched teeth, Cassie said, "This elevator's no good option now, the stairs, either."

Hector dabbed at a last droplet of blood on Virginia's cheek and said to the ashen actress, "Darlin', please tell me you still have your room key on you."

Back in the Welles' hotel room, reloading her gun, Cassie said, "Hec, I don't call this progress. All of them will be soon headed to this room, if they aren't already on their way up."

Hector thrust his forty-five drown his waistband at the back. He set to work at a window latch. "So we'll leave by the fire escape. Not likely they're guarding that."

"Brilliant," Cassie said.

Hector said, "More like tragically necessary. I'm no fan of heights."

Hector pushed down the ladder from the second floor to ground level. It banged against the concrete with far more noise than he'd anticipated.

Christopher ended up wrapping her arms tightly around his neck as he made his way down the ladder. Police lights splashed one end of the alley. Cassie said, "Like it or not, we're going to have to exit where we came in, close by the hotel's main entrance. Let's just hope they've all at last gone into the lobby."

Hector said, "You three wait here. I'll see to getting us some kind of wheels." He handed the little girl back to her mother; Victoria was still looking stricken.

"I'm not feeling good about taxi cabs," Cassie said. "Mr. Hoover's crew isn't building confidence on my part, and the FBI can trace a cab like nobody's business."

"Exactly why I mean to hijack a car," Hector said. "I want my hands on the wheel going forward. When you hear two short blasts on the horn, you all come runnin'."

Cassie said, "Two following us. Gray Olds and the black Chrysler Royal."

"Right," Hector said. "Traffic's just heavy enough to make out-horse powering and losing them an impossibility."

That frustrated him. The Chevrolet coupe he'd taken at gunpoint seemed to have some real horsepower but no room to run.

Hector said, "Police stations, secret sanctums or Superman, I'm open to suggestions, ladies. We need strategies or some close-by outside help."

"Harlem," Cassie said finally. "At least these monsters on our tail will stand out there again, like the other night at the club."

Not much, but it was something, Hector figured. He course-corrected accordingly, awaiting better options.

As they headed toward Harlem, Cassie fiddled with the radio.

A voice—*that voice*—"This is probably a meteorite of unusual size and its arrival at this particular time is merely a coincidence."

Christopher said, "That's daddy on the radio! It is, it is!"

18

THE POWER OF THE MIND

Hector managed a tight smile in the rearview mirror at the girl's mother. Victoria said to her daughter in a strained voice, "Yes, but daddy's just acting dear, he's pretending to be someone he really isn't."

Turning that statement over in his mind in ways no child could comprehend, Hector weaved in and out of traffic, extending their lead on their pursuers for a time, then losing ground—and then losing some more—in a flurry of horn-blasting increments.

Flashing lights ahead. Hector cursed softly. "Afraid we're coming to a full stop. Looks like some wreck up ahead. They may just overtake us on foot then."

Cassie said, "How do we get around that?"

From the safety of their CBS broadcasting studio, Orson and fellow actor Frank Readick were describing the huge metal cylinder embedded in a New Jersey field, the canister containing the first of waves of Martian invaders.

Not wanting to scare Christopher anymore than the tension in their voices might already be doing, Hector spun the radio dial, looking for Charlie McCarthy's show. Instead, there was some middling singer there. Hector turned off the radio. It was now about fifteen minutes after the hour.

Traffic was definitely slowing to the complete stop Hector had feared. Desperate, he palmed the wheel, cutting off an oncoming Packard. The driver hit his horn and shook his fist out the window as Hector blocked his path, skidding toward an alley.

The Chevy slid into the narrow channel between buildings, its right fender chipping bricks before buckling in a flurry of sparks. Hector righted the car, smiling at the horn blasts behind them—presumably those of the Germans now, still surely several car lengths away from replicating the suicide turn Hector had barely executed.

"We'll make one more turn up there," he said. "You three will get out after. Find a store or a bar and stay well out of sight. I'll give those Germans something to chase once they finally get untangled from all that traffic. In fifteen minutes—no more—we'll meet up again." Hector glanced over at Cassie. "Remember, no later than eight-thirty p.m."

Cassie checked her watch. Hector continued, "Question is where do we meet? You seem to know Harlem, Cass. Give me a destination. I do know there's a police station on 123rd Street. We're close to that, aren't we?"

"Sure, and that's great if you trust the police," Cassie said. "I know you love your churches for everything but worship, Hec. There's a parlor church maybe five doors down from that cop shop. How about we meet in there instead?"

"There then. Just keep them safe." Hector rolled curbside. "Skedaddle now."

Cassie said, "Please don't let them catch you, darling."

With the girls out of the car and the Germans again attempting to pursue him, Hector found mounting commotion on the streets around him. Even here, blocks from where he'd dropped the girls, traffic was beginning to become congested again. There were yells, screams. Some families clutching or leading pets were scrambling onto the streets, trying to wave down cabs or passing cars, begging for rides.

Frowning, Hector switched back on the radio, turning the dial until he thought he heard Franklin Delano Roosevelt, presumably breaking some very bad news which must be contributing to the growing terror on the streets. That famous voice said, "Citizens of the nation, I shall not try to conceal the gravity of the situation."

Hector checked his watch again. Eight thirty—he was looking to be late making his rendezvous with Cassie and the Welles women.

A family—a man, a woman and two children—stepped in front of Hector's stolen car. The author cursed and stood on the brake, wincing and waiting for a terrible series of thumps. But the brakes and the Chevy's Safety Silvertowns did their jobs. The man ran around the Chevy and beat on the driver's side window. He begged, "Please, mister, a ride for my family out of here? There isn't any time left! They're already crossing the river. For God's sake, say you'll take us from here. Won't you please do that?"

Hector had already decided to abandon his heisted wheels and make his way to the agreed-upon church on foot. Hector also figured if the German's caught up to the car and saw it occupied by this particular family, they'd sensibly push on with no more violence.

Cops, though, were likely another matter. He said, "The ride is yours if you want it, brother. But know this—it is stolen, a hot ride."

"I was going to steal one myself if need be," the stranger said. "Law don't matter none now, I figure. Not anymore."

The man's face was a confusion of gratitude and uncertainty. He said, "But don't you want to come along? To maybe *drive*? Mister, nobody should die this way and staying here means surely dying."

More confused than before, Hector slid from the car and shook his head. "If you need the car pal, it's yours. Drive it like you stole it, because like I said, I did that very thing. Don't get caught."

The man slid behind the wheel as his family piled in. He said, "Figure this time tomorrow, there won't even be cops, not if the army doesn't start doing better against these things. Thanks for the wheels, mister. We'll never forget what you've done here."

Brows knitted, at that moment—based on the panic around him and Roosevelt's brief statement—Hector was convinced Hitler must have invaded some other country, and in doing so, at last somehow dragged the United States once again into the turgid and bloody waters of feckless European hostility. Hector wished Roosevelt in hell, knowing the fey Democrat must somehow be responsible for all this fear and chaos. FDR seemed to be a master at cultivating a culture of fear, Hector thought.

From his surrendered car's radio, a last bit of described terror: "I'm speaking from the roof of the Broadcasting Building, New York City. The bells you hear are ringing to warn people to evacuate the city..."

The man who had accepted Hector's stolen car gunned the Chevy and took to the sidewalk with peels of rubber, sending other panicked pedestrians scrambling from his path.

As he tried to lose himself in the crowd, to get his bearings and find the right church, Hector heard more snatches from other car and window radios: "Streets are all jammed. Noise in crowds like New Year's Eve in the city. Wait a minute… Enemy is now in sight above the Palisades."

Hector pushed through crowds running the other direction, people streaming in and out of shops and buildings. A woman cried out, "Nobody should die like this! Nobody!"

More confused than ever, constantly looking over his shoulder, Hector made his way to one particular little church.

A lone voice calling from an abandoned car's radio, its sound receding behind him: "2X2L calling CQ… 2X2L calling CQ…New York… Isn't there anyone?"

19

HEART OF DARKNESS

Voices heard on the street, all of them talking about invasion, about mass deaths in New Jersey and some imminent threat to New York City. A woman cried out to another, "Don't you know, New Jersey is destroyed by the Germans? It's on the radio!"

How in hell had the Nazis struck a blow to the east coast of America, Hector wondered, and more piercingly, was this somehow his fault?

Was it tied in some way to the German pursuit of the medallion and the Spear of Destiny?

Hector saw police come running out of the precinct house, waving arms and yelling, "Calm the hell down! It's a goddamn radio show people, that's all! It's just a silly damn radio story!"

The novelist only half-registered the cop's screams. He pushed through more panicked citizens and police, bursting through double doors into the church only to find a congregation on its knees, pleading for mercy from "the invaders."

Dear God, was all this really the result of Orson's silly-ass radio show?

Hector could not quickly find or catch sight of Virginia or Christopher Welles, who, he cynically figured, would most easily stand out in present company.

Then he spied a familiar silhouette—a particular overcoat and hat. Hectored cupped a hand on her shoulder and said, "Cass? Where are the—" Cassie began to slump leftward. Hector just stopped her from tumbling from the pew. With a shaking hand, he felt for a pulse, found one and muttered, "Thank God."

A note was pinned to Cassie's coat. Looking around a last time, convinced calls for help would be lost in the congregation's doomsday hysteria, Hector instead ripped off the note and shoved it in his pocket. He lifted Cassie in his arms and kicked open the double doors, staggering out into the still crazier tumult of a Harlem neighborhood on edge of complete collapse. He made his way toward the nearby precinct house, figuring it was his best shot at securing fast medical attention for Cassie.

Something about the chilly air started to bring her around. Hector set Cassie down on a bench and stroked her face. "Are you okay? What in hell happened?"

She coughed and pressed her fingers to her temple. "My God but my head hurts. Chloroform, I think. There was something pressed to my mouth, then…" She looked around, said, "Oh God, Virginia, Christopher?"

"Yeah. Figure this will tell us." He pulled the scrap of paper from his pocket he'd found pinned to Cassie's chest.

It was written in shaky English script, the hand of a man writing in something other than his native language. "Phone HEM lok-7342 by ten p.m. or the little girl dies first."

"I'm surely not waiting until ten o'clock," Hector said. "Can you walk? Should I call you an ambulance?"

That earned him a look. He helped Cassie to her feet, said, "That coffee shop…"

The joint was empty for the moment—not many in this topsy-turvy neighborhood evidently wanted to spend their last minutes swilling java while waiting for death to arrive in the form of Martian gas weapons.

To that point, a voice on a counter top radio confided, "I'm obsessed by the thought that I may be the last living man on earth."

The attendant gratefully took orders for coffee and Danishes for Hector and Cassie. He jacked a thumb at the street and said, "Can you believe those idiots falling for this crazy Halloween gag? Jesus H. Christ, but some people are stupid."

Hector smiled in rueful commiseration and stepped into a mahogany payphone cabinet. He fed in coins, told the operator the number. An elderly woman answered. Hector said, "So what are you, lady, the New York arm of the German American Bund?"

She hissed, "Who is this?"

"Lassiter. I'm an hour early because I don't like the idea of my friends in the hands of *your* twisted friends any longer than necessary. So I'm giving you a heads up. If you haven't figured out already, get to a radio—this drama of Orson's has caused real mayhem in the streets. I expect Orson may well end up arrested for inciting panic before the night's up. I tell you this because I want your bosses or friends or whatever they are to you to understand things just went in crazy directions for all of us. This is something beyond the beyond. It's a complication none of us could sanely plan for. Patience and calm heads are called for now. Pass that along."

"I've had inklings of what you speak about. But no promises, Herr Lassiter. Call back at ten as you were instructed."

Seething, Hector folded back the phone cabinet's door and settled on a stool next to Cassie. As he warmed his hands against his coffee mug, a rare Welles' mea culpa was being offered up to a rattled world by the "Boy Genius" as his program's hour wound down.

Sounding more than a little shaken himself, the precocious impresario said, "This is Orson Welles, ladies and gentlemen, out of character to assure you that the War of the Worlds has no further significance than as the holiday offering it was intended to be."

The dark-skinned counterman said, "I told all those fools before they ran out of here it was just a silly old radio show." He wiped down the counter, *tsk-tsking*.

Still shaken by Virginia and Christopher's kidnapping—by his initial thought that Cassie had been slain—Hector sipped his black coffee and lit a cigarette with a shaking hand. He glanced over and saw Cassie wanting a light, too. He struck a second hotel match with his thumbnail and got hers going.

Hector drained his coffee and asked for a refill. Some announcer was promising the Mercury's coming Sunday production would be a trio of short stories. Hector wondered if the law would actually allow that show to come off.

The streets seemed to be calming just a bit—people getting word at last it was some hoax or confusion caused by those who'd joined Orson's program already in progress, missing all the disclaimers and the fact established at the onset that the story had been set one year from now, in a 1939 that promised a better economy and fewer war fears than this sorry year. Hector thought, *If only...*

Under the counter, Hector pressed a palm to her thigh. Cassie placed a warm hand over his, pressing it higher and harder up against herself. A little sexual shiver of carnal hunger on her part; on his, too. He wished he could do something about that. Instead he said to her, "If you think you can do it, we need to get to the studio. We need to get to Orson before the rest of the world lays claim."

20

FOLLOW THE BOYS

As their cab rolled up at 485 Madison Avenue, Cassie and Hector found the CBS headquarters engulfed by reporters from rival stations and myriad newspapers and news agencies.

Some bottom-feeding rag had already managed to get out a half-assed early edition with scream headlines. A young boy hawking the papers screamed, "Orson Welles—con man of the century!"

A pretty-enough female reporter, buxom and brunette, recognized Hector as he stepped out from the hack and paid their cabbie. She said, "Mr. Lassiter, I'm Anna Donaldson from the *Sun*. I love your stories. Tell me, please, did you have a hand in writing tonight's broadcast?"

Taken aback, Hector said, "Lord no. I'm just a friend of an actor inside. Are you all really here because of that silly show? I saw firsthand it caused a bit of a stir in Harlem, but I figured that was just an isolated misunderstanding."

The reporter shook her head firmly. "In Harlem… In New Jersey. Across other parts of New York… There are reports of more terror as far west as Oklahoma, if wire accounts are to be believed. This is the story of the century. This time tomorrow, I expect they'll be calling for Orson Welles' head, and maybe Bill Paley's, too. Tonight's broadcast may have fooled thousands. There are reports of attempted suicides all over the country. Bomb threats against this place have been made now that people know it was a hoax."

"It was a radio show, not a *hoax*," Hector said. "Hell, go ahead and quote me on that if you want. This was meant to be a silly entertainment."

"Drama, hoax—same difference now," Anna said. "Perception is reality. Isn't that the saying?"

Forcing his way into the lobby and throngs of shoving reporters, hand tight on Cassie's arm, Hector said, "What kind of goddamn fools believe a rocket could be fired from Mars—assuming there was anything actually capable of living on that rock—and reach the earth *and* conquer our armies, doing all of that in the space of twenty or so minutes? I mean, Jesus Christ, talk about suspension of disbelief."

Hector felt as though he was losing his mind. That even a handful of people had confused Orson's potboiler radio melodrama with reality was staggering to the novelist. The prospect many thousands might actually have been taken in—that some might have even chosen suicide in the face of alien domination or annihilation—that was beyond reason. Hector couldn't begin to get his mind around that terrible thought.

Cassie, clearly thinking along similar lines, said, "I can't believe it either. This is more than insane."

They were stopped by an elevator operator who put his hand to Hector's chest. "Mr. Paley's orders. Nobody allowed upstairs right now."

"I'm not a reporter," Hector said. "I was part of the writing team. Phone up Mr. Welles and tell him Mr. Lassiter is here. He'll vouch for me."

"Mr. Welles is pretty busy right now, as you might guess," the man, said. "I don't care if you're H.G. Wells himself, you're not going up there now, and I don't have access to a phone."

Angered, Hector dug around through his pockets and pulled out an honorary badge given him by a film connection back in L.A., one who worked hand-in-glove with the L.A.P.D. in shaping his B-movie police procedurals.

Hector flashed his fake badge at a different elevator operator but met with a different obstacle. "Sorry, officer," the man said, "but the whole crew is under lock and key somewhere upstairs, away from the actual studio. Christ, we're getting death threats, bomb threats, you name it. Hell, there's talk of you guys arresting Mr. Welles, for Christ's sake. It was just a damned radio show you know, nothin' deeper."

From outside, the call of more news hawks: "Riots in Harlem! Suicides across the country!"

Somehow knowing it would be picked up this time, Hector again found a pay phone and called the number for the Welles girls' kidnappers.

A voice, German, but a bit more facile with English than the rest, said, "Mr. Lassiter?"

"Yes."

"Sorry for the witch, but she struggled—she was armed. At least we didn't kill her, which would have been within the rules of war, you surely must agree."

"This is no war. Not yet. Are Virginia and the little girl alive?"

"Alive and quite well, if in a state of terror. But how could that be otherwise, Mr. Lassiter? Where is Mr. Welles? We require you two, together, to bring us the medallion."

Hector said, "We don't have it, but let's say we *did* have the medallion. You must know that Orson's not available now, and may not be for some time. You *are* aware of what happened tonight? I asked that traitorous old bitch who answered your phone to see you were all up to speed on tonight's events for this very talk. Hell, I can't even get near Orson at this moment and we're in the same damned building."

Hector was sharply jostled. Some short, bespectacled reporter broke the connection and tried to pull the phone from Hector's hand. The little man said, "Sorry brother, Fifth Estate. Breaking news trumps civilian need every time."

No hesitation at all—Hector put the man down with a single short, sharp blow. He flashed his badge at the reporter whose nose was now gushing blood. Hector said to Cassie, "Detective Smith, please see to this cretin. Get this joker booked for obstructing official police business."

Cassie pulled her gun and got it up under the reporter's chin. "Start walking slick. You should probably squeeze the bridge of your nose, meantime. That's a nasty break and I expect it'll bleed like crazy for some time yet."

Hector redialed the number. He apologized for the interruption, said, "The scene here, right now, is simply crazy. Some reporter took the phone from me."

"You should find a better place to call from then," the German said. Hector couldn't argue with that logic. The man continued, "I am now aware of the radio program, of the panic it has caused. I am more convinced than ever you Amerikaners are absolute fools. Perfect dummkoffs." A heavy sigh. "Anyway, call me again at midnight, precisely. Let's see how things stand then." A pause, then, "These are truly insane developments, Mr. Lassiter."

Hector said, "Jesus, pal, don't get *me* started about all that."

By nine-thirty p.m., Hector was feeling murderous. He finally spotted the pretty blonde with the cat's eye eyeglass frames and plunging neckline he'd met in the studio earlier in the evening, before what all the wags were now short-handing as "The Panic Broadcast" turned the world upside down.

From what he could gather, the effect of the broadcast, the actual so-called panic, had been limited to some pockets here and there, neighborhoods or public places—churches, notably. It had not had the widespread reach first feared.

Hector caught up to the sultry blonde and, flirting shamelessly, tried to gain passage upstairs to Orson. She smiled and said, "Sorry handsome, so sorry you weren't told earlier. The reaction's been just terrible, as you can see. As I'm sure you've heard if you've been down here anytime at all. Some of the cast hid in the ladies room for about an hour. We're still getting bomb and death threats. Men calling and threatening to break Mr. Welles' nose." Hector caught himself massaging his now bruised fist.

The saucy, four-eyed blonde looked around and then confided softly, "Mr. Paley is making his own threats against Mr. Welles."

"Believe it or not, this is a *real* emergency," Hector said, taking the pretty woman's arm and leading her to a quite corner. "There's trouble involving Orson's wife and daughter. So I really need to talk to Orson. I needed to do that at least an hour ago."

The woman fiddled with Hector's tie, leaned into him a bit so their knees touched. Her perfume in his nose, her hand on his waist. "Again, sorry, but the lawyers and business people took Mr. Welles, Mr. Houseman and a few others and snuck them out the back just after the broadcast ended. They took them, as well as recordings of the broadcast and all the scripts they could gather up. There is already all kinds of wild talk about lawsuits. About calls for new laws by congress controlling all broadcasts going forward. I mean, gosh…" She stroked his cheek. "I'm pretty shaken… hate to be alone tonight."

Hector let that last pass. "Do you have any idea at all where they were taken?"

"I wish I did." She brushed his cheek and said, "You look like a man who's had a long and hard day." He smiled and pulled back from her. "Looking to be a long night, too," he said, smiling, still flirting back, but just a little now, "but not the good kind."

He pulled out a fountain pen and a slip of paper. "I need your phone number darlin', the one where you can be reached tonight."

That elicited a smile bordering on the carnal. "Of course."

Hector almost corrected the record then, but decided it was probably more efficient in terms of results if he didn't.

Besides, you never knew when or which way the world might take a crazy turn. He often found himself in New York for publishing reasons. He scribbled down the name of a hotel he intended to check into within the hour and handed it to her. "If you do manage to make contact with Orson, have him call me there. Please impress upon him there's real trouble here for his family. Again, my name is—"

"I'm already a fan, Mr. Lassiter. I read all your books, I do that just as soon as they come out. Please feel free to call me, even when this emergency is passed."

"You're very sweet," he said. "Going forward, it's Hector, please."

"I'm Amanda." Buxom, blond and blue-eyed; Hector figured the Thule would just eat curvy Amanda up.

On the street, Cassie said, "That reporter is still bleeding like nobody's business. You've *got* to teach me that punch. You ruined him with a single swing."

"Just throw everything you own," Hector said. "Feel the punch coming up through your feet. It's really that simple." On a hunch, Hector flagged down a cab. He asked they be taken to West 41st Street, to the Mercury. After all, Orson had insisted he had to make a dress rehearsal before night's end.

There they found a theater troupe whose emotions ran the spectrum from shocked to angry. One actor said, "I wouldn't have believed it if I hadn't seen the news ticker on Times Square myself. Goddamned Orson! I swear he could fall into an open sewer and come out clutching gold watches. I'm convinced of that. That monster's uncanny luck…" Cassie looked liked she agreed with all of that.

Hector put the arm on several thespians. Not one had heard a word from Orson or Houseman since the broadcast ended.

As Hector and Cassie left the theater, a strapping, too familiar German blocked the path to their waiting cab. His accent was different than that of the German on the phone—the one for whom the Panic Broadcast's effects had confirmed his already low estimations about the worthlessness of all Americans.

Hector nodded and said, "Rune, I take it by now you know what's happened tonight, because of the broadcast?"

"I know, yes."

"The lawyers or the feds seem to have Orson," Hector said. "He's not at the studio and not here. And wasn't I calling you people at midnight, by agreement? I hope the Welles women are still in good and safe hands."

Hector had at last decided on a course of action. The only one, really, for a non-believer, which he truly considered himself. He was at last fully prepared to surrender the real medallion to the Thule in return for Virginia and Christopher.

Then things took an unexpected turn.

"What are you talking about," the tall German said, scowling. "We don't have any girls." Rune eyes narrowed, something clicking. "*Ah*. So, it must be true. There *is* a facture in our ranks. You're saying someone else, obviously German, has taken his family from Welles?"

Hector casually slipped his hands in his overcoat's pockets. "What's the matter, Fuchs, are you confessing there's a little uneasiness amidst your crazy coven? Friction between the Thule and, what's that other name some of you truck under, the Vril or some such?"

The big German smiled and said, "The Vril may have the women, but I certainly have you," a glance at Cassie, "and this dirty-blooded witch." He reached under his coat with his right hand. Hector didn't hesitate. He fired the gun in his pocket from its low angle. Scratch one more overcoat.

A bloom between his eyes: the giant German looked startled, then toppled over, blood spreading out fast from whatever was left of the back of the man's head. With a shaking hand, the man clawed at his necktie's knot a last time.

Footfalls. Maybe some trick of the eye: Hector thought he saw this tall figure running away. As the running man passed under a light, Hector could have sworn it was the very man who now lay dead at his feet—it truly looked like Rune Fuchs running from the site of his own murder, looking back over his shoulder, wide-eyed and snarling.

A couple of pedestrians screamed. Hector waved his fake badge, calling for order even as he urged Cassie into their taxi.

Hector pushed his gun up behind the cabbie's ear, snarling, "You drive on!"

The cabman said, "Which way? Drive to where?"

"Anywhere that isn't here," Hector said.

21

CHIMES AT MIDNIGHT

At eleven p.m., his hotel room phone rang, startling him. Hector scooped it up. Voice racing, obviously high on adrenaline, caffeine and lack of sleep, Orson said, "Amanda gave me your latest location. Hector, my God, what's going on? I can't reach Virginia. You're missing, and can you believe this night? This is the wildest kind of luck—a real career changer, almost certainly. Old man, Hollywood will surely coming knocking, now! That is if the lawyers don't sink us first. When Hollywood does call, I want you standing shoulder-to-shoulder with me. With your storytelling skills and my own not inconsiderable—"

It would *never* happen. As Hector had previously indicated to Welles, he had sometime ago read his young friend's contracts for writers. Welles' devil contracts required that all actual authorship be obscured by legally-binding agreement; all writing credit contractually was bestowed exclusively upon Orson Welles.

The concept deeply offended Hector.

Cassie was taking a quick shower. Hector took advantage of that fact to step in harder at his younger friend. "Goddamn it, Orson, put aside the career stuff for now. The Germans have your family—they've taken them *hostage*. They attacked

Cassie and Virginia after a citywide search. They got away with it in a crowd because everyone in the Harlem church where they were hiding was on their knees, praying for their lives that your goddamn invented Martians wouldn't kill them with their crazy heat rays. How that's for irony, kid?"

Hector heard Orson wet his lips. He heard Orson whistle, lowly. He said, "That's terrible. *Terrible*. And I am ordered into a meeting with attorneys in ten minutes. I'm under armed guard, Hector. The lawsuit threats alone are immense. At nine in the morning, I have to meet the world press. After that, if I'm not in irons, I swear that I am yours, old man. I'm certainly yours. But right now, I simply don't have my own liberty."

He couldn't believe what he was hearing. Hector said, "My God, your family, your wife and little girl, they're in deadly danger."

"I know, old man, so don't take that tone. I'm in misery to know this. But you must understand, I'm quite under lock and key now and by a corporation. Both Houseman and I are hostages in our own right. It was the merest luck that Amanda—the sultry blonde with glasses and endless stems who is terribly smitten with you, by the way—got word to me that you all were in some trouble. I see now the trouble is mine old man, and my stomach—already in knots—is now in an agony of turmoil knowing my family is in real jeopardy. Do buy me a little more time as I know only you can, yes, Hector? Use all your cunning to make sure they're not harming my girls. At noon tomorrow, I can meet you. Meet them. Meet *whoever*." A pause, while he assumed Orson checked a watch or a clock. "Why it's almost tomorrow already." Another long pause, then Orson said, "I assume it's your intention to surrender the real medallion in trade for their safety?"

"Of course," Hector said. "In exchange for *your* family's safety. I don't believe in any of this infernal mumbo jumbo, anyway, you know that. The goddamn Germans can choke on this goddamn chunk of silly metal for all I care. They can take this silly ass spear—if it even really exists—and they can jam it up their collective ass, sideways."

Orson snapped back, "What about those of us who *might* believe, at least even a little? You went to Spain. You saw! You would really surrender this terrible weapon to the fascists, Hector? What would all our lives be under the thumb of these monstrous Germans then? We should liberate the spear. It's like a Grail Quest…a once-in-a-lifetime adventure."

Some aspect of that argument did reach Hector. At very least, it could be grist for a novel. But with Orson's wife and child held hostage, the window on crusades and quests seemed truly closed.

Hector said, "Your family is being held by these so-called monsters right now, Orson. You goddamn be where I can find you and easily. I'll try to talk the Thule or Vril into a rendezvous at noon tomorrow if I can, damn it all. We'll make it the observation deck of the Empire State again. Plenty of security there and no way for them to effectively run if things should go crosswise at their instigation. That fact alone should encourage some restraint on all sides. They bring your family and they leave with the hokey medallion. It's really that simple as I see it."

"I don't think it's that simple at all, old man, not a bit," Orson said. "But you're right of course. We have to do whatever is necessary to save Virginia and Christopher."

Hector stared at the phone, wishing he could make himself believe Orson meant that last. It was delivered with all of the conviction of some of the young thespian's toss-off radio acting—Orson was literally phoning it in from Hector's perspective.

The novelist's wristwatch indicated he had thirty minutes before he had to talk to that other German, the one holding the Welles women—presumably, the more formidable Vril.

Negotiations didn't go well.

As Hector haggled with the new German on the phone, trying to convince him of the precariousness of Welles' own current predicament—of the reality of his unavailability until sometime in the afternoon—there was a knock at the door. Cassie, presuming it was their late order for room service food and drink, opened the door wide.

A gun was pressed to her chest. She was jerked out into the hall by one arm.

The German on the phone said to Hector, "Stay still, Lassiter! I know where you are. I desire more leverage. Don't attempt to follow my people. I've ordered my man to shoot the Rhineland bitch if you do *anything* in this moment. You remain on the line with me and continue calmly planning our rendezvous. You will do that, yes?"

Hector said coldly, "What other choice do I have?" Hector told him of his plan to meet on the observation deck of the Empire State Building.

The German said, "Why that idiot place? It will be cold, windy. It will be—"

"It will be safest for all of us," Hector cut in. "It'll keep us all honest and well-behaved, as I figure it. There is nowhere up there to run. Same problem with clean and safe escape if evil intentions should come into play. I figure we just all have to play nice up there, high above the unwashed masses, up high with the shivering tourists and gawkers and no clean and easy means of flight except over the side and down. So, do we agree it's a date at the ceiling of the world?"

Hours later, Hector stood glowering, arms crossed, as Orson jousted with the press, seeming at once earnest and calculating in a pale suit and askew tie, sporting unruly hair and the wisps of that little boy's first beard. Orson somehow managed to be simultaneously glib and defensive under the bright lights. Orson emphatically insisted he never envisioned his Sunday night broadcast as anything other than crackling good entertainment.

"Of course, we are deeply shocked and deeply regretful about the results of last night's broadcast," Orson said.

Some scribe asked if there shouldn't be some law to prevent anyone repeating Welles' hoax. Orson said, "I don't know what the legislation would be. I know that almost everybody in radio would do almost anything to avert the kind of thing that has happened, myself included."

After twenty or so minutes, Hector caught Orson's eye, pointed at his watch and nodded at the door. Visibly reluctant to leave the center ring of reporters, Orson held up a finger at Hector, signaling for more time.

The novelist lost all patience then. He called out, "Turn your goddamn cameras off, now! This press conference is fucking over!" His raw profanity would ensure compliance, he knew. Hector shouldered through surly reporters, photographers and cameramen. Hector took Orson firmly by the arm, jerked him into his wake. "Come on, *l'enfant terrible*. At least this one time, you're going to damn sure *be* on time."

Orson resisted Hector's pull as they exited the room of reporters, still shouting questions at the retreating radio star. Welles huffed, "Where are we going, old man? I deserve to know that much. I deserve to know exactly what you've agreed to, what you've committed me and my family to."

Hector bit his lip. He explained the rendezvous plan in more detail.

Orson railed again at the prospect of any time to be spent atop the Empire State. "My asthma, old man, remember? My infernal asthma. You always forget it. Anyway, you must wait long enough for me to recover my coat and hat."

Eyes nervously checking the rearview mirror, vigilant for tails, Hector drove them on through the chilly streets of New York City in another stolen car.

Staring straight ahead, moping, Orson said, "Where's your witchy girlfriend now, Hector?"

"She's a hostage, too. Collateral, so to speak, in exchange for saving your family. She should be with Virginia and Christopher by now. They took Cass from me at gunpoint at the hotel. At least your family has her with them."

"Hardly as though she's protection or real comfort for them," Orson sniffed. "She's just a fellow hostage, isn't she now? I mean, really, old man, you've hardly distinguished yourself as a protector these past hours. Your girlfriend, either."

Hector began to lose his temper. Orson saw and tried to head it off. "Just stating facts without judgment, Hector. Don't get defensive. Judge not lest ye bore the audience, yes?"

Hector took out his mounting anger at Orson by gripping harder at the wheel, laying on a little more gas.

Growing more nervous—a man who hated cars and had never himself learned to drive—Orson demanded, "Enough posturing—what's our *real* plan, Hector?"

His mouth was dry; his hands shaking. All of it from too little sleep, water or food. Hector said raw-voiced, "We play it straight, as I've said all along. The medallion in trade for safe return of your family. And now for Cassie too."

"You'd *really* give the Nazis all this power? This terrible weapon? I doubt Cassie's conscience would countenance that."

"Don't forget Cass first got into this for the money, as a job," Hector said. "At least at first she did that. And yes, I mean to do this to save not just her, but to rescue your wife and little girl. Anyway, you can't truly believe this fable about this old spear—even if it somehow did come in contact with Christ Himself, if there even ever was such a person. You can't really believe it could have any special power."

Orson sighed. "I suppose my mind is just more open to such things than yours is. I still believe in… let's call them possibilities. God, the Devil, even ancient Gods, potentially, if the case is made even a little. You see, old man, Christianity is built on the bones and symbols of now-dead religions that once meant every bit as much to their believers as all we hold dear means to us Christians. The so-called prophets were no different than we are as artists—quietly borrowing inspiration here and there like magpies."

Hector held his tongue about all that. He just said, "The Germans can have the goddamn lance for all I care. The Ark of the Covenant and the Holy Grail, too. They can take 'em all to some salt mine in Germany. Just symbols. Totems, at best. Seems to me that faith is the point, regardless what name you give your God. I'm not going to let Virginia, Christopher and Cassie die for some damned myth, for some mere metaphor."

"A mere metaphor," Orson repeated. "That from the mouth of a career author, a present-day myth-maker. Pardon me if I confess grave disappointment in you for that."

Hector counted ten. He took a deep breath. He resisted saying, "The disappointment is all mine, young man. You young, self-centered fool."

Instead, Hector said, "This is going to be straight trade, no tricks and no arguments. I'd spare you the view and the lung-troubling air up there, but they insisted on us both being there, in the flesh, for the swap."

Orson said, "It's my family whose lives are in the balance, along with your girlfriend's life of course. So absolutely, I must be there. I must parlay with them."

22

CIRCLE OF DEATH

Two strangers rode up in the elevator with Hector and Orson, getting on at the ground floor with the author and actor and staying on all the way up to the eightieth floor. There, they all transferred to another elevator in order to reach the eighty-sixth floor and its observation deck, tension mounting in the attenuated silence.

Significantly, although he was convinced the two men were shadowing he and Orson, Hector also got the sense the pair of strangers was not otherwise allied. On the contrary, they struck him as antagonists, if they were anything at all to one another.

As they stepped out into the fierce crosswinds of the observation deck, Hector and Orson saw a number of people were taking the view, arms resting on the slightly higher-than-waist-level wall. Many began to move from those walls when they saw Lassiter and Welles.

Factions defined themselves—five strapping Germans lined up to their left. Six more, with Cassie and the Welles family in tow, gathered to their right.

Behind the actor and the writer a voice, American, called out above the crosswinds: "Mr. Welles, Mr. Lassiter. We're the

U.S. government, and we're here to help." A pause, then a "You'll no doubt be relieved to know that."

Suppressing a groan, Hector half-turned. He saw ten men at their flank.

A few milling tourists gawked and looked nervous. The civilians were obviously, painfully trying to figure if it was better to vacate the observation deck or simply act as if nothing odd was going on.

The two men who'd rode up on the elevators with them chose their respective sides—one lining up with the group that held the hostages, the other with the contingent of self-declared government agents massing behind them.

Hector called above the wind to Cassie, "You three are safe and sound? No hanky-panky?"

Cassie was wearing what appeared to be some too-large, borrowed coat. She yelled back, "We're okay. They've behaved." She nodded at their German captors. "So far…"

"These government types," Hector continued, "friends of yours?"

"Maybe," Cassie said. "Just not at all sure. I know none on sight, anyway."

One of those men who might or might not be allied with Cassie said in a strong Boston accent, "You give the medallion to us, Mr. Lassiter. These Germans here, both bunches of them, can surely do the math. We out-number them, two-to-one. Got more guys at their backs, as you now see. We have much more firepower, too."

The nameless U.S. agent continued to prattle on, but Hector lost the thread, frowning as Virginia and Cassie's hats suddenly took flight.

Some Germans' and G-Mens' fedoras were similarly torn from their heads by the strangely shifting wind.

The women's hair—the little girl's, too—began to whip in an entirely new direction. It was as though the wind's direction had changed on a dime.

Then Hector saw them—three autogiros, each fitted with a mounted machine gun.

"They are ours," the German called out proudly. "Our Valkyries!"

Hector leaned in close to Orson's ear. "Looks like we're back to my plan, kid."

"*Your* plan," Orson repeated. He did that with an almost curled lip. Hector felt a little more of his affection for his young friend crumble.

Hector called out to the crowd, "Easy there, boys! I came to barter for the ladies' lives and I mean to do just that." He smiled at Cassie. "Sorry, darling," he called out above the roar of the wind, over the whip of the autogiros' blades. "Uncle Sam doesn't win this one. But from where I stand, it's a sucker's game, anyhow. Just fables and folly, fellas. Winner take nothing."

Hector steadied himself with a hand on Orson's shoulder. Balanced on one leg, he tore the bag holding the medallion loose from where he'd secured it below his knee.

Holding the authentic medallion in his right hand, Hector called out, "You send the ladies to me, and I'll roll the medallion to you."

The FBI agents said, "Mr. Lassiter, we will shoot you in the back if you try to do this."

"Roll it slowly," one of the German's said. "Gently. Nothing to damage it, or its directions."

Orson took Hector by the arm. Guns pointed from every direction shifted from Hector to Orson's heart and head. Swallowing, gathering his courage, Orson said to Hector, "Please. It's my family's life in the balance. Give me the medal. I'll make the exchange. With my connections to Roosevelt, even Hoover's thugs surely won't shoot *me*. Let it be on my soul if it should all bring the heavens down when the German's have the spear. Anyway, my girls need to see me do this. They at least need to see me try and do this. You must know what they must think of me right now."

"Don't talk crazy," Hector said, pushing away Orson's hand.

It was the closest Hector had ever seen Orson come to begging. "Please, old man, my wife, my baby girl—I *need* to do this. They need to *see* me do this, just as I said. Surely you of all people must see how that's so, old man." A hurt smile. "After all, you're my friend. My only true friend."

Hector hesitated. He said at last, "Then we'll do this together. Shoulder-to-shoulder, we walk toward those Germans."

Orson leaned in close, whispered, "Old man, it won't come as news I've been less than the perfect husband. Far less the father that I meant to be. Less the father than I should have been to poor Chris. Doing this, making this trade, especially when they later know the enormity of the stakes? Hector, it could go some real distance to repairing past transgressions."

Biting his lip, assessing Orson standing there with puppy dog eyes and gloved hand extended in expectation, Hector tried to weigh Orson's words and demeanor against that of an accomplished—even a megalomaniac—actor.

In the end, Hector just couldn't bring himself to think so little of his young, precocious and sometimes selfish friend.

Hector said, "I can truly trust you to do the right thing here?"

"Of that I promise," Orson said. "You can truly trust me to do just that very thing—that thing I think right."

With lingering hesitation, Hector passed the metal disc into Orson's hands.

"Thank you most sincerely, old man," Orson said. "You are my one and truest friend." The autumn light caught the diamond in Orson's dark eye. "I won't disappoint you, I swear." His blacked-gloved hand closed over the medallion.

Turning, holding the glittering piece of metal up for all to see, Orson yelled above the wind, above the continuing roar of the three aircraft engines, "Do you all know the tale of Solomon?"

Already regretting entrusting the medallion to the actor, Hector said, "Just make the goddamn trade and be done with it, kid. This isn't theater-in-the-round."

"Of course it is," Orson said. "It's *exactly* that. All the world's a stage, yes? And upon it we just strut and fret, am I not right?" Orson pressed on, louder, "Solomon, faced with two women, each claiming to be the mother of the same child, suggested the babe be cut in half so both of the women could claim a piece. When one demurred, when she rebelled at Solomon's unthinkable suggestion, he declared that woman the victor. Solomon figured she was clearly the true mother because of her intended sacrifice and so awarded her custody of the unharmed child. And then there is the tale of Alexander and the Gordian knot…"

All the while, as he spoke, Orson slowly turned around, speaking to all factions. "This is all a way of saying that, faced with making an impossible choice, the wise man simply cuts to the chase—takes the obvious, but unthinkable course of action. As a magician, I surely know something about sawing things in half."

Orson held up the medallion again, letting it catch the autumn light for all to see. Then, with a flourish, he turned his hand, letting the medallion rest on his outstretched left palm. He passed his other gloved hand over the disc, then raised both hands to show them suddenly empty.

Yells. Freshly leveled and cocked guns from all sides, all of them now trained on the young actor. Virginia screamed, "Orson, please! My God, no!"

Hector took a step toward Orson, then stopped as roughly half of the guns turned his way again. The American faction's leader screamed, "Goddamn it! We will not hesitate to shoot either of you. Give the medallion to *me*."

Empty hands held high, Orson smiled and said, "Please, don't overreact. Forgive an actor a moment of bad judgment. Forgive a magician the temptation to lighten tensions with a little harmless sleight of hand. A moment's amusement." He reached into his pocket, then extended his right hand, the medallion safely cradled there. "There, you see," Orson called out. "This bauble, this thing you all desire. Behold, look hard upon your false idol." His voice turned poisonous. "Do that, and *despair*."

Spinning, coat tails whipping darkly around him, Orson whirled faster, gathering force. He chucked the disc high into the air, hurled it right on over the edge of the world's tallest building.

Gasps.

Men—German and American—cursed in their respective languages and surged to the waist-high walls, trying to catch sight of the falling disc and its path to the earth.

Hector waited for some pedestrians' screams from far below or the angry blast of horns as the heavy piece of metal struck down some innocent civilian or crashed through the windshield of a car or cab.

From this height, with its weight, the medallion was more than a lethal object.

Hector also waited for the burn of a bullet, for the terrible vision of Cassie, Christopher or Virginia's head torn open by a cascade of retaliatory cartridges.

There was nothing but the sound of the wind and the autogiros' chopping blades.

Virginia Welles' eyes accused her husband. The actor seemed truly taken aback by that. Why that should be so Hector couldn't fathom. Hell, he wanted to chuck Orson off the Empire State right after the cursed medallion.

Cassie broke the silence—she had the presence of mind and foresight to strategically move the ball. She yelled out, "What are you all waiting for? You can't shoot the most famous man in the world right now. You can't shoot *anyone* and get away clean from up here. The medallion is now down there somewhere! If you're not going to go down and search for it, I certainly am."

A moment's hesitation, then a scramble to the elevators.

Hector, Orson, and the three women were left alone on the observation deck with a smattering of horrified tourists. Those last quickly began to flee behind the German and American agents of various stripes and allegiances.

Hector continued to study Orson.

The author shook his head and at last said to the actor, "You crazy, selfish reckless bastard."

Halloween was just one hour from arriving—the veritable witching hour looming large.

The four of them sat in Orson's den; it was testy in all directions.

The actor said, "You really must forgive me, old man. You really must, you know, Hector. I'm sure that Virginia has done so by now. I mean now that she knows the true stakes."

Virginia was ice: "I don't care about *stakes*. I care about Christopher. You put her at risk. You put both of us as risk with your little silly magic trick up there."

Orson swallowed hard. He managed a smile. "Anyway, the good news is bronze isn't durable at all. Falling from that height, the impact no doubt did terrible damage to the thing. The impact at least terribly distorted the medal, assuming any of them ever even find whatever is left. Most likely, the fall rendered it useless as a map."

"Off the point," Virginia said.

Hector's thoughts were elsewhere. He said, "And the fake medallion, do you still have it?"

Orson shook his head. "I guess you didn't notice the unfortunate tailoring of my coat tonight. Rather, its lack. I know I didn't until it was too late." An embarrassed smile. "You see, in our haste to make the rendezvous, it seems I apparently grabbed the wrong overcoat. It fit me like a tent, the sleeves nearly reaching my fingernails, as you apparently didn't notice. So far as I can tell, that copy you had made of the medallion is now in the hands of some confused newsman or equally befuddled Mercury player who has my coat." A long pause, then a shrug. "It really has been quite the confusing muddle, hasn't it?"

Cassie rose, extended a hand to Hector. She said coldly, "Either way, seems it's over now. The disc, such as it might be, is still in the wind, so to speak. All interested parties saw it pitched off a skyscraper and you and your friend are now off the hook." She hesitated, then said, "You and I? Much to discuss." She smiled at Hector. "You should treat me to dinner somewhere. Say goodbye to your *friend* and let's do that right now, yes?"

Hector wanted to be away from Orson too. He took her hand and said, "You pick the place, Cass."

23

HEARTS OF AGE

They were once more sitting at a table near the front of Café Society, Billie Holiday singing a too-resonant version of "My First Impression of You."

Cassie raised her glass, said, "In the end I'm convinced I was right from the start. Your young friend's a world-class jerk. I truly hate him right now."

"Not feelin' so warmly disposed toward him either about now, if you haven't gathered," Hector said. He nursed a Jack and Coke. He had no appetite for booze presently. That was a rarity these years.

Cassie was having a second red wine. "He got me fired, you know. That stunt up there cost me my job."

"I'm sorry," Hector said. "But I guess now that nobody has the disc—Christ only knows where the thing landed—they all stand down."

If so, it was not the worst news for Hector and Orson.

For his part, Hector figured the disc was probably resting on some parapet or ledge of the Empire State Building. At least once or twice, a would-be suicide had been thwarted in their fatal dives to the pavement—swept back and deposited upon some lower ledge of the building by the monstrous upward drafts of wind roaring up the sides of the skyscraper from the streets of Manhattan. Those colossal updrafts had rendered the building's distinctive dirigible mooring mast an engineering impracticality.

Hector continued to finger his drink, watching Billie slink across the stage as the band played on. "So what's next for you, darling?"

"I suppose, it's back to New Orleans," Cassie said. "Back to that little voodoo shop in the French Quarter. I have enough money to try and make a go of it again, for a time."

She took his hand, the one she had said told the story of his future. She turned his hand over to expose its palm and traced its lines with a long fingernail. "It's a wicked city, in a sense," Cassie said. "One that would tolerate the likes of us together, in ways that most other cities in this country won't." A cautious smile. "You game to try that, darling?"

Cassie looked around them at other couples. Some of those were clearly mixed, and some of those daring couples even held hands. A smaller percentage of interracial couples were actually presuming to exchange kisses in public.

She said, "C'mon, just answer. Think you might make it to the Big Easy, Tex?"

Hector certainly couldn't see visits running the other way—not since he'd begun to detect this growing white supremacy movement based on his new island home in Puget Sound.

He still had that little bungalow or shotgun shack in Key West, of course—Brinke's purchase, initially.

He could move back there, he supposed, another rare place in the States where their relationship would be better tolerated if Cassie might fail to "pass" from time to time—something that might actually be harder for her to do after a few months of deep bronzing under the Gulf rays. But that prospect, too, held complications from Hector's perspective.

Too vivid memories of Brinke crowded that island for one, as well as memories of the other woman who'd recently claimed a part of his heart down there on Bone Key, the vexing Rachel Harper.

Key West was just a too-small dab of sand in that way, far too crowded with painful remembrances, old and new.

And then there was Hemingway.

The prospect of Hector and Ernest presently not speaking yet living on that same postage stamp of an island? That would surely be a misery all its own.

Hector found himself focusing on her dimples as Cassie smiled sadly at him. "You're grasping for a polite way to say no, aren't you?" She looked away, looked to Billie. "It's okay. Really it is, darling. I told you before, you have everything to lose, Hector. I know that, I've made that clear before."

Almost as if it was planned, even on God's cruel cue maybe, a flashbulb exploded, setting both to blinking. Yet reflexes rose to the occasion: even as the little man with a camera began to dash away, Hector's hand lashed out and caught coattails.

Jerking the journalist and his camera back in his direction, Hector growled, "Okay, ace, which part of you should I break *this* time?"

The man's bandaged nose made Hector smile, meanly. The ambushing shutterbug was the same reporter Hector had assaulted at the CBS building the night before.

"Screw you," the reporter said. "This is my right. I know who you really are! A noted man like you crossing the color line with this dinge whore? That's same as cash in the bank for me."

Hector still had the man's coattails gathered in his left hand. The music stopped; other diners were watching. Billie glared. Hector was aware now that Cassie had a napkin gripped in one white-knuckled hand. She was shielding her eyes with her other hand, the one that should reveal her own future. Her cheeks were flushed. "Just let him go," she said through clenched teeth.

Aware it had also become a kind of performance now, even a position statement, Hector said to the reporter, said it for the room, "God help you if my being with this woman really constitutes news to anyone. And I'd argue I'm well within my rights to protect my privacy from parasites like you. I'm within my rights to do whatever it takes."

The novelist took another look around the room, then Hector tore the camera from the reporter's hands and smashed it several times against the table until it lay in pieces. That prompted a standing ovation.

But Hector realized Cassie was trying even harder to hide her face.

The reporter took a swing at Hector. The author caught the journalist's much smaller fist in his left hand and squeezed. Knuckles cracked and popped. The little man whimpered, then begged for mercy. Hector said, "You're getting off light, you rotten bastard. Before I make your smile or your tiny hands match that busted-up nose, you best vamoose."

The little man ran backward at first, tripping twice. He scrambled up the stairs to laughter and catcalls.

More diners applauded. Cassie looked more miserable than she had before. She rose and said, "I'm mortified, as I surely hope you can tell. Please take me away from here. Please do that now."

"We'll find another place," Hector said thickly. "A better place. I swear."

"I guess that would have to be Harlem at this point," she said bitterly.

They indeed ended up back in Harlem, to Hector's chagrin, at the Cotton Club.

Some want-to-be Ethel Waters belted out a mediocre take on "Stormy Weather."

Kneading her fingers and ignoring her drink, Cassie said, "I may want family, you know, maybe soon. I may want a lot of children. I'm pretty sure that I do. I can't tell how deep your intentions toward me run. If we go forward from tonight, will you react every time we're confronted like you did tonight, because you know it will happen, over and over."

She didn't even give him time to respond. Cassie plucked her napkin from her lap and slung it across her still-empty plate.

She looked him in the eye, and said, "Knowing you such a short time, I already love you, Hector. I truly do. But even those feelings aren't nearly enough to overcome what I know the world demands of the likes of us." A sad smile. "Sorry, darling, but there's simply not enough love in this world to make us work."

She showed him her back. Hector watched Cassie go—he watched other men watch her go.

A few seconds later, Hector realized the torch singer was pointedly singing her song to him. That made him squirm.

Feeling low, feeling angry, Hector drained his drink, settled his check, then wandered out into a hard cold rain.

He tapped a window with his knuckles and awakened a sleeping cab driver.

Sitting in the back seat of the cab, listening to the slap of the windshield wipers and some radio show festooned with longhairs attempting to analyze the deeper meanings of Orson's so-called "panic broadcast," Hector settled on a mean and carnal course to assuage his anger at the world and his bitter, immediate sense of loss.

He simply didn't trust himself alone tonight, so he asked his driver take him to the Stork Club.

Once there, Hector fished his coat pocket and found the very Aryan Amanda Noble's home phone number.

The blond, bespectacled siren answered on the third ring. Clearly he wakened her from sleep, but Amanda was quick enough to gather herself.

Hector said, "Is there any possibility, any at all, that you're free tonight, angel eyes? I mean, rather, free this morning? I mean right *now*." Hector knew he sounded desperate, but so what?

Amanda hesitated, then said, "I am free, though it's probably pretty bad strategy to admit that to a man like you. But facts are facts, right? And, anyway, it's only just Tuesday. Who has dates on Tuesdays at this hour? Good news is, the studio is still kind of closed down after all the mess from Mr. Welles' crazy Martian broadcast. So I don't have to go back in until Thursday. That's a lot of time for... *distraction*." A pause, then, "But honey, you frankly sound like twelve-kinds of hell. Maybe we'd both regret getting together just now."

"It's not been my best night," Hector admitted. "All tricks and no treats. So I'm indulging myself at the Stork. You up to helping me do that, darlin'? Still a few hours until last call."

A long pause, then saucy innuendo in her retort. "Day's still relatively young," she said. "Maybe it *still* could be your best night, Mr. Lassiter."

That was unlikely, but rotten as he was feeling, Hector wasn't above indulging that illusion with this pretty blonde.

Certainly, he would try very hard to make her think it was wonderful. He said, "Maybe more than maybe."

"Don't be a cynic," she said. "I'm very much an optimist. We'll try to make that quality rub off."

Right there, Hector committed himself to the notion of burying memory with this lusty, pale-skinned blonde in whose arms and tangle of long and eager legs he proposed to erase thoughts of Cassandra.

To his shame, and only at their end, had Hector remembered the classical allusion embodied in Cassie's first name—the beautiful, truly gifted seer cursed by Apollo so that her prophecies would never, ever be believed.

BOOK TWO

BLACK MAGIC

January 1948

"Robert Houdin was the greatest
magician who ever lived.
And do you know what he said?
'A magician, he said, is just an actor,
just an actor playing the part
of a magician.'"

—Orson Welles

24

THE ROOTS OF HEAVEN

A dreary opening to a new year, another birthday just days behind him.

Hector had come in with the New Year in 1900; now his own half-century mark loomed closer; it left him feeling… gloomy.

As this fresh and unpromising year unfolded, Hector found himself wandering the streets of Rome in a chilly rain, chasing a kind of ghost.

Gusts of wind jerked at his umbrella and bent back his hat's brim, making it feel far colder than the fifty-six degrees the morning newspaper had predicted.

From back home came reports of a devastating blizzard that had swept across the northeast. In Manhattan snow drifts were said to be exceed twelve feet. Desperate to dispose of all the white stuff, it was being dumped by the truck-full into always-warm sewers and already swollen rivers.

A part of Hector still wished he were back there, struggling against the elements with his countrymen in a clean and simple battle for survival instead of stalking his cold trail here, in pursuit of—how to put it?—well, yes, in pursuit of *himself*.

Hector was giving chase to some mysterious doppelganger or imposter who had been moving across Europe, seducing men and women, leaving behind staggering bar and hotel tabs and generally threatening Hector's own standing and reputation in Europe by posing as a financially and sexually profligate—and presumably polysexual—Hector Lassiter.

This bogus Hector Lassiter had led the real Hector on a far-from-merry chase across Europe for several weeks, his randy trail at last seeming to go cold in every sense in Italy.

Two days ago, frustrated by his dead-end search, Hector had been contemplating his return to the States when he saw a news item reporting his career-troubled younger friend, Orson Welles, was actually currently living in Rome, starring in some dodgy-sounding project about the black magician Alessandro Cagliostro, some film adaptation of a story or book on the man penned by Dumas, one of Welles' literary darlings.

Dumas and Welles were the only names associated with the film that resonated for Hector. The rest of the cast and crew were a mystery to him, and the director—a man named Gregory Ratoff—equally evoked no flicker of recognition from the Hollywood screen scribe.

It sounded like straight-up money work for the now thirty-something Welles, who was still struggling to get his life and career on track after the spiral that had begun in the wake of *Citizen Kane*, Orson's one great and fully-realized film as a director to date.

Orson was purportedly acting in this film about the black magician while somehow also editing his own film adaptation of *Macbeth* in Europe for looming release back in the States.

His perceived decision to abandon America and therefore greatly complicate completion of the Shakespeare film was doing nothing to repair Orson's pervasive image as undependable player in American film studio circles, both as actor and director.

Indeed, somewhere else, someone who was not Orson was still struggling to put the finishing touches on yet another incomplete Welles film project, *The Lady From Shanghai*, a film noir whose troubled production Hector had become unexpectedly entangled in earlier in the previous year.

Yes, looking back, 1947 hadn't been a banner year for either Hector or Welles.

After all, the year had begun for the two in exceptionally bloody fashion, with the still unsolved and nightmarish murder of Elizabeth Short, the so-called "Black Dahlia."

Beth Short's savage torture and mutilation murder had changed both men's lives and sent Welles, still a quiet suspect in her killing, fleeing from the States inches and hours ahead of a flurry of subpoenas, warrants and mounting interest on the part of the House Un-American Activities Committee and the FBI.

Welles was also running from massive debts and another divorce, too—the final settling of his troubled marriage to ginger-haired Mexican bombshell Rita Hayworth.

And now, Italy too, was seemingly turning on Orson after an all-too-brief honeymoon with the Italian press after his arrival in Rome.

Several months into working and living in the city—after being spotted looking heavier in the jowls and disheveled in posh places like Grotte del Piccione, or swilling veritable casks of chilled vino in Tor Fiorenza with a succession of buxom young Italian pretties—Orson was increasingly painted as the quintessential, vulgar "Ugly American" by the post-war Italian press corps.

Hector reckoned some of that was complicated or even driven by the fact the Italy was still justifiably struggling to overcome its guilt and distress in the rise and fall of Mussolini and its military forces' pasting at the hands of the Allies.

Orson's larger-than-life American persona was just going down too hard and too thick with contemporary Italians still mired in wartime recovery.

Once again, or so it seemed to Hector, Orson's timing, formerly seeming to be so effortlessly lucky in his crazy youth, was still badly off, just as it had been since circa 1947. Orson Welles seemed again to be, in Hector's estimation, in the wrong place at the very worst of times.

Hell, by way of most-recent proof, at least one Italian journalist had declared Welles in a paper printed the same morning to be no less than "the devil incarnate."

Angling his umbrella against the shifting wind and rain, Hector pushed his scarf up a bit higher under his chin—he had the stirrings of a sore throat, of merely a cold, he hoped—and picked up the pace a bit.

Everyone seemed to put a little hustle in their step as the weather worsened. Cursing, an older, stooped man was racing to collect an array of shoes he'd spread out under a canopy from the rain, but now his footwear was being dampened by the shifting winds.

So many shoes to collect in this soggy gale—a hot commodity on the black market in a Europe still struggling to find its own footing, so to speak, under the would-be largesse of the Marshall Plan.

Hector had seen it everywhere on this enforced tour of Italy.

Between searches for "himself," Hector had managed to take in a few sights of the country he'd not seen since the Great War and his long-ago stint driving ambulances for the Red Cross after a war injury effectively forced Hector from the field as a reluctant armed combatant. Chasing Pancho

Villa in Mexico months before, Hector had already lost his taste for military service.

As a civilian this time in Rome, he'd already wandered along the Via Sacra, staring up again at the Arch of Titus and at the Colosseum. He'd wandered further on the Sacred Road through the crumbling remains of the Forum, looking about as he remembered them from his youth.

But in a larger sense, to Hector's mind, Rome was now a troubling mix of scrambling peddlers, black marketeers, hurt feelings and all that beautiful, crumbling history that predated the equally present war-damage wreaked to its much younger structures.

Closing and then shaking out his umbrella, Hector ducked from the glistening Via Vittorio Veneto into the Doney Gran Caffé.

Hector handed his damp coat, hat and umbrella over to a striking hat checker who reminded him more than a little of a younger, bustier Marina Berti, only this pretty thing had a more American nose.

Hector looked around, taking in the warmth and grandeur of the place, hoping his elusive double hadn't burned him here, too. It would be consistent with his current flavor of luck if the mysterious bastard had done that very thing.

Orson was sitting at a corner table near the back. He held up a hand, and gestured with a fat cigar. He hollered across the room, "There he is! Do come sit down and dry off, old man!" Other diners frowned and scowled at Orson's disruptive, too loud greeting. Hector held up a quieting hand and moved the actor's way.

As the press indicated, Orson had put on a few more pounds, but he was hardly what Hector would describe as fat, or, to use the Italian wags' word for it, "corpulent."

Orson had a fresh bottle of pre-war Barolo and a wine glass waiting for Hector. They embraced and Orson said, "Do sit down, my dearest friend. Us crossing paths here and now, why that's the best kind of luck. Maybe the first good luck in a long time. At least it is for me."

Hector sat, poured himself some wine and they tapped glasses. Orson said, "You know a little Italian from the Great War, yes? So you handle the toast."

"*Per cent'anni,*" Hector said. "That means one hundred years of luck to you."

"And to you, too," Orson said, sipping. "You look quite well, old man, despite the horrors of this year."

"You look pretty solid yourself," Hector said.

Orson nodded and shrugged. "I don't feel that way. Still the dreaded insomnia. I hardly ever sleep. Every night is a *nuit blanche.* Don't think I've really slept since 1946. Still the conflicting obligations and horrors of domestic life tearing at me. I'm cutting *Macbeth* here, and it's a terror all its own—I confide that only to you. The studio is assuming I'll once again fail them, leave them with an unfinished work, but they're wrong. The problem is the film isn't maybe that good, and I say that as its creator. We must never delude ourselves from the fact that our shit is shit, yes, Hector? Some of this film is the best I've ever done, but as I cut it together, it just doesn't cohere. On whole, I fear I've missed the mark. Infuriating. Terribly demoralizing."

That was chilling news.

From what Hector had heard from sources back home, the Harry Cohen-guided cut of Welles' unfinished *Lady From Shanghai* was looking to be equally uneven. There seemed to be nothing in the immediate cards dealt by fate to change Orson's flagging fortunes. Unless this Ratoff piece was somehow a sleeper, things looked grim for Orson.

Sipping his wine, looking over the rim of his goblet, Hector said, "And this movie you're acting in here, this thing about the black magician. How does it go?"

"It doesn't go," Orson said dully. "It's a train wreck all its own, but one I'm savoring in a strange way because it isn't one of my own making for once." He looked around and dropped his voice a bit. "Not to say I haven't done a little spot directing on this one, just to improve the thing a bit where I can without bruising egos—I've done that as I've been asked—but the real director is a disaster and he's on the edge of nervous collapse, also something that resonates with me, but it's fascinating to coldly observe it from the outside. The production keeps shutting down for days at a time so he can collect himself, the poor wreck of a man."

Hector raised his eyebrows. "You're talking about this Ratoff character? And, by the by, what an unfortunate surname."

"For an unfortunate, if oft-times charming man," Orson said, smiling. "Born in Russia, so he has many of the same defects of character resulting from such unhappy accidents as wretched Houseman had. Difference is, Houseman has that dreadful but mostly understandable ersatz British accent. Ratoff? Much of what he says is a bewilderment to me. And his directing—that's truly mystifying. Still, his checks cash, and living here is rather fine, at least in terms of food, wine and the riper pleasures of the flesh. You should stay on a while with me, old man. I know I intend to, despite the brutality of the press here. After all, I can hardly return home yet, can I?"

Orson looked around furtively, and said, "It's true, isn't it? That I can't go back home yet?"

Hector sighed and sat back in his chair. He felt some measure of blame for all that, rightly or wrongly. He lit a cigarette with his Zippo and considered the legend engraved there, "One True Sentence."

Call it the Holy Grail for writers of conscience.

Hector said, "I'd advise strongly against a return just yet. The Dahlia stuff is still at fever pitch, nearly a year out, if you can believe it."

It would soon be, Hector realized then, exactly one year on January 15 since Beth Short's bisected body was discovered in a field where Orson once staged magic shows in which he sawed starlets in half—another piece of odd but potentially damning evidence that had made Welles a viable suspect for the Short murder in some daffier LAPD officials' eyes.

"Then there's the FBI," Hector said, "HUAC. And those damned surrealists."

"Yes, what became of them, those killer artists and art collectors?"

"Some are supposedly here in Europe and some in Mexico," Hector said bitterly. "I keep an ear to the ground for them. Deal with 'em as I can. For me, it's a marathon where those bastards are concerned, not a sprint. They're an ongoing hobby."

"You've always had the focus and patience I seem to lack," Orson said, contemplating his wine goblet and his reflection there, "even when it's wasted on something as vulgar as revenge. Anyway, we wrap filming here sometime around early February, I expect. I may move on to Vienna for a time. There is a part Carol Reed is wanting me for there, though I know little enough about it just now. And there's the final cut to prepare of *Macbeth*. I was just writing notes for an editing wire back home on all that. I think it's important they understand the witches don't really *prophecy* anything. The witches merely give Macbeth ideas that make things happen. Anyway, maybe I'll get it better with *Othello*. I may do something with that play next, you see."

The thing Orson should do next, Hector thought, was to focus on finishing one palpably commercial project. He needed to do that and do it well. He had to do that to get back some of the luster and uncanny momentum he had enjoyed between the Panic Broadcast and the release of *Citizen Kane.*

Contemplating his cigar's glowing end, Orson said, "And you, old man? What precisely brings you to Rome now, after so many years of avoiding Italy?"

"Hunting," Hector said grimly.

"Not hunting after one of those murderous surrealists?"

"In a sense," Hector said. "A performance artist of sorts, anyway. There's this man who seems to make a living impersonating me. Bastard's trading on my reputation and my good graces and credit, all the while chipping away at both in terms of his wake of broken hearts, unpaid bills and increasingly infuriating headlines."

"How very odd," Orson said. "This man actually pretends to be you?"

"Pretty much that simple. He seems to sleep with anything that moves and has all of my tastes in bars and restaurants, but no similar compulsion to pay his way like I do."

"This would make for a remarkable film," Orson said, palpably warming to the concept. "It's highly original, something really fresh, it seems to me."

Hector shook his head. "Maybe not so original as you think. Back in the day, when we were still talking, Hemingway went through something eerily similar."

That seemed to pique Orson's interest even more. "How so? What happened with Papa's double? What was he up to?"

"Much the same thing as mine is doing," Hector said. "Coasting on my name and good credit while bringing down my reputation on all fronts, including that of ladies—and I mean ladies *only*—man."

"Yes, but about Papa?"

"It was about 1935, I think, the year of the Big Blow that hit the Keys, when it all came to a head for Hem. This guy claiming to be Ernest was staying at the Explorers Club, signing copies of Hem's novels and generally cadging drinks and hotel rooms via Hem's reputation. This false-Hem actually turned up in Chicago, Hem's old town in his newspaper days, and kicked off a coast-to-coast tour of ladies book clubs, presuming to pontificate about Hem's novels and bullfighting books, the African book and all."

"That's amazing," Orson said, clearly delighted. "Papa must have been positively made murderous by it. I mean this attack on him and his machismo."

"To put it mildly," Hector said. "The thing that really got Hem's goat, just as you figured, was the fact this double was seducing young men as Hem. The rumors that stuff started of course, nearly drove Hem off a cliff and they dog him still, I hear. Rumors and whispers Hem is actually homosexual. Eventually, this imposter became so brazen—or so believing in his own deception anyway—he actually turned up at Ernest's boyhood home, even confronted Hem's mother there."

"What happened to this fake, fairy Hemingway?"

"Eventually, he was caught up with and found out. Turned out to be the dissolute and perhaps dangerously crazy son of some naval admiral. A real psychopath, Hem insisted. I think he ended up in the crazy house for all day."

Orson took that in. "So your double is here, in Rome?"

"Italy anyway, last trace I had. Seemed to be heading this way. Yet I seem to have hit a wall here, in this city."

"Sorry, Hector, but it is truly good luck for me—I mean your being here, whatever the circumstances driving it. But one important question first. Are you currently married or something?" A sad smile, "Or are you, to use a term you've used before, between the wars?"

"I'm presently unattached," Hector said carefully, "although why you would care baffles me." Hector did wonder about that.

"Coming to that now," Orson said. "You see, now with the real war over, and now that you are here, we can at last do what we might have done nearly a decade ago if circumstances had only been different."

Hector said, "You've lost me, young man. What might have been different ten years ago? I'm at sea, old pal."

Orson looked around again, then reached into his pocket. He placed his hand on the table. When he withdrew it, a familiar bronze disc lay there.

This knot in his stomach; a fast-percolating seethe. Hector said, "So you lied about losing the phony medallion all those years ago."

"About that, yes, old man. About that, and about throwing the real disc from atop the Empire State. Simple sleight of hand facilitated by a sleeve extractor secreted in my palm. That's the reason I wanted to go back home that night before the big broadcast. I wanted to fetch some prestidigitation items to facilitate the medallion's disappearance. I'll confess to having already settled on a course of action before I went home. The metal disc that went off the building was the fake you had prepared of course—sure you've already figured that was so. This is the real item, I assure you."

Orson's eyes sparkled. "It was simply too valuable to lose or throw away, Hector, you know that in your heart. And you also know my nature, my love of magic. Now, Mussolini is at last gone. The fascists are all but routed. All the key superstitious Germans are dead or on the run to South America or some such. Even Uncle Sam has moved on from his fleeting preoccupation with the occult. The Spear of Destiny can be ours now, old man. We won't use it as despots would, to rule the world, but merely to improve our luck as artists, yes?" A delighted smile. "A genuine treasure hunt! An actual quest for us latter-day knights errant! How can you possibly resist?"

The actor wet his lips. "I frankly meant to do it alone these past weeks, but it still scares me a bit and it involves a good deal of moving around which I can't always manage with my present film obligations. All of that, and perhaps travel to places buses and cabs don't go. I still can't drive myself, you see and so…" A smile and a shrug. Orson, Hector could see, was measuring his reaction to all that.

Hector sensed Orson knew he was losing Hector's attention and patience, maybe even losing his favor. Orson had said he wanted to go home that long ago night to see his *family*, playing to the novelist's sentiment. Now this revelation that it was merely to fetch some sleight-of-hand rig? That palpably galled Hector. Goddamn Orson anyway.

That famous smile again. "This will be a great adventure, Hector. At very least it will be that. A kind of heroic quest as I said, like… Like, *yes*, just like something out of H. Rider Haggard or the Arthurian myths. A novel for you, surely, and a film for me."

Hector sat there with his wine glass in one hand and cigarette in the other, contemplating the bronze disc and feeling this mounting sense of dread. He didn't believe in premonitions any more now than he did ten years before, Hector told himself, yet this escalating sense of menace and terror was undeniable.

"This is mad talk, you know that," Hector said. And yet? The idea of this strange treasure chase did appeal to some part of Hector. The spear meant nothing to him, of course, but the challenge of finding the thing? That was something else. And Orson was right of course, there likely was something in all of this to feed a novel or a screenplay.

"Maybe, but what's truly crazy is having the medallion here, in the very city in which its purpose lies, and not trying to *do* something with it," Orson said. "You can't deny the appeal of that. You really can't, you know."

Hector thought about that. Despite his own pressing quest for "himself," he couldn't deny the quirky appeal of making a little time for this other hunt—couldn't dismiss the prospect out of hand.

25

THE BLACK MUSEUM

They were roaming the streets of Rome, huddled close under umbrellas and continuing their debate about the medallion and its possible use to try and recover the Holy Lance of Longinus.

"Lord knows I have my flaws, my character defects, of course," Orson said. "Yet those flaws are the very ones I've *always* had. They are a part of my nature. But until 1942 or so, I was able to triumph in any field I turned my attention to—the stage, radio. Film too, at least in that first going, at any rate. Despite these flaws of mine, I once triumphed in every at-bat I enjoyed."

Hector stepped wide to miss a puddle. Orson blustered on through, succeeding in splashing the novelist's pants legs while wetting his own shoes. "It all went to pieces for me with that mess in South America, old man. My great regret and my first unfinished masterpiece, you know. My film I would have called, *It's All True*."

"You really blame that movie for your run of bum pictures?" Hector scowled. "You've never talked about that before."

"I've come around to the realization increasingly, but in its most potent form relatively recently," Orson said. "You see, old friend, I was intending to segment the film in discrete sections. One of those vignettes was to include a portion focused wholly on Voodoo." A cautious smile. "That inspiration was partly thanks to you, old man. You, or rather to that delectable young woman you were irrigating around the time of my Mars scare. You remember Miss Allegre."

Of course Hector remembered Cassie. He'd wondered about her from time-to-time in the years since. And, Jesus, *irrigating*?

"She sparked my interest in White Witchery," Orson said. "I studied up a bit on all that after making your lady-friend Cassie's memorable acquaintance. Voodoo, VouDon… Tarot and palmistry. It had always been there in the back of my mind of course, because of my grandmother, sure, but also because Cassie brought it all to the forefront again and with such convincing force. Anyway, I began to work on my film treatment of all that. The project—as all of *It's All True* seemed to do—continued to spiral out of control. At some point, it seems I somehow offended a particular voodoo priest. You see, I arranged with great difficulty to film an actual voodoo ceremony. We had protracted conversations with the head of the group, this *doctor*, and an advance payment was arranged. But someone at the studio was fired. Terms changed. As old film hands, you and I both know how these things go, but this voodoo doctor didn't understand any of that, none of the vicissitudes of the cinema, not at all."

Hector found himself watching Orson now and so nearly tripped over some street urchin for lack of looking ahead. He excused himself to the child, gave the boys some coins, then said to the actor, "Where on earth are you going with this?"

Orson watched his own feet. "I had to tell the doctor the film was canceled. The witch doctor told me this was deeply offensive, and that he and his group took it very badly. I said I was very sorry, and I was all of that. But that didn't spare me a voodoo curse, old friend. For years, I've toiled under nothing less than that witch doctor's curse. It sounds crazy to you, I'm sure. Hell, it's crazy to me, or at least to some stubbornly blind Western part of me. But there it is."

"For Christ's sake," Hector said. "That's *insane*. You must see it."

"No," Orson said. "Why must you call it insane? It's as sane as any other belief, as any other expression of faith."

"Voodoo? You dare call that crap a *faith*?"

"Yes, Hector. You see, a curse was put on me, and on my film. It's why despite all my efforts to the contrary, *It's All True* will likely always be the one film of mine that is never seen by the public. Since the curse, I've lost…" Orson looked for words, then settled on, "I've lost my Zen archery range, can't you see that?"

Hector lit another cigarette. He said, "What kind of curse is this you think you're under? How do you know it even happened?"

"It was hardly subtle," Orson said. "Quite the opposite, really. A *macumba* cursed my project. He drove a long steel needle with a red piece of wool tied to it through the entire script. He left it like that for me to find. The project was positively done for after that, old man. And me with it. It's never been good since, you know. *Never*. And I still don't know what I did to have evidently offended the *macumba*."

Hector cast down his cigarette; it sizzled in a pool of standing water. Neon glowed in the same rippling puddle. He said sourly, "So what, the Spear of Destiny is your corrective? Your panacea?"

"Why, yes," Orson said, "Exactly that. And I want you to be a part of this. I certainly wouldn't cut you out of this, you know that, old man. Together, as always, we proceed. We'll share in my good fortune."

Hector just laughed. "I want no part of this shared fortune aspect," he said. "First, I still don't believe in any of this mumbo-jumbo. Even less now than then, if possible. Secondly, even if I did buy any of this horseshit, I'd be a fool to join in on this silly gambit in terms of having or holding even a part of the spear. You do remember the rest of the myth, don't you, Orson? You remember about what happens if you claim the spear and then lose it as every fucking person in history eventually has?" Hector raised his eyebrows in inquiry.

"Death, *terrible death*, yes, old man, I know. But we all must die sometime, of course. What's that line from Shakespeare that Papa so loves? 'Every man owes God a death,' that is it, isn't it?"

"Yes, that's close enough," Hector said. "That is bloody well in the sorry ballpark. But there's dying in your sleep and there's dying bloody and crying out to your mother or God. I know which I prefer."

"But still you're dead after all that, old man. You're still dead and dust. And we've walked far enough." Orson whistled for a cab. Taking Hector's arm he said, "Simply too far to continue on foot, especially with this cursed weather."

Orson gave Hector this hangdog look. "So you're not in old man?"

"I didn't say that exactly," Hector said. "The *quest* aspect appeals to some part of me. No saying if we found the spear, we have to do anything with it, you know. We could just take a long good look at it and leave it there."

"So you're saying you're still not with me."

Hector shrugged, smiled. "It's crazy as all hell, but I'm not exactly firm on the next step of that other hunt I'm on. So I reckon I might spare a couple of days to tag-along with you. Hell, how many times do you get to go on an honest-to-God treasure hunt?"

They rolled to a stop before the imposing St. John in the Lateran and the Cloister.

Hector said, "Why in God's name are we here of all places?"

Orson beamed. "You declare yourself a skeptic," a taunting smile, "but I come to believe you may well actually have second sight of your own kind, old friend. This place is practically a museum as much as it's a church. It's also something else. You see, according to the wondrous medallion in my pocket, this place you arbitrarily chose years ago to make the Nazis start their search if they ever gained possession of your false seal? This place is in fact the actual starting point for our very real search!"

"Are you kidding me?"

"Not this time, Hector. No, old man, you somehow unerringly seized on the real starting point for our quest when you were manufacturing your bogus metal map all those years ago." He held up a gloved hand. "But hold on, for there's much more. We're going to go inside now. We're going to do that and then we're going to see if I might yet surprise you again."

26

SYMPTOMS OF BEING THIRTY-FIVE

The actor and the author entered the soaring nave of the chapel with all its arches and ivory and gilt; its reaching and grasping marble statuary.

A woman was standing with her back toward them, looking up at the altar.

Hector had this shock of recognition. He said softly, "Cassie? Really?"

She turned and smiled. Those dimples. Those pale gray eyes. "So good to see you again, Hector." The war years and their rationing, or perhaps something else, had conspired to make her look thinner. She wore a tailored suit and carried an overcoat coat folded over one arm. He noticed that coat also covered her hand. Hector wondered if she might not be armed for their reunion.

Orson said, "Turns out Cassie has been living in Paris for several years. I heard about that a couple of weeks ago. Since then she's been trying to lift the curse on me, at least to neutralize it. Now that you're here too, well, it occurred to me she'd be a valuable and essential third partner in our quest to recover the Holy Lance. We'll make it a three-way split of my good fortune, we three who've endured so much woe these past years."

Hector was very aware of the way Cassie was studying him, gauging his reaction to Orson's assertion about how she was helping him with his "voodoo curse."

For his part, Orson said, "You two surely have some catching up to do. You should do that *now*." He slipped a folded-over piece of paper to Hector. "Where I'm staying with the film crew. Call when you're ready to start our search. That is to say, phone me there, but not before noon tomorrow. Figure we'll all be wanting to sleep in tomorrow." Only a little innuendo in the actor's voice.

They watched him go. Standing in that imposing house of worship, Hector said, "Should I infer you like him better this decade?"

"Still not so much," Cassie said matter-of-factly. "Not really." A little beguiling shrug. "But now I somehow actually feel sorry for that man. And Hector, he *does* hold the key to finding the Spear of Destiny, after all."

A smile. "I'm delighted to see you again. I'm frankly surprised you're on board with the hunt…"

Hector smiled back. "Hell, me too."

The rain picked up as they took a cab back to her hotel, lodging paid for, or so she claimed, by Orson and the film crew of his black magic opus. "I'm a kind of film advisor, too," she said, sitting next to him in the cab. Hector studied her profile in the dusky gloom. She was still beautiful, but her hair was now longer and straighter. He wondered about that—the result of chemical efforts to that end? The manifestation of increased efforts to blend in? He decided not to ask.

The rain picked up. She said, "I'd ask if it's been a crowded decade for you, but I'm still a reader, still a fan. So I feel as though I know all that."

"A lot of it is made up in the novels you know. I *do* have an imagination."

"You surely do. But remember too, I took a good look at both of your hands. I even did it a time or two at very long leisure, when you were asleep at my side."

Hector was taken aback by that. "Really? You actually did that?"

A sheepish smile. "I did. I was infatuated with you back in the day. With you and your legend. And you were a worry, too. And that unbelievably long lifeline of yours? My God, I've yet to see anything ever to match it."

"Here we go again." Hector remembered this time to check her left hand in the early going. He saw she returned the study of his naked ring finger.

"The idea of Orson Welles privately holding the Spear of Destiny is insane to me," she said. "Almost as scary as the lance falling into Hitler's hands or Mussolini's.

"It's hardly that bad," Hector said. "I mean, Orson's a liberal, maybe just this side of a communist, but despite some flickering political ambitions, the genius is just an artist in the end."

"Welles could lose the spear," Cassie said. "That could be bad not just for him—the death curse attached to it—but for the world too, depending on who then assumed control of the Lance."

Hector just shrugged at that. He still thought it all crazy superstition. He said, "Tell me about your life these past years. Orson evidently kept tabs. To my shame, I didn't. When did you come to Europe?"

"Just after the war," she said. "When the Nazis were gone, I came back. Some of my happiest days were there, old school days. I wanted to make Paris my home again. When I got to Paris, I quickly caught traces of your trail. Whispers about stuff you did with the resistance, with the OSS, in taking back Paris. Guess we just missed one another there. Probably just as well, I guess, as I hear there was another woman. Another marriage."

Rearview mirror stuff. Hector *had* married again about that time, to a good woman, but the wrong one in the end.

He traced the pressed crease in his slacks. "Have to ask, is there then a Paris branch of that New Orleans voodoo shop?"

A wistful smile. "Not quite," she said finally. "I give card and palm readings. I play spiritual advisor. No potions and no spells. Well, some special efforts here and there, like present exertions for your sad-sack actor friend, but that's a fraction of what I do these days."

Hector said, "Let's talk more about that. You truly don't believe Orson's under some kind of curse?"

"Again, I'm not comfortable talking much about this with you. I know which side you fall on regarding all things supernatural. Let me just say this. What Orson described to me about his time in South America, about this voodoo threat he believes he's under, it is an accurate depiction of a certain kind of an all too-potent and real curse. And *macumba* are dark witches as you'd probably think of them. They are the kings of black magic."

She paused and took his hand. She looked at it afresh. He said, "The future's that hand, yes?"

"Like I said, I know your past."

"Anything change from what you've already seen coming for me?" They were slowing for a stop in front of her hotel.

"Pretty much all is as I remember," she said. She closed his hand and squeezed it. "God, I've missed you, darling. Your novels in the in-between time have been a comfort, hearing your voice in my head as I read your words, but of course it's not like having you here in the flesh."

That last word resonated between them. "Let's get dinner," he said. He hesitated. "Should caution you to keep your distance though. Think I'm coming down with a scratchy throat. Maybe a cold. Hell, maybe something *worse*. Just feeling more run down than I can remember these past few days."

"I've got a strong immune system." She pressed her palm to his cheek. "And I'm not hungry. Not at all. If you are, I'll watch you eat." A raw smile, too easy to read.

Tracing the lines in his hand, she said, "Hector, I know what I want, and I want that right *now*. I'd have you in this cab, right here, even with that terrible little man driving us," she whispered huskily in his ear. "What about you? Would you have me, right here, right now?"

Hector whispered back, "I'd have you in bed, just as soon as realistically possible."

They'd started pawing one another in the elevator.

Inside her room, with the door closed and hastily locked behind them, it was a scramble to strip down that resulted in a split hem up the back of her tapered skirt and some popped and lost buttons from his shirt.

Frustrated by the intricate confusion of her silk under things and garter belt, he'd ended up tearing her panties to get her out of them, leaving just her stockings and belt— her sexy black garters—wholly intact.

It made her somehow even more erotic to his eyes.

She held her blood-encrusted fingernails up between their faces after, and said, "God, I'm *so* sorry. As if your poor back needed more damage."

"It's okay," he said. "I've thought a lot about you since 1938. Thought about how it might have been if we'd tried to make a go of it."

"We were right not to try then," she said. "It's a little better now, at least in some places. Here in Europe, like we've discussed before. Still, I don't think we could have had a family, even then. Not with a happy ending. Not with the war looming."

"You never married? Never had children?"

"No and no," she said. "Never found the right man. And… There's something else you might as well know now, particularly after what you'd probably call our recklessness tonight. You see, I wondered, all those years ago, particularly after a couple of our other reckless moments during that crazy autumn a lifetime ago. There were no consequences from any of that, you know. No pregnancies, I mean. So I had some tests done later. Seems I can't… *you know*."

"I'm sorry," he said.

Cassie wasn't having it. "It's probably for a good reason."

More fate and predestination—all that claptrap Hector couldn't fathom or countenance. But he held his tongue. Instead, he stroked her breast; kissed her there, suckling. In time he worked his way up to her throat and found her mouth. He pulled back just long enough to say, "There is adoption, you know."

"Wouldn't be the same for me," she said. "I know that's terrible, selfish even. But it's how I really feel."

She traced the line of his jaw, his cheekbones. "I've wondered a lot about the child we might have had. It would have been a girl, I'm pretty sure."

He couldn't help himself. "That more second-sight?"

"More like simple intuition," she said. "Still none of your own? Children I mean."

Hector said, "Nah. Just not in the cards. No pun intended."

"Just wait," she said. "Your time is yet coming. Lucky for you, the clock doesn't run out for men like it does for women, not like that." Thinking of the time, she checked the wall clock. "And, now, I am positively starving for food. You take a lot out of a woman, though I doubt that comes as news to you, either."

"I could eat, too. Shall we dress and head down?"

"Not on your life," she said. "We're going to continue destroying this bed. I vote for room service."

"After, are we really going to look for this silly relic with an eye toward claiming it? I'm on board, to use your phrase for the thrill of the chase — the lark of this crazy crusade to find the thing, but not to have and to hold, so to speak."

"I've already signed on for the ongoing search, Tex. But not to just gawk at it and walk away. As much as it can be a tool for terror, I believe it can be used for good, too. But still you don't believe that, do you."

"Heathen I am—skeptic you know me to be—of course not. How could I?"

"You may have held on to all your doubt in that way, yet you're not the man you were in 1938, not at all," she said, studying him.

"How could I be?" He caught himself looking at his palms again. He closed his hands, made fists. "Ten years and another war. More scars. More ex-wives. Some might call it all more proof in the futility of all faith."

"But you?"

"I said some might call it that."

She stared at her hands. "That's almost funny. The world's closer to tolerating the likes of us, at least in some places, but you? Why are you in Rome now, Hector? With everything I think I know about you, I know it's not for this search Orson is intent upon continuing. Orson was thrilled to learn you were already here, so I know you didn't answer some request of his to drop everything and run to Rome."

"No," he said. "About that you're right. I happen to be here for a search of a different kind. Meeting Orson here was a mere accident, just as you say. Or I believe it so."

He told her about his double.

When he was through she said, "And people tell me *my* life is bizarre." Cassie said, rested her chin on his chest, and said, "It could only happen to you."

27

THE CREEPER

"Almost feels like second nature," Cassie said as they moved around the hotel's bathroom nude, sharing spigots and mirror space as he shaved and she applied her makeup. "Almost feels like we've always been doing this."

Or maybe it was just because both were practiced at sharing such intimate spaces with others, Hector figured more cynically. There were only so many variations on a theme, after all. He said, "Maybe we should have been doing just that."

"We've been over this already," she said. "Anyway, I don't believe for a minute you'd have missed the company of all the women you've known in the between time, and I mean more than just Duff. You come by your reputation as a lady man's honestly enough. Besides, I earnestly think you need all of them—need *us*, since I'm of that legion of women—to feed your writing."

He pressed a hot towel to his face. With a muffled voice, he said, "What's all this about so many other women? You don't still have access to my FBI file? Do you really know stuff about the past ten years beyond what I've elected to confide?"

"Just have access to your hands these days," she said. She stroked his freshly shaven, still-warm cheek. "You truly loved some of those women since. I'm sorry they didn't last, those love affairs." Some of the women either, he thought.

"You've still not told me much about that part of your life in the time since."

He watched as Cassie weighed her words. She finally said, "Haven't exactly been chaste, if that's what you mean. But not in love, either. Never in love. Not like you were."

That old whore regret—she and Hector were too well-acquainted. He wrapped his arms around Cassie, gathered her close to his chest. "Let's not screw this up this time."

She drew the back of her hand across his cheek again. "A man who favors a close shave. No surprise in that either. Let's take this new round as it comes. Enjoy this time together, whether it's a just few days or longer. Tell me, where are you living now?"

"Still have that little place in Key West, but I mostly rent it out for money still," he said. "I live in New Mexico, right on the Rio Grande, or, as the Mexicans call it, the Rio Bravo. Having said that, I lately find myself thinking a lot about Paris. And about the days there before I was me, so to speak."

A funny smile. "When you were unknown, you mean," she said, "before you were someone that a crazy man might feel compelled to impersonate? Is that what you're saying?"

"Yes," Hector said. "Everything you've said."

"Could you live in Paris again?"

"Yes," Hector said after hardly any time at all, surprising himself. "I really think I could now. The time there during the war was… good. Maybe I could reinvent myself. Be the writer I thought I'd be when I was there when I was young and learning. Reaching more than I feel that I do now in my writing."

"I don't believe you've ever stopped reaching. You're not the kind." Cassie pressed her cheek against his bare chest. The hair there tickled her nose. "You really mean that, don't you? About starting over some day?"

"With all my heart," Hector said. "If I ever find the courage to do it."

"But it's not there for you just now?"

"Not now, not yet, no." He tried to make a joke of it, to lighten the mood. He said, "Hell, first I have to stop this other joker from being me."

Her teeth teased her lip.

She leaned in, kissed his cheek, once, again. Her fingers traced his lips. She kissed his other cheek. She bumped foreheads with him and said. "I ordered up some food. "You want something in your coffee, or do you prefer it black?"

"Your books are sadder now, darker," Cassie said. "The dialogue is not as, well, it's not as glib as it once was, not like in your earlier books."

"Afraid you're not the first to say it."

They were walking along Via Frattina in a still-drizzling rain, window shopping under a big, shared umbrella.

"If it truly is darker, my stuff more serious, it's just a function of age and a life lived I reckon," he said. He studied her reflection in the glass of a couture shop's window. "God but you're still a beauty," he said. "Stuff like that was designed for a pretty body like yours."

"But not for a bank account like mine," she said. "You're such a con artist in some ways. Always the silver-tongued devil."

"Nah, I'm not like that, but my granddad is," he said. "He can make you believe anything."

A shift in tone of voice, drifting from his right arm to his left, taking that arm instead, she said, "We're being followed, *again*. I do hope you're armed, *again*." She hadn't watched him dress this one time and so she wasn't certain about any weapons he might be carrying. He felt her checking under his left armpit. She whispered, "Thank God," as she felt it suspended there.

He checked the reflection in the glass again. The man was of average build, maybe six-feet, even. The stranger was clean-shaven, likely fortyish. Something there in the way he moved—the man didn't seem Italian or even European. There was something distinctly American about the stranger, just based on sight and comportment.

Hector said, "I'm thinking G-Man, specifically FBI. They're of a piece in their sorry way. Or Hoover's sorry way. Doesn't make much sense, though. They don't have jurisdiction out this way, not a spit's worth."

"So what do you want to do about him, if anything, Hec?"

"Just leave him be for now, I think," Hector said. "If we decide on anything else, and if it means using a gun, I'm not sure the ending would be a happy one for me. Not here, not in this place." He'd bought a gun cheap on the black market, just in case things with his double got rowdy. In case he ran into any other old friends.

"Probably too true," she said.

Sirens in the distance, an ambulance. Cassie asked, "Do you still have trustworthy FBI friends? Someone you could call to check on that man behind us?"

"Maybe, but I feel like I've burned many FBI bridges this past year, partly thanks to my actor friend. I kind of helped Orson escape the bureau's clutches last winter."

Cassie wrinkled her nose, said, "HUAC? Orson's in *that* kind of trouble?"

"That and some other kinds, I'm afraid," Hector said.

"And you?"

"Trouble nearly always, it seems, manages to find me. But not with HUAC, not for me. I'm good there."

Cassie was even more alarmed looking after hearing that. She said, "Oh God, you didn't *inform*, did you?"

"Dear God, no," Hector said, his back up. "Not at all. But my politics, what little I have of them, well, it seems they're in season this year."

"One of *those*, huh? Well, I can forgive you that, I guess."

"No percentage in this kind of sorry talk," Hector said. "You know what they say about religion and politics. So let's get back to the hotel. I want some more time with you out of your clothes before we start this scavenger hunt. I don't read palms, don't believe in foreordination, as you know, but I can already predict this probably ending somewhere wide of where any of us expect."

28

THE CRADLE WILL ROCK

Hector pulled the covers up over Cassie. She nestled in deeper, smiling in her sleep.

Naked, he stood by the window, looking down on the street. He lit a cigarette and ran a thumb across the engraved words on his Zippo.

That old word game it alluded to set his mind to running faster—one man starts a sentence and another tries to quickly finish it, straight and truly as possible.

Their shadow, the mysterious American, he was down there on the street, taking refuge in the recessed doorway of a barbershop. Hector resisted the urge to wave. There was probably at least one more in the lobby, or, to be more efficient, maybe one more man staking out the couch at the end of the corridor just outside near the lift, watching their door. That would make far more sense. It would certainly be more efficient, if not at all subtle.

Hector glanced at his phone. Orson was probably awake. Hell, he'd admitted he was still prone to the intense insomnia that had plagued him last year through the trauma of the Dahlia murder and beyond. Now here was Hector, suffering his own *nuit blanche* or white night, despite the toll their torrid lovemaking had evidently taken on Cassie.

Bewitching Cassie. She'd confessed to him before falling asleep that after exhausting all that he'd written, she'd reluctantly turned her reading attention to Brinke's novels, now safely back in print, thank God, despite the war years' severely enforced paper rationings.

Hell, half of Hector's own books were presently still out of print according to his most recent publisher's form letter—being held back "to help the war" that was so long over.

"I loved her books," Cassie had confided. "I'm sure I would have liked Brinke, too."

Hector was pretty sure that allure would have been mutual, and perhaps even have run deeper than Cassie might think, given Brinke's bisexuality. In the end, more than once, Hector and Brinke had shared similar tastes in women.

The temperature must be dropping Hector thought, as the rain turned to sleet before his eyes, the stuff making more noise as it struck the fogging glass. Music reached him from some distant room—*Winter Winds*.

Hector rested a hand briefly on a radiator coil to warm and to steady himself, as he was overcome by a sudden wave of nausea. He prayed it wasn't the flu. Maybe in addition to nausea, it was simply nostalgia he told himself. That particular song took him back in raw ways to Paris—he'd finally made the connection.

They claimed loss got easier with time, but as Hector settled deeper into his own middle age, he found he thought more often of Brinke and missed her even more; he even found her taking up a kind of permanent residence in some part of his head.

Hector ground out his cigarette and brushed his teeth. Shivering, he slid between the covers, spooning up tight against

Cassie's long, bare body. He cupped his hand around her right breast, moving softly against her. She pressed her hips back against him, then stretched and cooed as they became one.

Despite their joining, she said, "You can't possibly be up to this again." She turned and wrapped a leg around his waist, even as she said it, guiding him back inside her.

"It's a problem if I am?"

She smiled and said, "Way you've worked me up already, it's definitely a problem if you *can't*."

Cassie and Hector stood off a distance behind Gregory Ratoff's director's chair.

Orson was garbed in black velvet and shiny baubles that recalled that infernal medallion that dominated their talk and actions these hours. On the black fez that topped Orson's head there was pinned a shining Masonic symbol. Hector thought his friend was just on the edge of over-playing his role as the notorious *wizard* or *warlock*—the novelist wasn't too familiar with the historical figure Orson was playing and so figured either term was close enough.

Orson had understated director Ratoff's accent: so far, it was utterly impenetrable to Hector.

The lights flickered. Thunder rumbled and shook the cameras and some glassware set up on a banquet table. Ratoff looked to his sound man. The technician drew a finger across his throat.

Orson presumed to call "Cut," then added, "Thank beneficent Christ for this blessed storm!" He then dared to go further: "You know the weather here. I say that's a wrap for the day, eh Greg?" The actor savagely ripped off his latest false proboscis—Orson still rarely appeared on film with his natural, God-given nose.

Hector counted seconds between the next dimming of the lights and the ensuing rumble. Orson was probably right, he decided—the worst of the storm was to come and definitely bearing down on them, approaching with real speed.

The actor strode toward them, dangling his false nose in hand, and said, "Give me a few minutes to wash off the rest of the silly war paint. I say we go straight off to our search now."

"First, we've got a fresh shadow to lose," Hector said. He drew his sleeve across his damp forehead. He was overcome with this fresh wave of dizziness. "Do point me to a starving actor I can pay to distract the man following us when we take our leave from here," he said thickly.

Standing again in the grand nave of the St. John in the Lateran and the Cloister, Orson said, "Damn it, there are paces to be measured. It's clear the search begins right here, at this place of worship, but the *measurements*? Where do we start here, specifically?"

Both men looked to Cassie.

Earlier, when it was just the two of them, Hector had said to Orson, "I'm surprised you brought Cassie in on this. Figured it would gall you enough to have me as a partner," he'd told Orson. "Three-way split seems even more unpalatable from your perspective, at least based on how I read you."

"Oh, you're not wrong," Orson had said. "But Cassandra's a necessary evil, especially with my unusual enemies and current precarious situation with the forces of darkness. Also, I figured you could bend her to our will." The implication of that statement had made Hector bridle—namely, that Orson implied by extension he could bend Hector to his own will.

Cassie looked around the cathedral again, then said, "There are two logical places to start from, as I figure it, not that either of you has asked me outright. The threshold at the front door is my first choice. It's the least ambiguous place in which to start. I say we try that first."

Orson said, "And your second theory?" A half-smile. "I mean, since we're already here…"

"The altar," she said. "But it's such a long way back there and so spread out, and Mr. Rosenblum's time was so limited by all accounts that I incline away from that as the start." She shrugged her padded shoulders. "Of course, I could be wrong."

"No, it makes sense to me," Hector said. "Let's start right out front."

As they walked back out into a driving rain, a sodden and legless man crouched on a wheeled board begged money from them. Orson ignored the vagrant; Hector dropped a couple of low denomination notes into the man's crudely carved wooden cup.

"Right sentiment, but the wrong action, Hector," Orson said, sour-faced. "With the economy in its present state, with tourist dollars being so essential here after the war, the police actually punish do-gooders like you more often and harshly than they do the panhandlers you all would help. They don't want to encourage beggars, don't you know. You're lucky no police saw your donation just now. They might have arrested you on the spot."

The medallion's map led, or seemed to lead, away from the church to a railway station lunch counter and a particular stool. From there, they made their way to a public fountain.

By Hector's reckoning, they had four more sites to arrive at before they reached the presumed hiding spot of the Holy Lance. Standing and staring at the fountain, fishing his pockets for coins to make silly and sentimental wishes, Hector said, "I presume they don't arrest you for doing this, too?" He felt very tired now. He thought he could lay down and go to sleep on the spot if his friends would only let him. He couldn't remember the last time he that he felt so drained, so weak.

Orson just shrugged. Cassie said softly, "Fellas, our shadow has found us again."

Orson said, "You mean that man over there? That one looks like FBI to me. God knows, I've seen my share of his kind lurking these past few years."

"That's what Hector thought, too," Cassie said. "I think we have to confront that man. We certainly can't continue a search with him dogging our heels."

"Agreed." Hector pulled her close and hugged her tightly. As he did that, he slipped his gun into her pocket. "Let's split up," he said softly in her ear. "You two head to that café. I'll continue on somewhere, as if moving to the next point. You double back and follow at a distance. We'll get the drop on this guy in a few minutes and soon have our answers with some luck."

"Won't you need your gun?"

"Got a knife, too," Hector said. "I think this little chat will likely go better close in. Besides, he might have friends, in which case you can maybe do more with that gun to help the cause than I can."

Things went more or less to Hector's impromptu plan. His scheme bought him five minutes alone in a darkened alley with this most recent shadow.

Knife to the man's throat, a feverish Hector dragged an arm across his beaded forehead and said, "You *are* a Hoover minion, aren't you? FBI, yes?"

The man wet his lips. Panting, breaking a sweat in the rain to match Hector's own odd perspiration, the stranger said, "Agent Tilly speaks well of you, Lassiter. Ed says you're one of the smart ones as Hollywood types go. And a Republican to boot."

"What's your name, agent?"

"Special Agent Mosley Horton."

"Funny, Agent Tilly has never spoken of you to me," Hector said. "So you might as well be anybody at all for what I care just now. That fact in mind, why are you here, following us? And why are you so far out of your range to boot, to borrow a phrase."

"I'll remind you I'm a government agent, Mr. Lassiter. Therefore I'm under absolutely no—"

"What you're under is *no authority*," Hector said, cutting him off. "You're under no authority whatever, not way out here on the wrong side of the ocean, fella. I'm former OSS, and *I've* got more juice and rights here than you do. If you were CIA, I might just be a little worried. But you're only FBI, in Europe, and so all your powers stopped at shore's end back home. Here, you're just another maybe luckless tourist who could succumb to death by misadventure in some Italian alley."

Hector pressed his knife's edge harder against the man's throat. "On that note, are Mr. Hoover's secrets really worth your life, Sad Sack?"

"You can't be serious," the agent said. "You just can't. And be careful with that knife. You look quite ill..."

With a cold smile, Hector said. "Under the weather or not, I've still got the edge, so to speak. If Agent Tilly's really told you anything at all about me, you most certainly know better than to think I wouldn't cut your throat and leave you to bleed out in this infernal Italian alley like some luckless and car-struck doe."

Spraying spittle, the man said, "I'm off-duty, for Christ's sake. I mean, mostly off-duty. I mean that I have *family*. I mean, my daughter, Mina, she needs braces. And my boy, Chester? Chet's getting older so there's college to think of. I mean, I only…"

"So you're here for Hoover on *special duty*, if you will," Hector said. "And at some special pay rate, trying to help make ends meet at home? What on earth is possibly worth Mr. Hoover going off the books and sending your kind so far from home and out of your obvious depth to chase the likes of me, special agent?"

"Mr. Hoover has been director since 1924," the FBI agent said. "Nobody's held the position that long. Despite Mr. Hoover's protestations and continuing success, President Truman's becoming increasingly loud about wanting to replace Mr. Hoover…"

Hector shook his head. "Hell, practically every president since Coolidge has wanted that little frog-faced monster out on his fat ass and rightly so. Hoover's fucking evil. To that point, purportedly your boss has consistently succeeded in blackmailing ensuing chief executives into perpetuating his dubious reign."

Hector indulged a way-out-there leap in logic. Presumably, Hoover was surreptitiously as superstitious as naïve young Orson claimed to be.

Could that be it? Could Hoover really be as crazy as to think possession of the "Spear of Destiny" could somehow perpetuate his unholy regime as FBI director until God or the Devil at last called the little monster home?

Hector elected to go darker in his treatment of Hoover's latest stooge. He said, "You really love your children? You *truly* cherish your health?" Hector raised his eyebrows. "If you do, then you report that you failed here. You tell your overlord that Rome was a very dead end. Convince him Orson and I bore no fruit for him in that way." Hector bit his lip. He said, "Hell, it's been years since anyone cared about Orson, me and that… *thing*. What's got you all freshly going again on it now?"

The G-Man looked around to make sure they were still alone. He said, "For ten years, these German types—ex-Nazis, I guess—have watched that church you and Welles both finally visited today *and* yesterday. This legless beggar watches the church for the Germans. He's done that for years. This part sounds crazy to me, too, but Mr. Lassiter, I hear for ten years, *we've* watched these Germans watch that church. Today, I guess it was just my turn. And just my sorry luck, I suppose, that you finally came along."

Ten years of overseas surveillance of some hoary cripple running watch on a church in exchange for presumed chump change? Hector actually shivered afresh.

Jesus, Hoover must really have the bug *bad*, he thought.

Hector pulled away his knife. "Do you have any grasp what it is exactly that Hoover is looking for? Do you really have a sense why he would want this thing?"

"It's not for me to judge," the agent said finally.

"So I'm to infer you know just enough to know it makes your boss even loopier seeming than some already believe him to be. If I were you, pal, I'd look for another line of work and I'd do that pronto. If your boss is that out of touch with the simple ground, I'd expect some heavy-duty shake up, top to bottom, in your agency soon. Any new head of the FBI would be well-advised to engage in wholesale house clearing. All it'll take in the end is a president who can keep it in his pants and not stray from his first lady. That's *all* that's needed to see Hoover out on his ass. Either way, are you prepared to stand down here, right now?"

"What do I really tell the director?"

"Nothing too far from the truth," Hector said. "Orson lost interest when the questing didn't prove easy. Say I mocked Welles for a fool and for his ever believing in all this hokum. Report to Hoover we've all started plans to leave Rome empty-handed. It's all perfectly in character. And, as it happens, it's all true."

29

THE SILENT AVENGER

Once again in full costume as the dark wizard with his false nose, moustache and goatee firmly glued in place, Orson said, "Maybe you have and maybe you haven't put the FBI out of the picture, at least for now. I suspect we both know Mr. Hoover isn't easily shaken off. But it seems there's a new threat, old man. I found this on my bed when I got back."

Orson tossed something—some little wad of floppy cloth at first glance—Hector's way. The writer caught the scraps on the fly. "What the hell, Orson?"

"It's a fetish of a kind," Cassie said, taking it from the novelist with a cautious hand. "An avatar. What I guess you might call a voodoo doll. The bottom line is our friend has been freshly hexed. You might be next, Hec. So, like Orson, you're going to wear one of these around your neck. You'll sleep with it under your pillow."

She held up a black bag about the size of a small change purse and suspended from a length of twine. "Put this around your neck, please. Do it now. It should rest over your heart in order to be most effective."

Hector scowled. "What the hell is this thing?"

Cassie said softly, anticipating his rebuttal, "It's a hex bag."

Hector rubbed his nose. "Thing reeks and I already feel sick to my stomach. What's in it?"

Cassie popped the cork on a bottle of champagne. Orson had ordered up a case of the stuff to "stave off the doldrums." The crew happened to be currently filming in the grand ballroom of their venerable hotel so Orson didn't have far to travel.

She filled three flutes with bubbly. "You really don't want to know the answer to that question, Hector. Put it this way, when you shower, I'd suggest refrigerating that bag in an ice bucket, however briefly. They might be a bit gamey in just a day or two otherwise."

"Gamey in a day or two? It already stinks." Hector, accepting his glass with a shaking hand, looked to Orson. "Tell me you're not wearing one of these right now under all that." Orson's hand reflexively moved to his chest.

"Well, I'm not going to," Hector said. He drained his glass, feeling desperately thirsty for some water. "And I'm certainly not putting one under my pillow." He tossed the bag to Orson. "Here, twice the protection. Although I wouldn't count on getting any dates going forward, kiddo. Not with those things on you."

"This is not a good idea," Cassie said. "Not smart at all."

Hector shrugged it off. "Well, I'm a staunch non-believer, as you well know." He held up a hand even as he reached for a refill of his champagne with the other. "I appreciate your effort to ward me, I do. But you were right about me all those years ago. I'm afraid that now I'm even more the cynic and hardheaded maverick than I was back when. Just my nature you might say—a point of view I suspect Orson would support. If I was to let in any doubt about my doubt, if I was to begin to believe as you two do, it would surely damage me, down deep."

Cassie was visibly given pause by that admission. He was, after all, essentially throwing her own words and observations about all that right back at her.

"I remember telling you that," she said. "But I was maybe wrong. Almost certainly I was in error. When you have a voodoo master coming at you like the one you might be facing—like your friend is certainly up against—then you don't have the luxury of not believing anymore. I simply can't indulge your narrow-mindedness this time."

Jesus. That set Hector's teeth on edge. "I don't accept that," he said. "And you're being hurtful, painting me as some naïf."

"It's my life's work you dismiss, Hector," she said. "It's my faith you're spitting on, that you're waving away at like it's just some pesky gnat or the like. Believe me, I wish it was different for your sake, but there's something terrible coming and you must prepare. You must take precautions."

Orson muttered, unable to stop himself, "By the pricking of my thumbs, something wicked this way comes."

Welles threw the second bag back to Cassie. She held it out to Hector by its string. "This little nothing in your eyes *can* protect you. Just maybe. I have powers, but the kind of warlock who did this, I don't know if I can stand against his kind of power, not for long." She frowned and placed the back of her hand to Hector's damp forehead.

Orson raised his glass. "Believe her, old man. Or don't believe while still *acting* like you do. I can give you lessons there: I feign conviction every sorry day. What harm can come from complying with this lady's wishes? Do it in that context."

"Do it because I love you and because you still care for me at least some little bit," Cassie implored. She took her hand away from his forehead and said, "You're burning up."

Hector took the bag again. If he wore it, it would only be a matter of believing it to be a sham.

Conceit?

Arrogance?

Close-mindedness?

Maybe it was so from Cassie's perspective, but Hector didn't accept any of those possibilities. He was steadfast in his belief that all this supernatural business was so much bullshit.

He looked to Cassie a last time. A sad smile. "You didn't actually kill something in order to make these did you?"

"Of course not," she said. "*I* didn't killing anything."

Hair-splitting and dime-store semantics, the author thought.

Cassie said, "You should lay down a while. You look terrible."

Director Ratoff seemed to have recovered his stomach for work after lunch. In his thicket of an accent, Gregory made clear, more or less, his intent to push his cast ahead into the small hours of the next morning in order to regain lost ground.

That enraged Orson. "You're changing the rules!" Tearing at his makeup, ripping off his false nose, he said in full Shakespearean bellow, "Tickle us, do we not laugh? Prick us, do we not bleed? Wrong us, shall we not revenge?"

Under his breath, Orson spat out, "You goddamn hack!"

A long pause, then, he called out in his loudest voice, "Hell is empty and all the devils are already here!"

Hector endured an hour more of watching the filming, waiting for a chance to put his arm on the film's regretful lead.

At last afforded a moment's aside with Orson between lighting changes, Hector said, "Two alternatives. You give us the medallion and let us push forward a bit while the FBI is apparently still at bay, or you catch up with Cassie and I later in some bar or restaurant along the way. I'm not sitting through a minute more of this wreck. You're right, Orson. This movie is Grade Z, even now, and maybe headed down from there on the ladder of low art if such a thing is possible."

"Tell me." A hesitant smile, then Orson said, "And, I *must* be with you for the last of the search, for all kinds of reasons. When I'm done here, regardless of the hour, I'll find you two and then we'll get underway starting our search."

"I'm not that flavor of night owl," Hector said, struggling against some sense of vertigo that threatened to drive him to his knees. "Got a few years on you, kid, and tonight, I'm feeling every one of them, somehow. I also like a hearty breakfast. So don't call before eleven a.m. We'll resume the search at the fountain. Having said that, you do have the medallion some place safe? In case more FBI or some diehard Thule or Vril come looking right here on set?"

Orson looked horrified at that prospect. "You do know how to cast a pall, how to damage man's calm."

"You're probably safe enough in a big crowd like this," Hector said. "But I *would* take some extra precaution getting back to the hotel."

Orson chewed his lip. He checked to see if Cassie was looking, then he hugged Hector.

The writer felt something slipped into his coat.

The actor said, "I *have* been reckless carrying it, curse me for a fool. And I'm trusting you not to do something crazy with that medallion in my absence. Go as far as the next-to-last stop, if you can, I beg you. But save that last step, please, old friend. I want to be there when we get to that big X that marks this particular spot."

"I promise. And trust me to handle it all with appropriate caution."

Arm-in-arm with Cassie, the medallion secretly in his pocket, Hector escorted her from the ballroom.

Hector steered his sultry seer from the impromptu movie set straight into the path of a walking corpse.

30

MURDER BY THE DEAD

Waiting for a lift, Cassie buttoned her coat and said, "You *did* get to talk to Orson about taking more precautions, about protecting the disc?"

"I did and I *did*," Hector said as they made their way from the ballroom-cum-film set.

Hector coughed, rubbed his throat and swallowed a few times. He just needed hot tea and some honey, he told himself. That and some solid sleep.

He said in final answer to her question, "He is and he is."

"That's at least a little relief," she said. "I know you think me the perfect fool—think it more every minute for all of this—but while you two talked, I consulted the cards. It's bad, honey. Such threat and terror as I've never seen in a reading. This city's going to become a place of dread and fear before it's all over, It's going to happen and soon if we don't change courses."

The elevator door opened and Hector wrapped an arm around Cassie's shoulders, escorting her into the cage.

The old elevator operator smiled and said something in Italian. Hector was too many years away from the language to be much good just now, even in a situation as simple as this one. He also felt freshly dizzy, so he just shrugged and pointed down at the old man.

The elevator operator nodded and smiled and fiddled with his finicky lift and got it going with a shudder that might have terrified Hector if only he were sharper.

Hector said dully to Cassie, "It doesn't matter what I think about how you arrive at these premonitions. If you have fears, a sense of something bad to come, I know I best take precautions. You're at very least attuned to signals and the world in ways most aren't. Please keep sharing your reservations."

"It's not just observation and deduction," she said sharply. "I'm not just a kind of Sherlock Holmes or something. It's also not something as ethereal and insulting as so-called *women's intuition*, if that's what you were implying."

The elevator jerked to a final stop at the ground floor and the door opened before the cage had even settled.

Three men stood awaiting the cage. One was quite tiny, perhaps a midget or dwarf. His black hair was slicked back from a widow's peak. The little man was dressed all in black but for a gold chain with a medallion—a lightning bolt imposed over a swastika. He said, "Ah, Lassiter! Just the man I need to talk with… and *robustly*. How lucky I am, eh?"

The second man was thin and about six-feet tall. He was brown-eyed and had thick brown hair.

The third man was the one who most got Hector's attention. He was a too-familiar, imposingly tall blonde with now opaque eyes—formerly blue eyes but now hidden behind what almost could be taken for a dense layer of cataracts.

It was the spitting image of the giant Thule, Rune Fuchs, whom Hector had shot between those cloudy eyes a decade before, the author figured, trying to make sense of it all, trying to figure out how the man could be standing before him now after that surely lethal headshot.

To that end, there was no wound to be seen on the giant's forehead; no scar from that impossible to survive shot.

But there was something else that was off about the man. And then there was this smell… No, Hector thought, not just a smell, a stench.

Cassie gasped, rooting her pocket for the gun Hector had given to her.

The brown-haired stranger was clearly reaching for a gun of his own.

The elevator's accordion cage door was still closed and latched from the inside. Hector accepted the gun Cassie handed him. Raising it, he snarled at the old operator, "Close that damned door! Do it now and get this thing going back up!"

Hector's tone of voice seemed to overcome any language barrier. The brown-haired man was taking quickest aim from the other side of the cage door. Hector fired first and the stranger's face caved in. Blood-sprayed the faces of the little man and the big blond man.

The tiny man screamed and bolted.

Expressionless, the blond man jammed an arm through the mesh of the cage, fouling Hector's aim at the retreating little man.

With his other hand, the giant Thule grasped at and tore open the old elevator operator's throat. The old man crumpled to the cage floor, blood gushing from his ruined neck.

Cursing, Hector put two shots into the giant's chest. The big man staggered back a step or two, but didn't fall. He reached for Hector's throat next.

"What the hell," Hector muttered. "What's it gonna take to put this sucker down?" He was taking fresh aim at the giant's forehead this time.

Cassie got the door closed and threw the elevator into upward motion. One of the giant's fingers was sheared off before he could pull his arm back out of the rising cage; the digit fell to the floor and lay there. There was no blood coming from the severed finger, Hector noticed.

"Think your bullets might have to be silver to stop that thing," she said. "Which floor?" Cassie didn't say it like it was a joke.

"Any floor," Hector said, leaning back against the cage wall and staring at his gun, trying to figure out how the giant blond Nazi could have sustained two shots to the chest, let alone that long-ago shot to the face.

But then, like the severed finger, there'd been no blood from his most recent chest wounds, either. "Go higher, all the way to the top," Hector said.

"What, you mean we're heading to the roof from up there?"

"Yes, exactly that," Hector said. "We can get up there much faster than those bastards can climb all those stairs."

He jammed a fresh clip into his automatic with a trembling hand. "I swear I killed that man ten years ago," Hector said. "And his eyes? They looked very strange to me. Still, his surviving those shots to the chest just now? He must be wearing a vest of some kind. You know, bullet-proof. Surely it was like that."

Cassie wasn't having it. "After all the wars, all the combat zones and all the hospitals, after your recovery efforts in the Great Keys hurricane, you're telling me you really don't recognize the tell-tale smell coming off that man?"

Hector took over operation of the elevator. He indeed meant to go all the way to the top. From there they'd make their way to the roof of the old hotel, he'd decided. They'd move across adjacent rooftops Hector figured, finally descending street level from some other building several-doors-down from the hotel. "Smell," Hector said, resisting the memory of that odor coming off the blond giant. "What are you saying?"

"He is dead already," Cassie said. "I've heard of this, but never seen it in person until now. Might not have believed it possible myself if I hadn't just stood witness. That little man, the midget, he's a *Houdon*—the operator or string-puller of the z—"

"Christ, don't *say* it," Hector said.

"Of the giant Thule's *zombie*," Cassie insisted. "You still don't believe, not even after what we just escaped?"

"Less than ever," Hector said. He bit his lip. "Still, the bastard is below us, and Orson's here, too. We need to drag Orson away from this set for his safety. We need to finish this search for the spear. We need to do that tonight. This was looking like a heady lark, but now people are dying again." Hector stopped several floors below the top in order to fetch Orson.

Soaked through from traveling over rooftops and climbing down staggered walls in the driving rain, Hector, Orson and Cassie shivered in an upstairs hallway of a wholly different hotel, awaiting another elevator. Orson's dripping black greatcoat obscured the costume of the black magician that he still wore underneath.

To Hector's mind, Orson had too readily and too quickly accepted Cassie's assertion they were running from a supernaturally animated cadaver.

"Bullshit," Hector said finally, not caring what Cassie thought about his crude refusal to back down from his skepticism. "Just bullet proof vests and bad hygiene, that's all it is."

"And that bullet you put in his head years ago," Orson said. "Explain that away."

"That's tougher, but trust me I'll be working on it. Hell, you're a magician, you tell me how the trick is done."

"I'm not sure I'm wrong about silver bullets," Cassie said. "Need to get back to my room, I have some books there on warding against these kinds of creatures and—"

"*Later*," Hector said. "I'm serious that tonight we take this hunk of metal and we follow it to journey's end. You two can have the damned lance as far as I'm concerned, as I've always said. I'm not laying a glove on it. But seeing the deranged types that are still scrambling to lay hands on the Lance, I've decided they simply can't do that. We find it first, then my plan is to push on from this place come morning. Resume the hunt for myself—my double I mean—or cut my losses and head home. I've got some deadlines looming, other commitments. And frankly, I feel like hell."

"We're all going to catch pneumonia," Orson said, patting his sodden coat.

"Hell, I think I'm already halfway there," Hector said.

It was true that he felt even more feverish. His throat was far rawer than before. God, like he needed a cold, or worse, the *flu*. Having lived through the flu epidemic of 1918, Hector, like most of his generation, still lived in abject terror of the latter.

God, how he *was* shaking with the wet and cold. He decided it was best they indeed go back to the hotel. Orson and he were close enough in build the actor could probably make do with some extra suit of Hector's.

Rather than rely on any more cabs, Hector secured a rented, tan Maserati. As Hector drove to their next stop, Cassie read by the light of a flashlight from a book on African

Voodou. "Forget what I said about silver bullets," she said. "We're going to need salt. It's like being in purgatory, only here with someone else pulling your puppet strings."

Orson seemed to be hanging on her words. Hector just ground his teeth and drove on through the rain.

From the fountain, the map led them to the Pyramid of Cestius and on to the foot of the Spanish Steps. From there they were directed to the Trevi Fountain. With her flashlight, Cassie again checked the notched edge of the medallion and said, "Looks like we're nearing the end. From there, we'll be counting footsteps again, I think."

The last major location proved to be the Catacombs of San Callisto—home to something like a purported half-a-million corpses.

Confident they were without tails—alive or "zombified," and thinking of the latter, Hector couldn't resist a little dig. He said, "Better hope nobody said any witchy words over all the dead in this joint. Don't think there'd be enough salt in all the mines of northern Ireland to put all these stiffs back down."

Cassie shot him a look. Orson just said, "Let's this finish this. Clearly we can't wait to go in with the tourists, so—"

"So we have to break in," Hector finished for him. "Holy Christ, breaking into a burial site that holds dead popes? Talk about risking bad luck."

False starts; strange sounds. The scuttle of rats and the cloying silence of all those rotting dead around them.

In 1924, Hector had ventured into the catacombs of Paris, though not by choice. It was where he'd acquired all the whip scars on his back that so appalled Cassie, just as they did all the women before her. He found himself shaking again as they entered the dank cold of the tombs. This time, Hector thought his shivering had nothing to do with the illness he felt insinuating itself in his lungs and bones.

The medallion map at last led to the room housing a statue of the "incorrupt" and prone body of Ste. Cecilia. Below her right index finger, almost as though her statue were pointing there, they pried at a lose paver and found a void. Unable to stop himself, Orson reached into the shallow hole. As he did so, he said, "There's no way to hide a spear or anything of length in here." His famous bass voice echoed eerily off the walls, evoking memories of his early career interval as the mysterious voice of The Shadow, the invisible avenger frighteningly attuned to the evil that lurks in the hearts of men, and presumably of women, too.

Digging around in the hole, Orson at last pulled out another medallion, smaller than the first. He shone his light on it. One side contained another map, similar in construction to the medallion that had led them to this place. This new medal also had notches along its edges. On the flipside, or "obverse" face of the new medal, there was an image of St. Stephen's Cathedral.

"I guess we're not through here," Orson said. "Not by a longshot."

"No," Cassie agreed. She frowned at Hector. "My God, you look terrible, darling."

"Really not feeling too well," Hector admitted. "Terrible, actually."

"We need to get you out of here," she said. "Someplace warm and dry."

31

SOCIETY OF THE LIVING DEAD

Hector couldn't remember the last time he'd been really sick. And he couldn't remember being sick quite like this: he was shaking so hard he could hear the bed springs squeak. His teeth and jaws were starting to ache from impact with one another. He was at once freezing, yet soaked through with sweat.

At some point, eyes closed, he heard testy voices. He heard Orson saying, "Take the goddamn thing then. I'm through with it, finished with all of it, Goddamn you all."

Later he heard Orson say to an accusing Cassie, "What difference does it make now, now that I've established to their satisfaction neither I or Hector have the spear and I've given them the real medallion to conduct their own search? Let the idiot Thule or Vril or whatever these Germans regard themselves to be trace the first map back to that empty hole in the floor of those catacombs."

Doctors—Hector was aware of them coming and going, too. One with a professional-sounding voice, speaking English but heavily inflected with Italian, said, "This is very strange, not like flu, at all. More like, I don't know… Typhoid, dengue? I've never seen anything quite like it. I hope it isn't the first indication of some coming epidemic. I confess I really don't know how to effectively treat this. His body can't sustain this fever for much longer..."

After the doctor left, Hector heard Cassie say, "I think it's up to me to save him. I think this is something that's been sent against Hector."

Orson's resonant baritone had an odd tremolo: "A curse or a hex?"

"Yes," Cassie said. "I truly think that's so. This has been made to happen to Hector, I'm convinced of that."

Rebelling at that absurd notion, trying to claw air, to speak or call out to get attention, but having no result with either, Hector lay there, screaming inside, but to Cassie and Orson, looking terrifyingly motionless, looking like a dead man.

Hector came to with the sun in his eyes. He could hear birds chirping, a radio set low—a shortwave, he suspected, for it was playing an obscure American tune—Sister Rosetta Tharpe and "God Don't Like It."

Some of our members gets on a drunk
Just to speak their sober minds
And when they raise the Devil, Lord,
They put all the blame on shine

Hector forced himself up on his elbows. His back and shoulders cracked. He was in a hospital, he could see that much.

Still, there was this strange smell, overcoming even the odor of his stale sweat and sour breadth from his mouth that tasted of days of having been violently ill. This mystery scent was overcoming even the usual antiseptic smell typical of all hospitals, European or American.

Looking around, trying to get his bearings, Hector seemed to remember Cassie's voice in his ear, soft. Then something was held up to his dry, cracked lips. Her voice coaxing, "That's it, let it out darling. You get all that nastiness, all that poison *out*." Words in something like French followed, but not French—not any version known to him.

He sniffed the air again, tracing this other, stranger stench to his pillow. He felt under there and found this ratty, foul smelling little burlap bag. Disgusted, he tossed it across the room. Just that small effort made him dizzy; his field of vision was a shimmer of floaters and glittering spots of color.

Blinking, looking around, Hector saw a pitcher and a glass. With shaking hands, he poured himself fresh water. He called out and said, "Is there anybody there?"

He thought he heard a call back. As he sipped the water, still looking around, he saw a newspaper resting on the stand by his bed.

Blinking his eyes afresh, rubbing some dried crust or sleep from them, he focused at last on a headline on page three, to which the paper had been opened and folded back.

It was an English-language paper.

At the top of the page was a headline that immediately set Hector to wondering if he was truly awake. Reading that scream headline, he wondered whether he was really even *alive*:

Novelist, screenwriter Hector Lassiter dead at 48
Author found strangled in hotel room in Vienna

BOOK THREE

THE THIRD MAN

Vienna, November/December 1948

"Every true artist must,
in his own way,
be a magician, a charlatan."
—Orson Welles

32

THE POISON DEATH

"Do you miss holidays in the States? God knows, this place doesn't exactly feel festive, not even when there's snow." Cassie held out a gloved hand to stop some flurries in their slow-motion fall.

The giant carnival wheel was still today, just no paying customers, Hector figured. And it would surely be miserable to go up there anyway in this biting cold.

A lonely truck rumbled by, hauling more rubble to somewhere; the city was a warren of impromptu scrap yards and slag heaps. Post-war Vienna: like so much of war-scarred Europe, Hector thought the city might be a generation or more rebuilding. And then it would never be the same. It was like moving through Eliot's Wasteland. Here, the loss of old structures and statuary seemed more acute to Hector, more the pointless waste.

Hitler had said of Vienna, "This city is, in my eyes, a pearl. I'll give it the setting it deserves." Too often we speak our plans and God—or the Devil—laughs.

In terms of his own ruined body, Hector felt oddly attuned to the ravaged city. It was nearly twelve months since he'd fallen so very ill back in Rome, yet he was still struggling to recover his health almost a year on. As he did that, Hector was also trying to trace the last steps of his dead doppelganger; still spreading news to the right parts of the world that the one true Hector Lassiter still drew air, was "still vertical and published," to use a writer chum's term for remaining in saddle or still "north of the dirt," to use one of Hector's phrases for the same happy state of being.

"Holidays—Thanksgiving and Christmas," he said, reflecting, "I don't think I've spent those two with family of any kind, not since I was a little kid."

Cassie drew closer, freshly troubled he still seemed to lean so much on her as they walked, still needing her unremarked-upon support in that way across longer distances. It was worrying to her that this once vital man's man was still recovering from the terrific toll to his body by his self-described flu.

Surely enough, giving Hector some lucky cover for what Cassie regarded to be his mistaken self-diagnosis, a flu epidemic was indeed raging across Rome even now, but that scourge had hit the city many months after Hector had taken ill.

No, Hector's case was something else entirely. His malady, Cassie had decided to her own satisfaction, was the result of a very powerful and malignant Voodoo priest's curse. Probably the work of that mysterious little German man, she figured.

In confirmation, she'd found a jar filled with Hector's nail clippings, discarded cigarette butts and a chicken heart in a sealed mason jar under their hotel bed back in Rome the first night after he'd become seriously ill.

She had never confided to Hector about that discovery—he was simply too steadfast in his doubt about all things supernatural and would have dismissed it as macabre nonsense. She was frustrated the writer was such a headstrong naturalist, despite all he'd seen in his storied life that should have convinced him otherwise a hundred times over. Stray hairs, a scrap of fingernail—these could be made weapons against their source. Cassie was quietly frantic herself to find a scrap of fingernail somewhere in their hotel room. She'd broken the nail, she guessed, opening and closing a suitcase, only noticing later when it began to hurt. Since the attack on Hector, her life had become a sustained search for Hector's and her own shed hairs and nails.

Anyway, Cassie had been far too preoccupied saving his life to debate with Hector then about supposed flu bugs and the like. It had taken all her stamina and skill simply to hold all that foul black magic ranged against her man at something like bay.

Hector would never know the days and nights she sat at his bedside, giving him tonics, stuffing myriad spell and hex bags under his pillows, slowly nursing him back to health while laying down salt trails at hospital window and door every night.

That last was to keep evil loas and the zombie of Rune Fuchs at bay while Hector recovered, while Cassie and Orson contrived to find a secure hiding place for the second medallion until Hector was better and it could be used.

Their plan had become one of waiting for Hector to recover so the three of them, "We three Musketeers," as Welles sentimentally put it, "can complete our quest together as it clearly is meant to be."

Holding tighter to his arm, leaning in still closer in hopes Hector wouldn't realize just how much support she was giving him, Cassie said, "You and Brinke never shared a Thanksgiving or a Christmas together?"

Painful silence. Hector said, "Time wasn't on our side. No Thanksgiving. No Christmases. We had Valentine's Day,

Independence Day." A catch in his voice that shredded Cassie. "We had a Labor Day together. And then…"

She knew too well how that story ended. If Hector ever finished his book about all that, the world would know it too.

"You and I," Cassie said, firm and sure, "are going to spend this Thanksgiving together. Christmas, too. Yes? Here, perhaps in Paris. In the Alps or even in Germany, I don't care which city or place we do it in. I don't care where so long as we're together. But we will do that, won't we?"

"Yes, definitely," Hector said. "We surely will do that." Somewhere behind them there was the echo of laughter on rain-slicked cobblestones.

Five a.m. was Hector's usual writing time. Cassie was in the bedroom next door, in a deep sleep, long lush eyelashes twitching with her dreams.

Hector sat with a notebook, pen and a pot of room service coffee—some extra strong, wake-the-dead Viennese blend—dreaming while awake. He was trying to write fresh fiction but instead found himself once again turning over the scattered and sorry rocks of another man's life, a man who had desired to be Hector Lassiter and been killed by someone for daring to impersonate the author.

It seemed that Hector's double was born Andrew L. Parker, son of Miriam and Jerry Parker of Steubenville, Ohio in 1906. There was not much after that to be found on the lad until Andrew changed his life's direction.

After adopting the slightly older novelist's persona, Andrew had cut his profligate, headline-generating swath across post-war Europe, including that last, jarring headline that greeted

Hector upon waking from what doctor's described as a near coma.

Hector Mason Lassiter, dead at 48.

Jesus.

No man should live to read his own obituaries. Hector's had run the spectrum of hagiography to downright character assassination.

A few too-candid remarks from so-called friends and sometimes lovers ensured they were no longer regarded as such by the resurrected novelist.

In time, Hector got beyond all that, simultaneously cutting back on liquor and cigarettes to hasten his physical recovery. Making a point of daily exertion, he felt himself coming back, regaining strength and muscle tone, but it was a painfully, frustratingly slow process.

And he remained frustrated in another respect. Hector couldn't get a firm handle on who this Andrew Parker had been in terms of deeper detail, even after the man had contrived to become Hector. He couldn't get at what had impelled the stranger to adopt Hector's persona when so many other men's identities might have been claimed.

Hector couldn't find his answers here in Vienna, anyway.

Maybe the clues to all that lay back in Ohio.

When he talked of heading back to the States to take up his search for more dope on Andrew there, Cassie balked. At first Hector thought her resistance had something to do with lingering racism in the States. Here in Europe, they were left alone for the most part, left to just be together without remark or accusing gazes. They were never turned away at a restaurant, or at a club. She was never ordered to the back of a bus or denied the use of a water fountain.

And when he signed a hotel registry, "Mr. and Mrs. Hector Lassiter," no eyebrows were raised, no hotel dicks loomed, ready to run some shakedown on a morals beef or to drop coins to some scandal rag for a quick-cash kickback and resulting headlines that might end a career like Hector's back in the States.

No, like Orson, like Cassie, Hector couldn't say he truly missed America himself.

But there was that other thing binding Cassie and Hector to Europe, to Vienna, particularly—that thing for which Hector had no patience whatever.

Cassie and Orson were still fixated on finding the damned Roman spear. Before his health collapsed, Hector had of course bought in to the chase for the chase's sake—it was like a dry-run for some caper novel waiting to happen. But now that he was little more than an invalid? Hector's heart might be in the quest, but his legs were a different matter.

Yet his comrades in the crusade for the Holy Lance remained indomitable.

Orson had accepted a role in this new film, *The Third Man*, penned by no less than Graham Greene, in order to fund his ongoing search for the holy relic as well as some self-mounted film project.

Cassie, too, was still fully invested in the myth of the spear and its power.

Hector stared at the nondescript name again: Andrew Litner Parker.

Well, adios, Andrew. We hardly knew ye, you luckless son of a bitch.

Too bad you had the misfortune of being born with a face that looked so much like the real article's mug,

Hector thought, raising an imaginary glass to his dead double's memory.

The only thing Hector thought he did know—and this, too, was mere supposition—was that Hector's picaresque life that seemed to so entice luckless Andy had almost certainly been Mr. Parker's fatal undoing.

Old Andy had evidently been just close enough *in situ* to the real Hector that one of Hector's all-to-real enemies had erred and killed Andy in his stead. Hector was sure of that much—the fool's death hadn't been a result of anything Andy had done other than pretending to be Hector. It wasn't some lover's tryst gone bad—Andy/Hector hadn't been found choked to death in some tangle of sheets or in some men's room somewhere with his pants down.

No, Andy had been found tied to a chair, fully dressed, and choked to death with a length of cord cut from an electric light and twisted tight with—a piercing touch—a couple of number two pencils.

Maybe it had been the Thule or Vril. Maybe the Nazi film-maker Werner Höttl or possibly one of those murderous surrealists. They all had reason to mean Hector harm.

Whoever had done the deed, Andy perished because he had been swamped in the backwash of Hector's lurid, larger-than-life legend.

A scream from the street below—male or female, Hector couldn't tell which.

Was a time, he'd have run to that scream. Now his back simply wasn't in it. If he over-exerted himself he coughed, and when he coughed he still saw spots and felt like someone was sitting on his chest.

His last doctor in Rome said it might be spring of forty-nine before he felt fully himself again.

Disgusted at his inability to find the words, Hector sat back in his chair and cast down his pen.

There would be no fiction writing tonight—he could already tell from the way his mind raced in every direction except the one that would result in words on paper it was fruitless to push on now.

Despite the extra-strong coffee, he felt beat to the wide.

Hector sighed, struggled to his feet, then stripped and slid into bed.

Cassie kissed his cheek, said, "How did it go?"

"It didn't."

"I'm so sorry." Another kiss on the same cheek. "The words will come again, I know it. And soon." She tried to move his head from the pillow, to gain access to his other cheek. Probably she figured he didn't remember her long ago caution about just such kisses, he thought. Either way, he didn't oblige her urging to get the other side of his face. She studied his pale blue eyes and said carefully, "Sleepy?"

"Nearly always these days."

Another scream outside. She shivered and felt Hector's muscles tense at the sound from the street. "Easy there," she said. "Not your fight, not tonight. Not until you're entirely yourself again."

"Yeah," he said, raw-voiced. "Wonder when that will be exactly."

He fell asleep to the distant sound of more screams.

Yes, he thought, even as the darkness enveloped him, *You are far from yourself, old pal.*

33

THE MOST DANGEROUS GAME

It wasn't so long ago, sitting in Los Angeles and talking about a cabal of killer artists, Orson had tried to talk Hector into turning all that madness with the surrealists into a film. "Ben Hecht will write it, and we'll get Joe Cotten to play you," Orson had said.

Now, to further dizzying effect beyond his usual recent bouts of lightheadedness, Hector and the very actor who might have impersonated him onscreen were seated across from one another amidst the ruins of Vienna, snug in a café in sight of the Prater Amusement Park and the Wiener Risenrad—the park's giant Ferris wheel and still the largest such wheel in the world. Half its gondolas were gone now, the result of more war damage.

Hector sipped his espresso, then broke off a corner of a scone. He liked Joe Cotten—the actor remained solid, charming, every-inch an American.

Joe was playing the lead in *The Third Man*, cast as an American pulp writer who comes to believe his childhood friend Harry Lime—the latter to be played by Cotten's longtime friend Orson Welles, of course—might still be alive. To his horror, it also slowly dawns on Joe's character that his dear friend is a black marketeer of coldest calculation, an actual villain of the blackest stripe.

Joe was hopeful his many years of friendship and playing against Orson on stage, screen and radio would inform both parts with rare resonance.

Impeccably suave with his brushed back waves of sandy-colored hair and tailored herringbone overcoat—like Hector's, a coat worn indoors against the chill of the under-heated café—Joe Cotten drummed fingertips on the table top.

"He's two days late arriving, you know," Joe said. "He's not doing himself any favors with that. My God, how he frustrates me with these pointless… *episodes* I guess we'll call them."

Hector watched Joe fidget. He said, "Orson would probably just say it's his nature, like that's all the explanation that's required."

"But off the point," Joe said. "You should see the desperate letters I was writing him about trying to save *Ambersons* while he was down there in South America on that other farce of a film for Rockefeller. The letters I wrote about trying to save *Journey Into Fear* from the studio hacks. Those letters probably damaged our friendship. Don't think we've ever been quite the same since. I love the man, I do—I revere the artist—but both Orsons also exasperate the daylights out of me."

"Hell, don't get me started," Hector said. "Do you know he told me the South American film, *It's All True*, that and everything since, has been undone by a voodoo curse? I think he really believes it's so."

"I've heard that story, too," Joe said. "Absurd. And you know it didn't happen to Orson, not at all. It was Dick Wilson who met with the alleged voodoo priest. It was Dick's copy of the script that was cursed with that spike through its page." A wry smile. "Though in light of all that, I have to observe that Dick's luck hasn't been so good since, either. But he's still intensely loyal to Orson, despite it all. That says something."

Hector signaled for two more coffees. The first had lifted Hector's spirits and pulse, had him feeling fitter and maybe sharp enough to whip a ten-year-old in a fair fight. Some tough guy to be sure.

"Shall I go to Rome and try to fetch him for you all?" Hector asked. He hoped Joe said no. Hector still wasn't up to that kind of travel. He feared his contemplated travel all the way back to the States might actually put him under the earth.

The actor shook his head. "No, I hear he's on his way. Lured here somehow, or so I'm told, after a silly gambit involving a magician of rare skill and a promised private performance for Orson the Magnificent." Joe finished his first espresso. "Enough of this Orson talk. Let's stop his ears from burning. What's your next novel, Hector?"

"Struggling to find that," Hector said candidly. "Reading anything yourself?"

Another funny smile. "A potboiler western called *The Oklahoma Kid*. By a 'master of suspense.' And what a swell cover it has. All guns and sneers. You know, there's a bit in this picture that reminds me of you more than a tad."

"Oh?" Hector settled up their bill as the waiter delivered their fresh coffee. "How do you mean?"

"Some interlude where my character—my novelist, Holly—is being quizzed by some sinister character in front of a book club of old lady types. I—you—I mean my character, is being cautioned about the danger of mixing fact with fiction. A dangerous game, this mysterious man says." Joe toyed with his cup. "Hector, it seems to me that with each new novel you write you increasingly blend the two—fact and fiction—

as well as to highlight that fact in the work itself. It's like you almost mean to tear down the fourth wall."

"Hell," Hector said, "find me a single book of fiction that doesn't have its share of fact."

"Anyway, thanks for the breakfast and the company," Joe said. "Nice to talk to someone from back home. A man with at least the trace of a Texas accent. If you see Harry," an embarrassed smile, "I mean *Orson*, if you do that before me, please get his broadening ass to my hotel. I'll take it from there and get him to Mr. Reed, our British gentleman director."

"Certainly." Hector drained his last coffee at a pull and rose, steadying himself with a hand on the table as another brief bout of dizziness threatened his balance. He had to remember to take it easier getting up and down, to not move so quickly that every motion triggered a head rush. Hector pulled tighter his warm, big overcoat and put on his fedora. He buttoned his coat and followed the actor out in the crisp November air as he pulled on his leather gloves.

Joe gestured at the big old Ferris wheel yonder. "We film there soon, you know. Have a big scene on the ride."

"Very picturesque," Hector said.

"Let's hope," Joe said. "My humble opinion—and all apologies to Mr. Graham Greene whom I usually revere—the dialogue for my confrontation with Orson on that wheel could frankly use some work. It's a pivotal scene, and probably Orson's most crucial. Right now, it lacks, well, let's call it *punch*."

Hector shrugged, his breathy icy in the air. "Maybe the actor will fix it. Certified genius, right?"

Joe laughed. "So he says." A beat, then, "I mean, so they all say. It's how he's perceived anyway."

The chill air hinted of snow. Anywhere else, Hector figured he'd be right about a coming storm.

But here? He'd smelled the snow in the air of Vienna for more than a week, but no more than a few light flurries that left no trace on the ground had fallen in that time.

The wind whipped at his coat tails and made Hector tug his hat lower on his brow. Kids chased after him, begging coins, tugging at sleeve and coattail.

The city was divided among allied overseers, quartered essentially, so eventually tiring of the urchins, Hector flashed his passport and simply crossed sectors, just trying to lose the begging children who couldn't roam the city at will.

Money was running a bit lower, and it was harder to access funds from Vienna, this city where he'd stayed on far too long already for his taste. Hector figured he could maybe solider on another four weeks—just make Christmas—before he'd have to move on to some other part of Europe, England or France, where he could more easily access money by wire and mail from back home.

Hector once again pulled his collar up against the wind, slowly making his way back to the hotel and Cassie. The wind chased brown leaves; his shadow was lengthening. Footfalls—his and another's. Hector paused to light a cigarette, looking back as he did so.

There was a slim silhouette in one of the few working streetlights. Male, tall. That's about all Hector could discern in the growing gloom.

A passing car blocked Hector's view for a moment—someone who could still afford fuel. When the vehicle had passed, Hector saw the silhouetted man was gone or blended into shadow.

Hector cast down his unwanted cigarette. Some impossibly wrinkled old woman stooped and snatched it up, gratefully sucking down its smoke. Zither music came from a bar; Hector almost succumbed to its zinging siren's song.

Why didn't he feel like going back to Cassie and their bed?

Why didn't he feel drawn to spending time loving and lolling in the warm sheets with Cassie?

He knew he was again on the verge of some realization—probably an unhappy one, but one that would come eventually anyway. Rather than push it away this time, Hector decided it was better to keep walking, to allow the bloodhound in his head to follow that destructive scent to its natural end.

Maybe it had something to do with a kind of foresight. Unlike Cassie, he couldn't see their future—wouldn't presume to guess at it. It wasn't her mixed race that was an issue, not that at all, Hector insisted to himself. No, it was the very fact of her superstition that was a wedge between them. The longer they were together, the more impossible Hector found it to write.

Now, coldly thinking back—having murdered a morning with Joe discussing film, literature, talking about art in general—Hector was struck with an epiphany. It was a potentially fatal one for Hector and Cassie as a couple, he realized.

Yes, it indeed all came down to her damned superstition. It was all about Cassie's spooky acceptance of predestination and fate, of this crazy belief in foreordained events etched on a man or a woman's hands.

Honest belief in any of that precluded serendipity, invention and all the happy accidents that kept creative types like Hector infatuated with their craft.

Nine months together, and he'd written the fewest number of words he'd strung together since 1920 or thereabouts. Disaster.

He realized instinctively he needed to get back to the States as soon as possible, to get back in touch with the ground there.

He would poke around Ohio, learning some more about this mysterious Andrew Parker who'd died pretending to be Hector and, maybe in the process, Hector would find his way back to fiction, write a novel about a man who became another man and died for his trouble. Hector's own headlines would sell that novel, no sweat.

Hector sighed and looked back over his shoulder again, almost hoping something—someone—might be gaining on him. Something to feed his creative beast with a necessary sense of uncertainty and menace, restoring creative sparks stripped from him these past months of convalescing and having supernatural claptrap shoved—sometimes literally—down his throat.

But there was nothing back there but more storm clouds on the horizon. Even those were probably just another false alarm, just like the smell of all that heavy snow that couldn't seem to fall.

A hand on his shoulder; something at his back. "We really are losing our touch, aren't we, Mr. Lassiter," a voice filled with menace said.

34

MAN, BEAST AND VIRTUE

"Is this a robbery, or something worse?" Hector waited for the answer, gloved hands raised.

A tall, dark figure swung into his path. It was a big man, imposing and nattily dressed. It took Hector a moment to recognize him. Orson hugged the author to his chest and said, "Old man, so good to see you again! Forgive the theatrics but I couldn't resist. Just me being me, yes?"

"To the bone," Hector said. "You just got in?"

"Just. Have an early day tomorrow." Orson smiled, dark eyes twinkling in the moonlight. Hector looked up, smiling at the moon. Orson liked to say how much the moon meant to him personally, claimed that his moods closely attuned to its phases. "Up for a nightcap first? Some catching up?"

"Definitely," Hector said. "Yes, please. We must do that and right now."

Despite the actor's required early morning set-call, Hector and Orson sat up many hours, drinking and discussing writing, acting, and all things creative. In the end, all of that deep talk about the act of creation only firmed Hector's darker theories about what was holding back his own writing.

Hector at last wandered into their hotel room at two in the morning, exhausted in the good old, dissolute way, slightly drunk and somehow freshly aflame with new notions about potential writing projects.

He stripped again bedside and crawled in next to Cassie. She said softly, "The hour's wickedly late, or early, rather. Where on earth have you been?"

"Café Marc Aurel, then a bar or two… Walking and talking the day and night away." She heard his cockeyed smile in his voice. "Had breakfast with Joe Cotten, then for hours roamed and haunted the stacks of a bookstore full of books whose languages I can't read, but it was good to smell the old paper and leather. Took in a string concert. And, walking home, I ran into Orson. Time got away from the two of us from there."

"Sobriety flew, too, I see. Still, I'm glad you were able to make your way through a whole day and night on your own… and even soldier on into the start of another day. Probably sleep like the dead tomorrow, but there you have it. Got to take the rough with the smooth, right?"

She drew her thumbnail across the side of his hand, trailing across his "love affair lines," as her occult books he'd secretly browsed over during his recuperation had called them. She said, "So we start the final search again tomorrow, since your stamina seems there again and Orson is here now?"

"Possibly. Subject didn't really come up this time. Frankly, I don't want to encourage any distractions in Orson. Joe Cotten's much more in-tune with Hollywood politics than me, and I get the strong sense from Joe that Orson's career rests on the knife's edge back home just now. He desperately needs a victory. This picture seems the best shot for that from my perspective. I refuse to foul things up for Orson with this madcap treasure hunt."

"It's my quest, too, you know, and I don't take it so lightly, not at all."

"I know. I apologize." Hector stretched out an arm. She curled into a familiar cuddle. Destructive as he now viewed her strange "trade" to his writing—now that he regarded Cassie as almost a kind of anti-muse—he was still dreadfully fond of her. "You're no longer on Uncle Sam's nickel, he said. "You're a free agent. So what is your real ongoing stake in this quest exactly? What do you hope to gain in discovering this particular flavor of grail?"

Her long silence was an indictment. She finally said, "After all the roadblocks thrown down before us, all the things that conspire to make us ultimately impossible as a couple, you really have to ask?"

Hector took too long responding—he knew that. When he did, he said, "Orson really does needs to focus on this role. Shouldn't take too long for him to finish up here. I've seen the script and he should be able to wrap up his bits of business in a mere couple of days here before they all head back to England to finish up at the studio for the interiors and such."

"And you, Hector? Are you staying on for the holidays as promised?"

"I'll help you find this thing. I'll do that if you're sure it's what you want."

They were both aware of his dodging of the second part of her question.

"Thank you, Hector." She stroked his chest. "How are you really feeling?"

"Better, a little stronger," he said. "But I pushed too hard today… *yesterday,* now, I guess. Feel freshly beat to the wide for certain." She could hear it in his voice.

Cassie's hand strayed south. Her hand was warm—all of her seemed to radiate a strange heat. "Can you make me feel wonderful now, despite all that? Please make me tingle? Don't you want to be one person for a while again, while there's time?"

Despite his deep feeling of fatigue, Hector found himself up early, showered and out again on the ruined town. He sat with Joe and then Orson at the Cafe Marc Aurel. The place was, both remarked, an actual future setting for Joe and Orson's characters' last, ill-fated reunion.

Orson was characteristically last to their little breakfast party. While they waited for Welles, Joe had confided to Hector their friend had tried to drop out of the picture overnight.

Joe sensed it was cold feet—some sense of tension of working for another accomplished director, particularly one of Carol Reed's renown and accomplishment. At Joe's cunning urging, the British director had appealed to Orson's populist bent, imploring him to think of all the working men he'd be putting out of a job if he truly bailed on the project.

Orson grudgingly relented, but was still resisting spending much time in the city's sewers for a climactic chase scene. Given Orson's asthma, Hector could see the actor reasonably seeking concession on that point.

Even as they ate, work was purportedly already hastily underway at Pinewood Studios to construct a warmer, more sanitary sewer set for Orson to run through to his character's forlorn end.

Joe had an earlier first call than Orson and so excused himself. He looked at his watch, looked at Hector and said, "Please make sure that Mr. Welles isn't far behind me, okay?"

"Do my level best," Hector said.

Alone again together, the writer and actor tapped glasses. Orson said, "You survived our little alcohol orgy I see."

"Yeah, okay. I'm better, but short of fully fit. I'll get there."

Orson nodded, drummed his fingertips on the marble countertop. "And you and the dusky lady? I meant to ask last night, have you proposed to Cassie yet?"

"No," Hector said. "Fairly certain that's not in the cards." He winced at his own bad, unconscious joke. "That was awful, and not intentional. I meant to say—"

I know exactly what you meant," Orson said. "You're worlds apart in every sense. She's not your real type, of course. I fancy I have a handle on the women who you're most drawn to. She simply doesn't fit that rarified template."

"Tell me one thing," Hector said. "Are you here for the film, or is this role just an excuse and paycheck to fund leg two of this quest for the spear?"

Orson took a deep breath. His brown eyes darted left to right and back again before at last focusing on Hector. He couldn't tell if the actor was seeking the right words, or rather, the right lie. He said finally, "Why, both, old man. They're of equal importance to me. Of equal weight, I suppose. At least in this moment. Or maybe not, frankly. The older I get, the more I find I can change my mind on a dime. Is it the same for you, old man?"

"Quite the contrary," Hector said. "Longer I stay alive, the more I find I just harden into the man I've always been."

Orson considered that, then picked up the book that Hector had brought along to read if he felt he needed moments of rest in his day. It was a French translation of a biography of Byron. He said suddenly, "Do you know the best service anyone could render to the arts, Hector? Destroy all biographies. Only art can explain the life of a man, and not the contrary."

"Forgive me, Orson, but where the Holy Lance is concerned, you sound like you're wavering."

"Belief is an exhausting thing," Orson said. "To really embrace a faith, one must make certain commitments, take the effort. When you were so sick, I watched Cassie working what she regards as her magic. I suppose I wonder if I can keep up the steps, the effort that possessing that spear seemingly requires."

Orson hesitated then said, "Sacrifice is a word I keep coming back to in relation to all this, and to your lover."

"What do you mean?"

"Cassie told me the damnedest tale about a rite she participated in to stall Hitler and thwart some German cult called the Black Order," Orson said. "Has she shared the story with you?"

"With me? I'd be the last person she talk to about anything like that."

"Seems in the summer of 1940, near New Forest, a coven of British witches gathered as they have before to perform a rite to protect British sovereignty, only this time against Hitler's forces. Cassie was a part of this rite, she told me. They all went out into the forest, nude and slathered with some strange oil, they all took some kind of mushroom and then danced in a circle holding hands… It seems to be utterly effective a human life had to be sacrificed. The oldest coven member volunteered himself for that."

"Jesus Christ," Hector said. "Please tell me Cassie didn't wield the blade."

"I wondered about that too… I asked, she didn't answer, which, I suppose, in its way is an answer."

Hector just shook his head.

Orson tried to make light of it. "Anyway, Hitler never invaded British shores, so the magic must have worked, yes?"

As promised, Hector did everything he could to rush Orson through a hasty breakfast and on to the set.

They were walking that way, toward the film crew's next location, Hector checking over his shoulder now and then for one of the city's far-too-scarce taxis.

Orson said, "I still hate the way things are in the United States, even if I could go back today. Did you hear what the bastards did to the Josephsons? Leon was subpoenaed by HUAC. It destroyed their business. By all accounts, it's still like a witch hunt back there. We're the wise ones, old man, safely enjoying the fruits of the old world while home burns itself to pieces."

Possibly all too true, but Hector had also heard the Greenwich Village club in which he'd wined and dined Cassie their first night together had become increasingly leftist and overtly so, a vaunted hive for fundraising and left-wing firebrands, a watering hole for outright communists. He said, "It's not the time to be loudly political back home, that much we agree upon."

Their footfalls fell like gunshots on the nearly empty, damp streets that wound between the tall, still-standing old buildings.

Orson pointed at the skeletal silhouette of the great Ferris Wheel behind them. "We film there, you know."

"So I've heard from Mr. Cotten. He's worried the dialogue is a little flaccid for that scene."

"And he's right," Orson said. "But don't worry. I'll think of something. When a director hires me, I try to stay out of their way in terms of my own directing impulses. Writing, contributing ideas, that is a different matter. You've been here quite some while, chasing your own ghost, so to speak. Have you ridden the thing… the big wheel?"

"Nah," Hector said, "not crazy about heights, remember?"

"Yes, and me either," Orson said. "My fear of heights is slightly milder than yours, I suppose. I managed okay filming that big ledge scene in the rain in *Journey Into Fear*, after all. A man was killed there the very next night. Slipped and fell to his death." That put Orson in mind of something else.

He said, "On this matter of your recently presumed death. It sent poor Marlene into a terrible state. I hear Hemingway went on a week-long drunk before he got word it was all a mistake. Anyway, this business of your imposter, it still fascinates me. I'm still thinking it would make for a remarkable film."

"Nothing too compelling there I can find yet," Hector said. "Just some average man who was tired of himself, I suppose. Poor bastard rode my coattails right into a coffin."

"Having such a man so drawn to your life rather than his own is just the price of living such a romantic existence as you seem to excel at doing," Orson said. "This story still could be film-worthy, you know."

"Romantic? Anyway, I need to write the book first. You can option that." Hector frowned. He took Orson's arm and stopped him moving. Orson frowned back. "What's the matter?"

Hector waited, then said, "Nothing, I reckon." They started walking again. "How did things wind up on that last film you were acting in? I hear they're actually calling it *Black Magic* now."

"That's right," Orson said. "And a disaster? My God! Making that picture went from being merely an amusing train wreck to a truly catastrophic derailment that will probably end more than one career. Hopefully not mine, but almost certainly others. A stand-in was badly hurt after you left, a cameraman died of a strange heart attack. Then there were these absurd stories in the press that we were somehow vandalizing the Quirinale Palace, which got the Holy Roman Church whipped into a holy dander. The story was, I'd damaged an ancient door in the throes of some angry fit. Lies. All lies."

Orson waved a hand and said, "But enough of that tedium. Like all post-war cities, I hear this one is replete with fuzz palaces populated with these remarkable and beautiful women forced into prostitution to make ends meet." He read Hector's expression and course corrected. "Anyway, shall we test these claims?"

"We certainly shall not," Hector said, running a count in his head of Orson's divorces, trying to remember if one was still pending with Rita Hayworth, or if it had been consummated.

"Curses."

"You have a film to make," Hector said. "I've got a feeling about this one. It could be huge for you. Anyway, you're seldom alone, abroad or anywhere else. Don't tell me you don't have some woman here with you."

"With me, old man," Orson said. "Yes, for the moment, she is with me. A comely and willowy thing called Katherine. But I don't think this one has legs, so to speak. She might even be a studio spy. Lord knows she wouldn't be the first."

Hector frowned and took Orson's arm again. They stopped for a longer interval this time.

Nothing.

"You're getting paranoid, old man," Orson said. A smile. "But hard not to do that in this beautiful wreck of a city. Something really sinister yet seductive about this place." His smile became uncertain. "Would you tell me, have you come over at last? After so many months with our delectable seer, after your close call, have you at last been swayed to her side of belief?"

"Quite the contrary," Hector said. "In the early going, Cass perplexed me by knowing things I've since learned are in fact in my FBI file. How the bureau got wind of some of this stuff I have no goddamn clue, but it is indeed in my file. Hell, if anyone's a witch or a warlock, I suppose it's J. Edgar or one of his minions. And I've watched you do mind-reader stunts before. You know how this kind of thing is done. Just a trick."

Orson bridled. "In a magic show, yes, it is merely a trick. But Cassie is something else, I believe that. What you're claiming is absurd."

"You can't really believe she can see the future, Orson."

"I can believe it, and that's just for starters. And anyway, women hate magic as we men think of it. Magic isn't for the ladies. They don't like to be fooled. The very fact that this one dabbles in the dark arts proves she's legitimate, the real thing, not just a conjurer."

"I can't even begin to argue with logic like that," Hector said, exasperated. "Hell, it's not even close to logic."

"Forget her knowing things about you then," Orson said. "What about that resurrected Nazi, the one who nearly killed you both in that elevator in Rome?"

Hector rubbed gloved hands up and down his arms briskly. Since he'd gotten sick he seemed always to be cold. He wondered if he should rethink his resistance to the Florida Keys. After all, Hemingway was long gone from there now. Bone Key was very much on all the tourist maps again, but Hector could perhaps again comfortably be a big fish in a small pond there. If nurturing his fame was an objective, it certainly made sense. He was still identified with the island in his readers' minds. It was a canny next home, if he wanted to keep building his legend… while maybe drawing more suicidal moths like Andrew Parker to his destructive flame.

If he wanted all that, if he could live with it, it could be a sound next step.

"The resurrected Thule is just another bit of misdirection—if not premeditated," Hector said. "I'll confess I stewed about that one a while. So I did some digging and learned something. As a magician, you should appreciate this. Turns out that Rune Fuchs, whom I killed definitively, I maintain—killed with a shot between the eyes—"

"Yet when we saw him again in Rome, there was not so much as a scar," Orson cut in. "But then they can do miracles with mortician's clay."

"But they didn't need any miracles for that one," Hector said. "You see, Fuchs was a twin. I'm convinced that *Günther* Fuchs was the man we saw in Rome. The one with the bum eyes and a bullet proof vest that I shot into, over and over."

"You keep telling yourself that," Orson said. "Cassie insists it was a living corpse that attacked you in that elevator. An animated cadaver who tore out some old man's throat with a dead, clutching hand. Cassie insists on all of that, and I agree. I'm sorry, old man, but I do stand with her on all that."

Hector took his friend's arm and held a gloved finger to his lips to shush the actor. Orson whispered, "You have no sense how truly hard it is to stay still when one is dieting on Benzedrine, old man."

Hector said, "*Shh!*"

Footfalls in the distance. Heavy and uneven. More like the echo of a giant's stagger.

Orson said, "You have a gun, don't you?"

"I do."

"Then we confront him?"

"I'm not that chipper, remember," said Hector. "I say back to the hotel for me, lousy as it is with its lobby-lurking international spies and abundant skeleton keys. That's for me. For you, it's a hotel-called-for taxi to take you to set. You okay with that?"

"I'm much more than fine with that, Hector. Next time we meet, do ask me about how I improved on Graham Greene, by the by."

"Greene's considered one of our great current writers," Hector said. "How can you mock him?"

"Oh, come now, Hector. The goddamn pantheon is a perfectly legitimate shooting gallery." A wicked smile. "Anyway, your cue, old man, your trick to remind me of the anecdote about how I out-greened Greene, will be to mention, *yes*, a cuckoo clock."

Hector said, "This Benzedrine you're living on… that's crazy. It'll kill you dead in time."

"Don't be a goose, everyone is using it," Orson said. "Hell, Carol's living on the stuff so he can oversee all three units. Tired as you are, you should take some of mine. Get some of the old energy back. Stuff does wonders. Judy Garland swears by it."

Alone again, Orson safely deposited in a taxi, Hector wandered the streets a while longer, watching to see anyone who might be following. Very soon, he again caught sight of a tall, gaunt silhouette—he had a brief glance of a giant, then lost him again in a swirl of sunlight and shadow.

He bit his lip, dwelling on the other uncovered fact he'd not shared with Orson, the one that undermined his explanation for that tall, terrible man back in Rome whom Cassie insisted was a walking dead man.

Hector was truly certain he had successfully killed Rune Fuchs. He was also certain that Rune indeed had his twin, the one named Günther. Having established that to his satisfaction, those same sources also insisted that Günther Hess could not possibly have staged that elevator attack back in Rome.

Purportedly, Günther had been killed in a car crash with another man's wife in 1946.

Staring down the street behind him, Hector weighed all that.

If the brothers Fuchs were twins, maybe there was a third man—a triplet? It must surely be so. It was Occam's Razor, after all—embrace the simplest, most obvious solution for it is almost certainly the one that is true.

Certainly it was easier to subscribe to a trio of murderous brothers than black magic and corpse resurrection.

35

THREE OF A KIND

Hector found Cassie dressed to go out, eager to escape the confines of their hotel. The phone rang. To Hector's chagrin, it was some reporter, wanting to talk about the mysterious and dead ersatz Hector Lassiter.

"I've been moving around the city, talking to men and women who knew the man," the reporter said, only a little innuendo dripping from his voice on the word *knew*. He raced on, "I'd like to get your take on it for my article. I mean, it can't be coincidence you're here, Mr. Lassiter, or I'll call you Hector, yes? I assume you came here to conduct your own investigation?"

"It's Mister Lassiter, and it would seem a safe enough assumption under normal circumstances for my being here, yet you might be surprised," Hector said. "Tell me what you've learned about this character who would be me."

"This other Hector—the other *Mister* Lassiter—was said to be charming… if vexing," the reporter said. "Also very passionate and very, very articulate. 'Boyish' is a word that comes up over and over to describe him. 'Very American' is another term that's been used."

Given more time, Hector would have indulged the journalist, maybe even tried to coax some contacts from the scribe so Hector could conduct his own debriefing of these people who had run up against the false Hector—who had come to spend time with shadowy Andy from Steubenville, Ohio.

Still the newspaperman could perhaps be useful. While he was presumed dead, Hector had been given accidental quarter by foes old and new—given recuperation time by Thule and Vril.

Now resurrected, Hector decided to try and defuse local interest in himself—and, by extension, in his friends. He decided to try and do that with a dab of volunteered intelligence.

"This is on the record," Hector said. "Please tell your readers I've been years in Europe, mostly, as a war correspondent and post-war novelist… and sometimes journalist," he said. "I'm here right now largely by accident. Just a stop-over and a weigh-station on my way home. Been too long away from the good old U.S.A."

He felt Cassie's gaze on him. He gripped the phone harder. "No," he said in answer to some question she couldn't hear. "I truly miss America, despite some current concerns back there… Expatriate? In the early 1920s that label might have fit me. I was in Paris then, part of that Modernist scene, surely enough. But I am, first and last, what I am and have always been. I'm an American."

Cassie listened as he completed his impromptu interview. For his part, as he spoke, Hector saw Cassie and himself from outside, figured they made a fine image for some Hopper-esque painting: two people, sexually intimate yet worlds apart, standing in a hotel room in coats, hats and gloves, one talking on the phone to a stranger, but also talking to that intimate stranger in the hotel room with him. Hector was calculatedly using the reporter to say to Cassie all the things he couldn't bring himself to put directly to her.

Hector at last hung up the phone, then sat down on the foot of the bed, a bit weak in the knees. His stomach was upset and he pressed a gloved hand to his belly. Cassie took a seat at the hotel room's writing table, her own gloved hand resting close by Hector's long-languishing portable typewriter. There was a thin layer of dust on its keys. Deplorable, he thought.

She said, "So you're truly going home for certain?"

"*After* the holidays," Hector said. "I have to get back there, I see that now. Have to get in touch with the ground there again in order to find my voice. I'm convinced of that. And I do want to see for myself what it's become like since the war. Guess I just miss home."

Home hung there in the silence between them.

"You could come with me," he said. "We could spend Christmas in the Keys."

"I could, but it's not home for me anymore, if it ever truly was." Cassie stood and smoothed her skirt. "I can see you're not feeling well. I suppose we're not going out after all."

"No, I want to go out, I just presently feel…" *Guilty* was the word he couldn't put out there.

A sad smile. Cassie said, "Please don't look so gloomy, Hector. I've studied your hand more than I suspect you ever have. I came in to all of this long ago knowing how this ended for us, believe that. I knew I was never going to grow old with you, that I wasn't going to be the woman who maybe one day will come to rue that extraordinarily long lifeline of yours."

He tried to lighten the mood, to play along. "You saying you know who that poor woman is?"

"Of course. Pressed, I could perhaps even give her a name."

Hector quickly held up his hand, palm toward her. "Please don't."

Hector tripped on some uneven cobblestones as they made their way to the Strauss monument in the Stadtpark, what proved to be the first location indicated on the second, smaller bronze medallion.

She said, "Are you tired again already? Feeling weaker?" Cassie offered him her arm.

He took it but said, "I'm fine. Just all the busted pavement giving me grief."

"We're being followed, you know," she said. "Are you up to trouble if it finds us?"

"I've been followed for days already that I know of," Hector said. "Started near Casanova the other day and has never let up."

"Who's following you?"

"One man, or one I could see anyway. Thin and tall. That's about it for now."

"How tall?"

"Pretty tall," Hector said. He let that stand.

"This man, this giant," she said, "he keeps his distance?"

"So far he has," Hector said, wondering where she was headed with this.

Now that imminent separation was a stated thing between them, Hector anticipated some stepping up of her occult proclivities. She'd modulated them up to this point, Hector figured, but why bother to do that now that their parting was near? He wasn't far off the mark, as it developed. He didn't feel smug about guessing correctly about all of it; rather, it horrified him to see how deeply her odd beliefs truly ran.

"It's Rune Fuchs," she said. "We both know it's so. He's keeping his distance right now because of the salt packets I've hidden in the lining of your coat, because of the granules of salt I've sprinkled in the cuffs of your trousers every morning."

Salt.

"That explains all these little white spots I keep brushing off my knees these past months," Hector said barely able to keep tones of ridicule from his voice. "These traces of white stuff I keep finding on window sills and at thresholds is at last explained." He made no effort to hide his exasperation in the end.

"Yes," she said cooly. "I did it to protect you."

"This simple table condiment keeps this thing at bay, you're saying."

"Yes, his kind."

"And to kill this thing? That requires salt, too?"

"You must fill its mouth with salt, then sew shut its lips," she said. "We'll have to do that."

It was all Hector could do to play along. He said, "Doesn't that present a pretty knotty puzzle in the execution? If salt repels these things, how in hell did you get close enough to one with more salt in order to kill it?"

"They have rest periods," Cassie said, not looking him in the eye. "There's an hour or two at dusk when they're inert. That's when you can get close enough to do the deed." She shook her head. "Please stopping looking at me as though I am the world's biggest lunatic."

Best just to let that go, he figured. And yet…? Hector said, "You'd maintain there's still a string-puller for this thing, right?"

"Yes," she said. "I'm convinced that is still the little German man we saw in Rome, the midget. You can't pass over ownership on a zombie—only the person who raised him can control Fuchs. I've been able to learn that little warlock's name. He is Pavel Maslak. He's Russian, not German, at least by birth. Seems to have once been affiliated with Rasputin."

"This Pavel looks way too young for that," Hector said.

"That's another thing," Cassie said. "Maslak's birth date seems impossible. He'd have to be at least a hundred by now, yet looks thirty. They say he underwent some kind of rite of immortality and…"

Hector tried to tune her out. They were at last again in sight of the Russian sector. A massive scarlet banner emblazoned with the image of Stalin loomed large on the horizon. Cassie said, "The wheel's nice, but to have to see that face every day in order to reach the park? Too high a price to pay."

"Old Joe does look like Hitler but with more moustache and a stronger hairline," Hector agreed. "At least a better barber."

"That's a terrible joke."

"Everything seems a terrible joke these days," Hector said.

"Yes, but not the funny kind."

From the musician's memorial, they pushed on to the front door of the Casanova Club. The next stop seemed to be the Weinhaus. The trail led from there back into the Russian sector and finally to the Prater Amusement Park.

"Crazy and so appropriate that it ends here," he said.

"Not quite here," she said. "There's a last bit of information. And, anyway, I thought we were waiting for Orson to finish this."

"We are," he said, "but what's the last bit of data?"

"Red, twenty-five," she said. Shivering while looking around, she said, "What does that mean? Something to do with roulette, maybe?"

"Doubt it," Hector said. "Anyway, we need Orson before we can do anything with that last clue."

"He's still really invested in this then? You made it sound like movie considerations trumped anything else for the man."

"That's so in my book," Hector said. "I think I care more about the state of his career—that Joe Cotten and I do—than Orson does himself. *The Third Man* surely should be his priority. Either way, I expect Orson will be with us for the last, for better or worse."

"When?"

"Just as soon as we can make it happen," he said.

Orson met them in the hotel lobby, ruddy faced and exuberant. He clapped gloved hands and said, "Any luck with the rest of your search?"

"Reached journey's end, in the bleakest sense, I'm afraid," Cassie said. "Unless you can make sense of 'red twenty-five.' Seems to be a final clue to the object's location."

Orson frowned and said, "Roulette perhaps? Do they have working casinos here in Vienna these days? Did they ever have casinos here?"

Cassie bit her lower hip and said, "I don't know about before, but now? Seen no signs of that kind of entertainment. Doubt there ever was a gaming place like that at the amusement park, which is where the map officially ends, by the way."

Hector listened to them, watching as a tall, gaunt shadow insinuated itself on the glazed, etched glass of the hotel lobby's large, decorative window. Backlit by a guttering, solitary streetlamp, the shadow seemed even more grotesque. Cassie and Orson's backs were to the window and the sinister-looking shadow on the glass.

Irresistibly tempted to test Cassie's crazy remedies, Hector took a step toward the window and was startled to see the shadow fall a step back in concert. Surely it was a coincidence, Hector thought, yet unable to bring himself to take another step forward and watch for any subsequent reaction from the shadow.

His friends looked at him with concern. Cassie said, "Are you feeling ill again?"

Orson didn't wait for an answer. He said, "You're still convalescing. We should go to the dining room and get some food in you, old man. God knows I'm starving."

"You two go get us a table," Hector said. "Order for yourselves. I'm going to take a fast shower and then I'll be right back down."

She pressed her palm to his forehead. "You do feel slightly feverish."

"Simple shower will fix that, I'm sure of it," he said.

Just in case Cassie came up to check on him, Hector really took that shower, once more disappointed by its low pressure and the fact it never really got as hot as he desired. But then the city was partly in ruins, its infrastructure still compromised.

He checked his fresh clothes for packets of salt or other Cassie-supplied occult accessories she might have placed in them. Finding none, he forwent his overcoat with its salt fortified lining.

Salt-free, Hector rode the elevator back downstairs. The gaunt shadow was still out there. It seemed to be leaning against the street lamp, judging by the shadow's posture. Hector wondered to himself if alleged zombies often struck Maurice Chevalier-like poses in the Viennese night.

Careful to stay out of line of sight of the restaurant, Hector slid outside. Startled, the tall man leaning against the light post dropped his cigarette and reached under his coat.

"Don't." Drawing first, pointing his gun between the man's eyes, Hector said, "please don't." The man was about six-five, blond, blue-eyed and all too-familiar looking. Hector shook off a fresh shiver and said, "Your last name Fuchs?"

"That's right." No surprise in that German accent, but this man's accent was more cosmopolitan, even watered-down-sounding, than Hector remembered for Rune Fuchs.

"Let's have a first name," Hector said.

"Klaus."

Well, well.

"You the last of three brothers, triplets I'm guessing?"

A nervous nod. "Why do you care?"

"Just indulge me. You the last son?"

"Yes…"

"Mother still alive?"

"Yes…"

"Then for the love of God, go home to her, kid. Don't break your mother's heart again. No point at all in dying for some goddamn fairytale like at least one of your brothers has done. You're caught up in a fool's pipedream. Hell, we both are. What do you say we both just stand down and each of us goes home?"

Confused but grateful-looking, the tallish young German began to retreat, walking backward, then turning and running into the night.

Quite cold now, Hector shivered again and rubbed his arms. He watched as Klaus passed by a stooped, heavyset woman and her child. The kid was holding the strings for a dozen or so helium-filled balloons in his tiny hand. The two must be returning from the amusement park after a chilly day's work, Hector thought. Jesus Christ, trying to sell balloons in that near abandoned carnival in this weather? Talk about optimism.

The woman seemed legless drunk, unable to find sure footing. She stutter-stepped, then staggered back. The child offered a hand, trying to steady his dumpy, drunken mother. Hector's heart went out to the kid.

Holding hands, the child and the woman pivoted, walking the other direction, following Klaus into the cold night.

A worried, honeyed voice behind him, said, "Darling?" Cassie said, "My God, Hector, are you *still* that hot? Do you want to give yourself pneumonia?" She held out his overcoat. He turned and she helped him on with the coat. He was grateful for its warmth, salt-packet fortification be damned. Sleet began falling, tinkling on glass windows and windshields and stinging their eyes. Cassie slid an arm around his waist and steered him back toward the hotel entrance as the ice collected in their dark hair.

She said, "Orson and I have racked our brains, trying to figure it out—you know, 'red twenty-five.' We're frankly stymied." Her hand was unusually warm in his. She smelled a little of fever herself.

"I'm not," Hector said. "Frankly stymied, I mean. I knew before we left the amusement park what it means. Pretty sure I'm right, anyway."

36

VOYAGE OF THE DAMNED

Whether morning, afternoon or at what in Scotland would be called the gloaming, Vienna presently always seemed to be shrouded in gray fog.

Orson had thrown some fresh fit about his day's filming of *The Third Man*, once again balking at having to run around in the city's vast and smelly sewer system.

"I again stressed my asthma," Orson said. "It has the virtue of being true, of course. They're feverishly working on sewer sets back in London. Whatever the case, I can hardly miss the denouement of our quest now, can I?"

"Don't you dare hurt your career by playing the prima donna," Hector said.

"I was far from the only one who objected to going down into that stinking, over-warm and terrible place, far from it. My God, the stuff floating by in the water that the crews are standing in—neither of you would do it, either. So I have a day, maybe two, for our search. We need to get moving, to use that precious time." Orson popped an anti-acid pill into his mouth. "That is to say if all of our hearts are still in the search."

Once again, Hector found himself wondering at Orson's devotion to the crazy cause.

"There's something terribly depressing about a bombed-out carnival," Cassie said as they reached the park. "Prepared to share your theory?"

"Soon," Hector said. "Let's take a ride on the wheel."

Orson said, "But you don't like heights. And I'm not crazy about them, as we both know. Bad enough I'll have to film here quite soon."

Hector paid an attendant. "There's a difference between being up high in an airplane, or in a car like this one, contained, more or less, a difference between all that and standing on top of the Empire State, which rather terrified me. Looking over the edge—hell, my legs were shaking. Years living in Paris, and in and out many times since, yet I've never set foot on the Eiffel Tower for that very reason."

An old woman and her shy child—the boy kept his head down so they could only see the top of his head—approached their wooden Ferris wheel car, painted garish red like all the others. "May we join you?" the woman said in a thick German accent. "There seems plenty of room," the woman said in her guttural English.

Hector said, "Sorry, but we need to be alone. Plenty of other cars and no crowds, right?" He closed the door of their car, then, put off balance by the sudden movement of the wheel, he sat down awkwardly on a bench.

Cassie and Orson remained standing, still steady on their feet. The actor said, "I haven't that much time, you know, old man. Why are we riding Ferris wheels?"

As they continued to climb, approaching the top of the wheel, all of ruined Vienna opening up before them, Hector pointed toward the forward facing window. He said, "The car in front of us—observations?"

"Wooden construction," Orson said. Then, the light bulb moment came. In his most sonorous tone, Orson said, "Each car on this Ferris wheel is painted bright red."

Cassie chimed in, "Red, and each one is *numbered*! The one before us is number one. So we need to ride number twenty-five next. That's the answer, isn't it?" Her excitement, at least, reached Hector, regardless of its silly, superstitious cause.

"That's the answer, I'm convinced of it," Hector said. "But there is a complication, I'm afraid, one that may well make recovery of the spear impossible."

37

COMPULSION

They were starting their second revolution, Orson said, "Why impossible, Hector?"

"The war's to blame, as it happens. At least, I think so." Hector lit a cigarette with his Zippo, keeping his back to the window. "When we get off this damned thing, if you count the cars, you'll see there are only fifteen. The wheel, the whole park, suffered bombing damage in the war like so much of this city. Before the war, there used to be thirty cars."

Orson shivered. "Where are the other fifteen cars, old man?"

"Some were blasted to hell and gone. Including maybe the very one we seek." Hector looked at the glowing end of his cigarette. "The rest I've learned are in a kind of junkyard of cast-off bombing debris. There's some field on the outskirts of town full of blasted statuary and discarded carnival attractions—the ones not a total loss from the bombings."

Cassie said hopefully, "And car twenty-five exists there?"

"We'll know in an hour or so, if we're still firm on really doing this," Hector said. He'd decided now to test further for some possible second thoughts about all that on Orson's part. The actor rubbed his arms and then sat down next to Hector.

After a time Orson said, "I've lost some of the zeal for having the Spear of Destiny, I must confess," Orson said. "Partly it's simply getting older I suppose. Also, the reality of its possible proximity and starting to think about the logistics of moving the damned thing around, place to place, from film set to film set. Working in Europe, as I seem always to be doing these years, the thing would be, I fear, *burdensome*, like Dorian Gray's cursed portrait. And what exactly is the definition of *losing* the Holy Lance? If it is in some villa in Rome, and I'm back in the States, is my distance from the thing an inadvertent death sentence? I doubt we get a rule or instruction book with the thing when we find it."

"That's the other thing to discuss before we close this out," Hector said, relieved they were again approaching the ground, if only fleetingly. "You've always talked of a three-way split," Hector said to the actor, "but seems to me only one person can truly possess the thing."

Orson sat up a bit straighter. "You've always said you don't want a part of it, even after recovery, old man."

Hector said, "And Cassie?"

"Suppose I always figured we'd work that out if it became necessary," Orson said.

Cassie, still standing, holding onto an overhead rail to steady herself, said, "And now it seems your interest is waning too, Orson."

"Or my fear—at least, my circumspection—is growing," Orson said. Their cage was climbing again, its last revolution, actor and writer both hoped.

"Then so far as a split of some kind, there's maybe no issue after all," Cassie said. "You help me recover the Holy Lance, and I'll assume all the consequences that ensue."

Orson shook his head. "The risk under those circumstances would certainly be worse for all of us, I fear. Truman already dared to use the atom bomb, and our next president is almost certain to be Eisenhower. My God, think about the implications of putting a weapon like the Spear of Destiny into the hands of a five-star general elevated to president." The actor raised his eyebrow. "Tell me, could me make a more calamitous mistake?" A strange smile.

"On the other hand," Orson said, "Look how everything came out for Germany and for Mussolini. And anyway, as artists, I think Hector and I would both agree adversity breeds creativity. Suffering fires the muse. Like the fella says, in Italy for thirty years under the Borgias they had warfare, terror, murder and bloodshed, but they produced Michaelangelo, Leonardo da Vinci and the Renaissance. In Switzerland, they had brotherly love, they had five-hundred years of democracy and peace, and what did that produce? The cukoo clock."

Cassie shook her head. They had nearly reached the top of the wheel for the last time. "I don't work for the government anymore, largely thanks to you two," she said. "The Spear of Destiny isn't going to fall into the hands of any politician, I swear."

"This would be for your own benefit then," Hector said. "That's what you're saying?"

"Me and people like me," she said carefully. "I told you that… you just didn't grasp the implication, I guess."

Hector still wasn't sure he knew what she meant by that. Orson weighed her words as they hung suspended at the top of the wheel—dangling there and buffeted by the wind as someone was let off the car and onto the platform directly below them. "Then you see this as a means of leveraging racial equality," Orson said. "That is what you're saying, isn't it?"

"In so many words, yes," she said, "exactly that."

"*That* I can endorse, then," Orson said. "That I'll still take some risks for."

Cassie looked to Hector. "And you?"

"How would it work exactly?" Hector asked. "How exactly does your recovery of the Holy Lance advance the cause of race relations?"

"Suppose I can't know that—let alone answer your question—until we see what I can do," she said.

Somehow all that sounded even crazier to Hector than the notion of the Spear tipping the balance of power in favor of despots. He said, "And if it does work somehow to that end, when eventually you lose it or it's taken from you as it has been taken from people throughout history—you'll die what, a martyr?"

"Worse things to be," Cassie said. "History travels on the backs of martyrs."

"But I didn't know any of them, didn't care about them and was never in a position to talk them out of sacrificing themselves," Hector said.

"And maybe that was all for the better," Cassie said. "This is my choice. What's your choice, Orson? Hector?"

"I'm prepared to help you, just as I said," Orson said. "The relic will be yours." He looked to Hector like some burden had been lifted from his shoulders.

It seemed to Hector to maybe also be disquieting evidence on the side of those Welles critics who contended Orson was not a "closer"—was in fact constitutionally incapable of finishing *any* of his undertakings, a perspective that seemed to be supported by the string of unfinished and mutilated Welles masterpieces littering the landscape in the wake of *Citizen Kane*.

Their descent was nearly complete. Cassie sat down between the men, took each of their gloved hands. "And you, Hector?"

He said, "If it's truly what you want? If you're certain, then I'll help you see it through, despite how crazy it all seems to me."

38

ANYTHING CAN HAPPEN

Securing taxis remained a vexing challenge in the war-ravaged city.

They returned to their hotel to get some warmer clothes for Cassie and to arrange for fresh wheels. Because Orson was required back on set in a few hours to film a pivotal scene with Joe Cotton, the studio had condescended to furnish a private car to carry the actor and his entourage of two to and from "lunch."

Orson was already wearing his Harry Lime suit, overcoat and hat. His make up needs were uncharacteristically minimal for this picture. Just this once, Orson was acting on film with his God-given nose.

Briefly passing them in the lobby on his own way to the set, Joe had confided to Hector his belief Orson was almost certainly turning in the performance of his career as the charismatic and charming but coldly evil racketeer Harry Lime. Hector was heartened to hear it.

As their bewildered driver passed the last of the city's viable restaurants, asking if they really intended to be taken to what was essentially a scrap yard, Hector watched for tails.

So far there was little sign of trouble, but single cars were so sparse that conventional tailing presented its own challenges. As they drove on, Hector tried to think of ways he'd run surreptitious, car-to-car surveillance under the same circumstances and found himself confounded by the challenge.

The scrap yard was bounded by a high and rusting fence; its gate was unsecured.

Still confused as to their interest in the place, their driver, a man named Viktor Ebner, exited the car with them. He was intent upon taking a short walk to have a smoke. "I won't go too far," Viktor promised. "As you'll soon enough realize, there's little to see in there. You won't be long, I'm telling you."

When he returned to the car about ten minutes later, Viktor driver was surprised to find they were still inside. He frowned at the back of his car—the trunk's lid wasn't secured. Lucky for him it hadn't come loose while driving, he thought. Clenching his cigarette between his teeth, he lifted and slammed the trunk lid down with both hands. He pulled up on it to make sure it was now indeed locked.

He next frowned at the fence line: a stretch of chain-link was peeled away from its support post. He didn't remember it looking that way on the drive up, but then he had also been preoccupied by his pretty lady passenger, stealing glances at her in the rearview mirror on the drive over.

As they had approached the gate of the scrap yard, Hector registered the bag Cassie was carrying. He held out a hand and said, "Please, allow me."

She passed him the bag but simultaneously reached inside. She extracted a large container of salt as the bag passed into his hands. In reaction to his expression, she said, "Just indulge me, please."

"Of course," Hector said. "Possibly bad for the birds though."

"Worse for other things," she said, finishing up her salt line across the entryway. She stowed the salt container back in her tote bag. "You may yet thank me for this, you know."

"Maybe I will," Hector said with little conviction.

Orson said, "Let's keep moving along. Remember, time is short for me."

Pointing, Hector said, "My source, a fella back at the amusement park, said that the cars salvaged from the wheel—whatever's left of the balance of the former thirty that didn't become the fifteen back at the park—are now scrapped somewhere at the back of this junk yard."

"That's almost like a kind of poetry, your phrasing, I mean," she said.

Hector said, "To the back, drift leftward and down the hill."

"Seems a long way to haul something that big," Orson said.

"The road twists," Hector said. "There's also a rail line running across the back of the yard—that's the way they get the bigger stuff moved here and deposited."

Fresh flurries began to sift down. Already feeling a bit winded, Hector pushed on, leading the way.

Soon, an old man came trudging their direction, waving his arms and calling out questions about who had let them in and what they wanted in his field of junk.

Hector introduced himself as a scout for the movie production team, then said they were seeking the discarded cars from the great wheel for possible use in filming the movie that was so dominating Vienna's newspaper headlines.

"But the real wheel is still standing you know," the old man said, watching for a reaction to what he must have thought was news to them.

"Of course it is, but that's not the way movie making is done," Orson said. "You see you can't get the cameras and lights up there on the ride. No, a car on the ground is much better in terms of stillness and just running power to the camera, in controlling lighting."

The old man pointed toward the back of his sprawling rubbish heap. "They're not in good shape, I warn you. But if you fancy one, then we can talk terms. You'll find me in the shack nearest the gate—the one with chimney smoke, of course."

"Of course," Cassie said. She turned to Hector and said, "Come along Mr. Reed, Mr. Welles, before the weather worsens."

It did seem as though they were losing the light, but several hours too early. Hector wondered if some winter storm front might be creeping in without proper prediction.

A jumble of red and black char lay ahead of them. Hector counted seven cars salvaged from the wheel, all of them in various states of destruction. Only one looked relatively intact; the rest all lacked their roofs. A couple of the cars were missing their sides.

"So far as numbers go," Hector said, "nearly each has at least one legible set of numbers still visible."

But none of them were numbered twenty-five.

Only one car, all but kindling, had no discernible number. Orson said, "Hardly seems worth checking that one. There's nowhere left to hide anything."

A soft curse. Cassie smiled ruefully. "In its terrible way, it's sickly perfect, isn't it?" she said, her voice filled with dejection. "The damned Nazis blew up the very thing that might have saved them. Hitler destroyed the very relic he spent years obsessing over."

"The least of his sins, in my view," Hector said.

The rubbish heap's caretaker was returning, waving a hand and calling out, "Hey there, any luck? Any chance this old man's Christmas might be more prosperous than the last?"

"Still talking amongst ourselves on that topic," Orson said. "Tell us, if a car from the wheel isn't here, then where might it possibly have gone?"

"Woosh," the old man said, pantomiming an explosion with his arms. "If it's not here or back on the wheel in the park, then it's gone to God."

A train whistle blew at the back of the scrap yard, drowning out the old man's next words. Arms still outstretched and waving, the old man shuddered, frowned. He took a false step or two, pulling his hands to his chest, then clutched at his heart and toppled over onto his back.

Hector was closest and saw the spreading red stain on the man's chest and hands—realized the old man had been shot. He was drawing his gun even as he turned in the direction from which the shot had to have been fired.

Above the train whistle, a female voice called out, "Drop the gun now Mr. Lassiter, or your witch friend will be the next we shoot."

Stalking down the hill behind them were three figures. One appeared to be a woman and her stocky little boy; the other was a tall, slender blond man—Klaus Fuchs.

The woman and child—his head still bowed—were the same ones they'd seen earlier at Prater, the ones who'd tried to share their car on the great wheel. The woman said, "I mean it, Mr. Lassiter, get rid of your gun."

Hector complied in so far as he lowered his gun to his side but he didn't let go of it. Somewhere out there was a fourth person—one with a rifle and a scope. For now, the trio and their hidden sniper held all the cards.

As he watched them draw closer, Hector wondered if the woman and child weren't also the same ones he'd seen carrying balloons the night before, staggering their way toward his hotel before turning to follow the retreating Herr Fuchs.

Just a few steps from them now, the child looked up sharply and Cassie gasped. Even Hector was startled to see the boy's face with its black moustache and goatee.

Hector was quickest to recover. He said, "Pavel Maslak, right?"

A nod. "Are you telling me this is where the search for the Holy Lance ends, Lassiter?"

"Afraid that's so," Hector said. He frowned at Klaus Fuchs, who seemed paler, more drawn than before. Something vacant in his eyes. "See you didn't run home to your mother after all," Hector said. "Unless this dumpy little German witch is mommy. Not going back was a mistake, Klaus."

Cassie said, "Don't waste your breath on him, Hec, he's a thrall now."

"A thrall?" Hector couldn't keep the edge from his voice. "You mean now he's a zombie, too?"

"A thrall, not a zombie," Cassie said. "More like hypnosis at work here."

The little man said, "Toss me the medallion."

"Hell, why not," Hector said. "It's just a paperweight now." He threw the little warlock the bronze disc.

The little man said, "*Red twenty-five.* You think that refers to one of these cars, then."

"Sure," Hector said. "Used to be thirty of them on the Prater's wheel. Since the bombing, there are fifteen. Sadly, the one we want is kindling somewhere, and evidently the so-called Spear of Destiny with it. I mean, I'm not out here for my health."

A mean smile from the little man. "What's left of your health, you surely mean. What this witch," he gestured at Cassie, "was able to maintain of your health against my attacks."

"Yeah, well, I'm coming back either way," Hector said. "By the way, are you two Thule or Vril? And who *is* the lady here, by the way?"

"We're neither Vril nor Thule," Maslak said. "My companion's name isn't of import to you. In fact, she insists on anonymity. If her real name were ever to come out, and her true age with it, there'd be a clamor for others of our secrets."

Hector had just about reached the end of his patience with all this occult stuff. Orson also seemed to have reached his limit. The actor said, "The car we need is presumed destroyed. We're no longer interested in pursuing this further, even if we could. We're going to leave, and leave you here with disc and the cold dead trail." Orson took a step and the ground erupted at his feet. The sound of the shot closely followed.

"Don't move again," Maslak said. "We're far from done here, and things are far from settled."

"Suppose that just might be so," Hector said. "I certainly have a question or two still hanging in the wind. Like your age. I hear wild tales about you, old son. How many candles on your birthday cake this year, Pavel?"

The little man thought about it and said, "True immortality of course can't be achieved, but let's just say lives can be made long enough to seem something like forever, Mr. Lassiter. Whether it's a blessing or a curse is open to debate after one has buried nearly everyone who mattered—all the ones lost to you because you can't age and die like a normal man.

And a note of caution if you think of hurting me now or sometime down the road of life. If you kill me, you inherit that blessing… that curse."

Hector was more than prepared to put that one to the test. He said, "Look, let's just all leave here without anyone else bleeding or dying like this poor old innocent man you've killed. Orson is right, the search is a dead end. The Nazis blew up the prize years ago. Let's all just stand down and retire to neutral corners."

The little man smiled and shook his head. "What a fool you two are, flummoxed and tricked by this self-styled white witch, as though there can ever really be such a thing. There is only one path and that is the left-hand path. Once feet are put upon it, there is no retreating, no turning back, we all become more the thing we always were. You're either with God, or you're with the Devil. If you practice the dark arts, even if you remained convinced you do it in the name of good, you still serve the Devil. This woman has betrayed you time and again, Lassiter."

Cassie just shifted her gaze between Hector and the tiny Russian. "Woman is the Devil's Door," Maslak said. "It has been so since Eve, and you, you writer with all your books littered with *femmes fatales*, once again have fallen prey to the whiles of a scheming, dissembling woman. Tell him, witch! Tell him the terrible truth. Tell this man what it cost to ward him against my spell, what bloody thing you had to do, to literally sacrifice—*who* you had to sacrifice to keep him alive and recovering against my hexes. Tell the hack writer about how you have tricked him and his silly actor friend here, how you've done it today."

The little man gestured at Orson. "Show the would-be magician, the parlor conjuror and ham actor how you tricked him. I want to savor his reaction—his real reaction, not the ones he manufactures on cue."

Cassie said, "Hector, Orson, they aren't going to let us walk away from here—you know that."

"No, I'm sure that much is true," Hector said carefully. "But they have somebody out there somewhere with a high-powered rifle and some kind of radio connection, clearly, so I'm still looking for next moves. While we wait for my next terrible epiphany, please address—or better, *refute*—this little monster's claims. What did you do to try and save me?"

Cassie's dark eyes pleaded. "I'll confess to this much, darling—a thing I do regret. While you were recovering, while Orson was wrapping up his film, I… I took a page from your playbook, I'd guess you'd say. I created a fake second medallion."

"The one we've been following," Hector said. "The disc that brought us here, it isn't real?" Hector shook his head. "On reflection, an amusement park ride does smack of a hinky place to hide something *so* important… so holy."

"That's right. Closure for you two, at last, I thought. Safe passage back to the other side of the looking glass, while I assume all the risks, just as we finally agreed I would at the end. Something to stop all those who hunt you because they think you and Orson are the surest key to reaching the Holy Lance."

Hector raised his empty hand in Cassie's direction. He said, "If you have the real disc on you, give it to them now."

"I don't have it here. Why would I? And they'd surely kill us if I did give it to them, Hector."

"I'll surely kill these two men and right here, right now if you don't," Maslak said. "After all, I've already begun killing you, witch. You were careless with a fingernail, my dear. That's more than enough for me to work my magic. Just a few words from my lips will bring it all down on you."

"Wait, please," Cassie said, looking stricken, holding up her hands. "The disc isn't here. Let my friends go, let them go back to the hotel, and let me talk to them on the phone to know they are really safe there. Then I'll take you to the disc." She looked at the ground. "And then… let the heavens fall."

Hector dismissed the little man's occult threats against Cassie, his pale blue eyes urgently searching the horizon of the scrap heap for signs of the sniper.

"Why would I trust you after the way you've played these silly artists, these men who regard themselves as friends?" The little man smiled at Hector and said, "I'll tell you what she wouldn't. She killed a baby as part of her so-called white rite to save you from my hex. I thought attacking you directly would make her more malleable to my will, you see. I always knew this would come down to a contest between myself and this tainted bitch, a contest between our respective brands of magic. She loved you enough to kill a baby for you, but not nearly enough to give me what I want. Not enough to surrender the disc."

Hector saw faint light glint on glass; saw the outline of a head and knew he'd found the sniper. But there was another man out there, one who seemed to be creeping up behind the man with the rifle. Hector thought about it. Their bored driver must have gotten curious and come looking. A chance?

Hector said, "Is it true? Did you really kill a child because you truly thought it might save me in some crazy way? Please, tell me no."

Orson's confiding of the killing of the old man to keep Hitler's invasion of Great Britain at bay gnawed at Hector. She killed Germans the night they first met. The act of murder wasn't a strange one to her, surely. But to *sacrifice a child*?

Cassie started to speak, faltered… She looked to Orson. She said to the actor, "You remember all those years ago, on top of that crazy building, you spoke of Solomon? Faced with two women claiming to be the mother of the same child, you said the King suggested that babe be cut in half so each of the women could claim a piece of the child. When one cried out in horror, when she recoiled at Solomon's unthinkable suggestion, he declared that woman the victor, you said. Then there is the tale of Alexander and the Gordian knot… That's the tale that resonates for me more right now, Orson. Rather than fretting, racking one's brain for an out, better to simply cut the knot."

As she spoke, Cassie had casually slid her hands into her pockets. One of those pockets exploded. A red bloom erupted from the forehead of the mysterious old German woman.

The little man screamed out, "Helena! No!" He snarled something at Cassie in a language Hector thought might be Latin. For her part, Cassie suddenly looked liked *she'd* been shot. The little man laughed as Cassie began to cough. Hector saw blood on her hands—he wondered if she'd been hiding some tubercular condition from him.

Hector quickly raised his gun and shot Maslak between the eyes. As he did that, he screamed, "Orson, Cassie, on the ground!"

As Maslak fell, Klaus Fuchs' eyes rolled up in his head and he fell to the ground too, like a puppet with cut strings.

A single shot rang out.

From the other side of the scrap yard came a call, "Hello there! It's Viktor! Mr. Welles, this man with the rifle, he is… how you say, *handled*. Are you out there? Are you well, Mr. Welles?"

Hector said to Orson, "You answer Viktor…" He fast crawled to Cassie, who was shaking and coughing up alarming amounts of blood—choking on it. Despite the cold, she was bathed in sweat. Hector rolled her over onto her stomach, trying to keep her from choking on her own blood.

Orson said, "Old man, she's burning up with fever, just as you were back in Rome when that little man put a hex on—" He hesitated and pressed a hand to Hector's shoulder. "Cassie… I mean…"

"I know what you mean, and don't say anymore," Hector said. "This is the flu or some virus she's got, it's running rampant all over Europe. Hell, she probably got it nursing me. Now she's hemorrhaging inside from it. We need to get her to the car and to a hospital before she bleeds out or chokes to death. We need to do that before Viktor sees these bodies. You two will take Cassie to the hospital, get her treatment started. I'll clean up here and follow fast." Hector bent down and picked up Cassie—already unconscious—hoping he had the strength to carry her the distance. As it happened, Orson soon took over, then their driver.

Orson said, "You should come with us now, you should—"

"Look around you," Hector said quietly to him as the moved Cassie into the back seat. "There are bodies to be disposed of. At least we're in a scrap yard to begin with—we have that much luck on our side. Plenty of places to stash bodies. Plenty of garbage to hide the smell come spring."

39

I'LL NOT GO BACK

Hector returned to the hotel dejected, exhausted. He had to walk nearly a mile before he finally found a taxi to carry him back into the city.

When he reached the hotel, Hector took a fast and not nearly hot enough shower to clean off the dirt and blood from disposing of the corpses. After, he dressed, wandered downstairs and caught a cab to the hospital.

Orson met him in the lobby, drawn and looking shell-shocked. He said, "I'm terribly sorry, Hector. It… well, the doctors can tell you more about what *they* think happened, but it spiraled out of control. Apparently she had some sort of pre-existing condition they think, and her fever was so high when we got here, at least a hundred–and-four. Her body just shut down. After such massive blood loss, there was nothing…"

Hector blinked. He said, trying to fathom it, "Cassie is dead? She got sick and bled out that quickly?" It seemed impossible. She'd looked in bad shape as he placed her in the car, but…

"Yes," Orson said. "But we know that warlock, or—"

Hector held up a hand. "*Flu*, Orson. She was hot to the touch before we ever got to that field, before that little bastard ever opened his mouth and uttered that damn incantation if that indeed was what all that Latin was meant to be. I just didn't register it when I was in bed with her, distracted as I was. And goddamn me for that."

Orson wasn't having it. He said, "Old man, we should really get you some help from another like Cassie. That little man said if you killed him you would inherit his—"

"Say one more word about any of this occult bullshit," Hector said, "And I'll put you on your ass, Orson, friend or not."

Orson nodded and said, "Either way, she's gone, old friend. We need to see to what comes after, now."

Hector nodded slowly. He said softly, bitterly, "Yes… all the usual loose ends."

Later that evening, Hector set up shop in a corner booth of the hotel lounge with whisky, notebook and a pen. He wrote until the shadows grew long, including the one cast by his bottle of whiskey that moved from the left to the right side of his table's top as the hours rolled along.

"Hector, are you okay?"

Orson sat down across from him. He looked from the bottle to Hector's notebook and presumed to ruffle some of the pages. He whistled low at the sea of ink staining sheet after sheet in the notebook. "The dam has broken eh, old man?"

"It would seem," Hector said, massaging his stiff and sore right hand.

"Cassie truly loved you, you know that, don't you?"

"Think she really killed a baby to try and save me?"

"Suppose we'll never know," Orson said. "I choose to believe she didn't."

"You *choose* to *believe*," Hector said. "It all comes to down to that crazy reaching for or running from faith in the end, doesn't it?"

Orson said, "What exactly do you believe in, old man?"

"Tonight, I believe I'll have another drink. Tomorrow? Then I'm going to get myself some travel arrangements made. I'm going home. How about you, Orson? After Britain, will you maybe brave the waters back in the States?"

"Of course not," Orson said. "I have certain baggage there, don't you remember?"

"Of course. Sorry."

Orson wet his lips, said, "Hector, you really shouldn't be alone tonight. Let's burn the midnight oil. Tomorrow I film my death scene in those cursed sewers. Come with me, watch us at work. After, we'll have a great dinner—on me—and I'll send you safely on your way back to Lady Liberty's ample yet lamentably milk-dry teats if that's truly what you crave."

They stayed on in the hotel lounge until breakfast, greeting dawn with a stomach-bursting breakfast and a bottle of vintage champagne.

As they finished with the last of their pastries, moving on to a second bottle of champagne, a small, balding man approached their table, cleared his throat and said, "Mr. Lassiter?"

"That's right," Hector said. "What can I do for you, Mister…"

"I am Theodor Forst, what I guess you might call a solicitor where you come from."

"Mr. Forst, what can I do for you?"

The little man bowed and handed Hector a small, heavy box. "Just sign for this. This is yours now, sir. Since she came to Vienna some time ago, a Miss Cassandra Allegre arranged that if she didn't call me every night at eight o'clock in the evening—if she ever failed to do that—then the very next morning, I was to see you were delivered this box. Last night, I receive no such phone call." A nervous smile. "I hope all is well with Miss Allegre."

Hector said nothing about any of that.

The little man handed him some papers and said, "To acknowledge your receipt, sir, just as I said…"

Hector scrawled down his signature and stared at the box as the balding little lawyer took his leave.

Tenting his fingers under his chin, Orson said, "You know almost certainly what that is, of course."

"Of course," Hector, more than a bit buzzed, said. "What else could it be? You want the damned thing? You know I couldn't care less about having it, of course."

Orson still staring at the box, wet his lips and said, "I'm being quite honest, you know. I want no part of it now. It seems to me truly a cursed thing to have to carry the Spear of Destiny through whatever remains of life. It's a kind of albatross to my mind."

"You know my sincere thoughts on all of that nonsense, too," Hector said.

"So what then, old man? Hector, what do we do with this accursed relic? Leave it here on the table? Toss it in some garbage can?" Orson rapped his fingers on the tabletop and said, "Or do we sell it to the highest bidder and see to our retirements in that way?"

Hector scooped up the box and thrust it in the pocket of his overcoat. He freshened his and Orson's champagne flutes. "As to this thing's fate, I suppose we await inspiration."

40

IF IN YEARS TO COME

Hector stood in the stinking, steaming sewers under Vienna, feeling truly warm at last, watching Orson—strike that, watching a mortally wounded "Harry Lime"—try and crawl up a winding iron staircase to escape his gun-toting former best friend the hack author and all of the sewer police pursuing him.

Somehow, the final interaction between Joe Cotten and Orson Welles wasn't quite pleasing director Carol Reed.

During a brief break, Orson took Hector aside and whispered in his ear. The novelist was very aware of the British director watching them.

Fifteen minutes later, Orson was again sprawled on that iron staircase. The thrust of the scene was such that Orson was supposed to give a faint but meaningful nod to his old friend Holly—strike that: to actor Joseph Cotten—an indication that Joe's subsequent shooting of Harry, or Orson, should be perceived as a kind of mercy killing.

When the moment came for Orson to send his subtle signal to Joseph to pull that trigger, this time, Orson looked instead to Hector. As he had been directed, the author held up the unopened box left him by Cassie. He raised an inquiring eyebrow.

Orson, puppy-eyed and contrite, gave Hector the subtlest of nods.

Hector didn't hesitate. On the actor's nod of approval, he flung away the box that was so precious to so many, the thing that and had cost unknown numbers of lives. He cast the medallion into the fast rushing, fetid sewer water.

Carol Reed, visibly moved by Orson's take this time, raised a hand to hold the moment, then said softly, "Cut and *print*. That was bloody marvelous, Orson. That was absolutely and truly goddamn transcendent, you magnificent bastard."

THE END

IT'S
ALL
TRUE

READER DISCUSSION QUESTIONS

1. Orson Welles (*Head Games*, *Toros & Torsos*) returns in this novel and at much greater prominence. If you know the other Lassiter novels featuring Orson, did this one change your attitudes about Welles in any way? If so, for better or worse?
2. Did you bring any notions about Orson, the artist or man, to this novel? If so, did your opinion about him harden or soften because of *The Great Pretender*?
3. What about the younger Orson Welles do you think so strongly draws Hector to the budding actor/director?
4. Orson and Ernest Hemingway are Hector's primary historical sidekicks across the series. Do you see any significant similarities between Orson and Ernest? What are their key differences?
5. This is the first Hector Lassiter novel to incorporate elements of the supernatural. How do you feel about that mild shift in direction?
6. The Spear of Destiny or Holy Lance was indeed coveted by Hitler and the Thule Society. Do you posit any belief in the spear's story and alleged power?

7. What do you make of key Nazis' obsession with the supernatural and their noted quest for certain religious artifacts?
8. Did you recognize a certain real-life supernatural aficionado and Nazi inspiration near the novel's climax?
9. Hector and Orson come to a shared decision about any further questing after the Spear of Destiny under the streets of Vienna. Do you agree with their handling of the problem of the spear?
10. The next Hector Lassiter novel, *Roll the Credits*, continues to explore the world of cinema and the rise of Nazism. What are your hopes or expectations for that novel?

ABOUT THE AUTHOR

Craig McDonald is an award-winning author and journalist. The Hector Lassiter series has been published to international acclaim in numerous languages. McDonald's debut novel was nominated for Edgar, Anthony and Gumshoe awards in the U.S. and the 2011 Sélection du prix polar Saint-Maur en Poche in France.

The Lassiter series has been enthusiastically endorsed by a who's who of crime fiction authors including: Michael Connelly, Laura Lippmann, Daniel Woodrell, James Crumley, James Sallis, Diana Gabaldon, and Ken Bruen, among many others.

Craig McDonald is also the author of two highly praised non-fiction volumes on the subject of mystery and crime fiction writing, *Art in the Blood* and *Rogue Males*, nominated for the Macavity Award.

To learn more about Craig, visit *www.craigmcdonaldbooks.com* and *www.betimesbooks.com*

Follow Craig McDonald on Twitter @HECTORLASSITER
https://www.facebook.com/craigmcdonaldnovelist

18368271R00182

Made in the USA
San Bernardino, CA
11 January 2015